BENJAMIN WHITE

By A. J. Butcher

BENJAMIN WHITE

a Spy High novel

A. J. BUTCHER

www.atombooks.co.uk

A paperback original from *Atom* Books

First published in Great Britain by Atom 2005

Based on concepts devised by Ben Sharpe
Story by A. J. Butcher

A CIP catalogue record for this book is available from the British Library.

ISBN 1 90423 336 8

Typeset in Cochin by M Rules
Printed and bound in Great Britain by
Bookmarque Ltd, Croydon, Surrey

Atom
An imprint of
Time Warner Book Group UK
Brettenham House
Lancaster Place
London WC2E 7EN

www.twbg.co.uk

For Dave
From that first day at Childs, no better friend

PROLOGUE

It was almost time.

Already, darkness was falling, and across the length and breadth of Boston, Massachusetts, people were preparing to head out and have fun with their evening. An intimate dinner for two, perhaps. Or a wild night dancing at a cybertronic club. An interactive holo-cinema. The Pleasure Mall.

Or slaughtering a hundred innocent civilians in the name of the revolution.

In his cheap hotel room, the cockroaches scuttling excitedly across the floor, as if they too were anticipating a night on the town, the man with the hooded eyes buckled the explosives around his midriff. The belt in which they were contained was light, slim; it would not impede the man's movements. It would not even be seen once he'd slipped on the waistcoat, black like his trousers and tie, and the jacket that still lay on the bed, half covering the pulse rifle.

The man with the hooded eyes completed his dressing. He stood in front of a cracked, stained but serviceable full-length mirror and inspected himself. Satisfactory. Very satisfactory indeed. No indication that he was carrying enough gelignite concentrate to demolish half a city block. No suggestion that he was anything other than what he seemed to be: a humble waiter. The man with the hooded eyes smiled.

Tonight's meal was going to be heavy on the flambé.

Elsewhere, a rather more expensive hotel room – the rumour of a cockroach here and litigation was a certainty – but a similar kind of scene. A young man was admiring himself in a sparkling polished mirror. Some, particularly those of the female persuasion, might have conceded that there was plenty *to* admire. The tall, athletic body, maybe, muscles in all the right places and places for all the right muscles. The blond hair, cropped short as if its owner meant business. The high cheekbones and steadfast square jaw, the same. The blue eyes that seemed to smoulder with intensity. 'Mirror, mirror, on the wall,' grinned the blond, 'who's the greatest secret agent of them all?' The mirror, not being personalised or programmed to do so, did not comment. Benjamin T. Stanton Jr did not care. He already had a pretty good idea.

It was just a pity he couldn't knot this blasted bow tie properly. Just as well that Cally wasn't around to relish his humiliation, but they'd thought it better to book separate rooms. It gave them space, and in more ways than one. Cally was no doubt at this very moment making herself look even more gorgeous than usual (if that were possible) in her own accommodation ahead of the dinner. She was probably having more success than Ben too. At least girls did not have to contend with bow ties.

A clip-on version would have been easier but had never been a realistic option. The little silk number that he seemed to be choking himself with now happened to boast one or two special features that made it more than simply decorative, and while technically Ben and Cally's attendance at the Maureen Lenehan Memorial Trust Annual Dinner 2066 qualified as a night off from their Spy High duties, it never paid to take chances.

And finally, success. The tie was tied. 'See?' Ben boasted to the mirror. 'A graduate of the Deveraux College can do anything. Eventually.' He shrugged into his tuxedo. 'Comlink, please' – more loudly, so the room could hear – 'connect me with Room 3096.'

'This unit is sorry,' said the room secretarially. 'There is no response from Room 3096. Would you like to (a) leave a message, (b) hold, or (c) discontinue your call?'

Ben frowned. No response? So where was Cally? He knew that initially she'd been reluctant to come with him – formal dinners weren't quite her style – but surely she hadn't done a runner at the last minute. His surprise would fall flat on its face – if surprises *had* faces. 'Comlink,' he said, 'what about (d) do you fancy coming out for a meal with me tonight?'

'This unit is sorry,' apologised the room, 'but it fails to understand the question. Repeat: there is no response from Room 3096. Would you—'

'C, c,' said Ben, 'but thanks for trying.'

He glanced at his watch. They still had plenty of it, but time *was* progressing. He'd better check on Cal himself.

Knocking on her door earned the same reaction as if he'd been rapping on a coffin lid. Nothing. It didn't matter, though. Hotel security was child's-play to anyone trained in covert entry and infiltration techniques at Spy High. Ben deactivated the door lock in less than ten seconds, eased himself into Cally's room.

Instantly, he knew what the problem was. He could hear it, emanating from the bathroom and punctuated by splashes.

'We're lost in music . . . uh-huh . . . caught in a trap . . . yeah yeah . . .'

Cally was in the bath. Cally was *singing* in the bath. What her voice lacked in finesse, it kind of made up for in enthusiasm.

'. . . no turning back . . . ooh-*ooh* . . . we're lost in music . . .'

Ben winced and grinned simultaneously. Cally in bath: major turn-on. Cally auditioning for *World Idol 2066*: forget the undercover placement in a nightclub.

He crossed to the bathroom door.

'I said we're *lost* in music . . .'

Pounded on it like a fireman warning of a blaze. 'This is the noise police! You are under arrest for being just about the worst singer we've ever heard. Unless you desist immediately, we're coming in to get you.'

'Ben?' A giggle from within. 'Is that you?'

'Sorry. We're coming in to get you anyway.'

In actual fact, Ben opened the door at first only a sliver, enough to reveal that yes, the intruder *was* him, enough to expose Cally reclining in the tub with only her head and shoulders visible above a snowscape of suds. Not a single freshly braided dreadlock was out of place.

'Did you break in here?' Cally protested playfully. 'Did you actually break into my room to lech at me in the bath?'

'No. Cal. Of course not.' Ben was shocked. 'I broke in here to remind you that the dinner is tonight, not next week. Leching at you in the bath, that's just a bonus.'

'Hmm. Sometimes, Ben Stanton, I don't know what I see in you.' She raised a shapely leg and indicated with her foot that Ben should hand her her robe.

'Yeah? Well sometimes, Cally Cross,' fenced her boyfriend, doing so, 'I know *exactly* what I see in you. But sadly, how about getting dressed? We don't want to be late.'

'We could always give the whole thing a miss and order room service,' suggested Cally, Ben knew not entirely frivolously.

'Bite your tongue, baby,' he said. 'Let me tell you now, this is one evening you are *not* going to want to miss.'

Across town, while Cally was clambering out of the bath, the man with the hooded eyes was fondling the electronic detonator like it was a precious stone. At last, unwillingly, he dropped it into his pocket. He was ready. His comrades were ready. Outside, darkness was falling. He needed to leave without delay.

It was almost time.

He'd go far, Tolly Porter's teachers had always told him. They'd never known such an instinctive scientific mind before. The sky was the limit.

Well, it turned out they were right about the first part, if not the last: 384,440 kilometres pretty much qualified as *far*, whisking Tolly out into space and leaving the sky a considerable way behind him. At the age of seventeen, and still seen very much as a child prodigy by his older colleagues, Tolly Porter was a key member of the scientific task force stationed on Moon Colony Armstrong. It might have been thought that such a position would make the teenager feel proud, privileged, or at least a little bit pleased. Only it didn't. If anything, his lunar life left Tolly suffering the pangs of disappointment.

Spy High was to blame.

When the janitor of his school had first revealed himself to be not so much a man with a mop as a man with a mission, a selector agent for the elite Deveraux College, Tolly's jaw had dropped. When the janitor had explained, further, that Deveraux was nothing but a front for a training establishment dedicated to producing the next generation of world-saving secret agents, and that Tolly Porter, kid genius, was in line for recruitment, his jaw had virtually struck the floor. That was probably why he'd found it difficult to speak when the janitor asked him if he wanted in. He only needed to form one word, though. Three letters. He finally managed a 'please' as well, because his parents had brought him up to be polite.

His brilliant mind had raced. Tolly Porter, secret agent. He'd been thinking girls, fast wheellesses, girls, incredible gadgets, girls, insane megalomaniacs with schemes for global domination, girls.

The reality didn't turn out quite as he'd hoped.

Because they didn't want him for espionage duties, at least not directly. He never got to wear a shock-suit or fire sleepshot or hang with Bond Team (and that Lori Angel had been *hot*) or go on missions. Maybe he shouldn't have been surprised. His brain might have been impressive, but the rest of him lagged a fair way behind. Glasses that made him look like an owl (he was too squeamish to have corrective optical implants fitted). Hair that kind of sprouted like moss on a tree trunk. Limbs that were a little too long and a little too thin and that never seemed to agree what they should be doing. In short, and Tolly Porter did not delude himself on this matter, he was a nerd. He knew it. The girls who always had prior engagements when he asked them out, they knew it. Jonathan Deveraux, the founder of Spy High himself, he knew it too. Secret-agenting had never been the plan for Tolly Porter. So why was he at Deveraux?

It seemed the organisation was expanding, developing new areas of expertise. One of these was EXIST. It was an acronym, they told Tolly unnecessarily. The letters stood for Extra-terrestrial Investigation and Surveillance Team. EXIST was going to be the planet's first line of defence against possible alien incursion. Its primary task was to seek out any evidence of extra-terrestrial activity or presence, past or present. Seemed Spy High in general, and Bond Team in particular, had had a little run-in recently with a militaristic master race called the Diluvians – it was all in the virtual files. Jonathan Deveraux did not want to be caught out again. EXIST would make an invaluable contribution to his – his *school's* – protection of the people of Earth. He wanted Tolly to be a part of it.

Hence Moon Colony Armstrong. So his job might not involve battling the bad guys head-on or braving certain death on a regular basis, but Tolly could at least console himself with the fact that he belonged to an organisation that did all that. Most of the time it worked. And besides, who knew? One day he might get a chance to *really* prove his worth.

Tolly Porter, secret agent. He still hadn't quite given up hope.

The call came through to his quarters. Professor Robertson. 'Sorry to interrupt your rest period, Porter,' she said, 'but the surface probe? I think you'll want to see this. We're in the command centre.'

Tolly was there in minutes. The white colony buildings took the form of a series of connected concentric circles radiating out from a central hub. The Earth shuttle's landing pad was here, with the base's command centre overlooking it. At the moment, however, those present had their attention focused elsewhere.

Professor Cassandra Robertson, a portly woman who looked as though she might have been more at home teaching classics at a minor public school in England, directed Tolly to the surface probe's monitoring screens. Tolly looked. To begin with he didn't notice anything unusual. The eye of the probe was transmitting back to command the kind of view of the lunar surface that he might have expected. The trundling little robot (if it had had fur, Tolly would have been tempted to give it a name and throw sticks for it) had been programmed to venture into previously unexplored regions of the Moon. The highlands, known as terrae, the most ancient realms of the satellite and characterised by innumerable craters, the legacy of millions of years of asteroid collisions. The probe was advancing towards one of them now: Tolly saw its lip as a darker streak of grey along the horizon of a world of grey. It was a big one, vast, though what it might contain was still minutes from discovery. The probe pressed on eagerly.

'I don't . . .' began Tolly. And then he did. It wasn't the visual information that was engrossing Professor Robertson and a clutch of his other colleagues. It was the probe's energy readings. They were off the scale. 'That can't be right,' he said. 'There must be a malfunction in the system . . .'

'There isn't,' stated Professor Robertson. 'Computer's checked. We've checked. The probe is in perfect working order, and somewhere in that crater is a source of almost limitless energy.'

'Analysis?' Tolly said.

'More intriguing still. Results of analysis: computer reports that the energy signature is of unknown origin, unknown nature.' She regarded her younger colleague meaningfully. 'I told you you'd want to see this.'

Robertson was not wrong. Tolly felt his heart pounding. If the computer failed to recognise the kind of energy that the probe was registering, it could mean only one thing. *Alien*. Tolly Porter, member of EXIST, could be on the brink of his first case.

'What are you saying?' Chief of Security Brankovic spoke for the first time. He used the slightly accusing tone he always reserved for conversations with scientists, whom as a breed he seemed to distrust. 'Are you saying we might be in danger, Professor Robertson? Should I sound an alert?'

'Oh, I don't think we need go to DEFCON One just yet, Chief Brankovic,' said the Professor calmly. 'Let's at least wait and see what the probe has to show us in the crater, shall we?'

And it was going to be any second now. Tolly watched spellbound as the probe inched its way up the rising ground towards the crater. Reach the top and it would command an unobstructed view of whatever lay within. Tolly reminded himself to stay cool. Scientists, even those secretly employed by the Deveraux organisation, needed to be guided by evidence, not imagination. Evidence the probe was on the cusp of providing. It gained the full height of the crater's wall. It toppled forward. Tolly didn't dare to blink in case he missed the first glimpse of . . .

The viewscreen went blank.

'What? I don't believe it.'

The data screens died. The surface probe had suddenly ceased transmitting.

'Total failure of all probe systems,' observed Professor Robertson with dismay.

'Was it attacked?' Chief Brankovic wanted to know. 'Can it have been destroyed by whatever that energy source is?'

'Disrupted, possibly,' said the Professor. 'Inadvertently. Shot at and blown up or something deliberately, however, which I assume is what you mean, Chief Brankovic, I rather doubt.'

'But you can't be sure, can you?' demanded Brankovic.

'A scientist requires proof to be sure, sir,' said the Professor tetchily.

'Then what are we waiting for?' It took Tolly a moment to realise that the animated voice spilling into the room like children into a playground was his own. 'Let's find the proof. Let's take a moon-hopper and get out there. To the crater. The energy's not radioactive and we've got our suits anyway. We should be safe enough.'

'That might depend, Porter,' said Brankovic, 'on anything that *is* out there.'

Mightn't it just, Tolly enthused inwardly. He prayed for aliens while the Professor and the Chief of Security decided between them that yes, perhaps a preliminary reconnaissance trip to the crater might indeed be advisable. Aliens, he begged silently, or at least secret weapons left over from the Moon Rush. Anything that would require him to contact Deveraux.

Tolly Porter, secret agent. He could make it yet.

Ben and Cally hailed a wheelless cab to take them to the Lenehan Hotel. Cally was now draped in a slinky red dress with a wrap for her bare shoulders and an evening bag by her side. Ben, who was into turn-of-the-century movies on the quiet, thought she looked like Halle Berry in her prime.

'It's a beautiful moon tonight,' she said.

'I guess so,' said Ben, 'if you've got a thing for barren hunks of rock hanging in mid-air.'

'Oh, Ben,' sighed Cally, 'the last of the great romantics. Come on, what say we ask the cabbie to shoot past the hotel and go for a moonlit walk in the park instead. I promise we can hold hands and everything.'

'Sounds good for later,' qualified Ben, 'but for now, business calls.' The cab pulled up outside the hotel's main entrance. 'You're not still worried, are you?' But clearly, Cally was.

'I just don't feel comfortable coming to an occasion like this, Ben.' She peeped out at the palatial hotel building and the lavishly attired bluebloods wending their well-heeled way inside. 'I don't belong. These guys, I don't know about being born with a silver spoon in their mouths. Some of them look like they had the whole canteen. Money all their lives. What's a girl from the street got in common with any of them?'

'You're dating one,' Ben pointed out. 'The heir to the Stanton fortune, no less.'

'You're different,' said Cally.

'I wasn't once. Not when we first joined Spy High.' Ben inwardly shrank from the memories. He'd arrived at Deveraux with all the arrogance of privilege intact, had spent most of the first semester imagining he was ten feet tall just so he could look down on the likes of Cally. He'd never have contemplated a relationship with her then, beyond her asking him whether he wanted fries with his order. How times changed. How people changed.

'You *learned*, though, Ben,' said Cally.

'Yeah,' Ben said, 'and if *I* can learn, so can anybody. Just give them a chance.'

'Hey, buddy,' interrupted the cab driver, 'is this a fare or a rehearsal for a soap opera? You getting out here or what?'

They got out. Cally supposed that Ben was right. The Maureen Lenehan Memorial Trust existed to finance projects that improved the life chances of the less fortunate among Boston society, the homeless, the destitute. She couldn't quarrel with that. The Trust's Annual Dinner which they were now attending cost five hundred dollars a plate, all monies going directly towards urban renewal in the very areas of town where she'd grown up. Cally couldn't quarrel with that, either.

So she smiled as the official photographer snapped her and Ben together. She smiled as they were shown to their table in the luxurious Liffey Room, chandeliers sparkling from the ceiling like stars. Smiled even as, from the high table on the platform where the Trust's representatives and officers sat, it was announced that dinner would be preceded by the speeches.

Gaped in shock when Ben was called on to give one.

'. . . making a special announcement on behalf of the Stanton Foundation, Benjamin T. Stanton Jr himself . . .'

'Surprise, baby,' Ben winked among the applause.

It seemed that the Stanton Foundation was establishing a fund, to be administered in conjunction with the Maureen Lenehan Memorial Trust, a fund to supply educational grants to young people from deprived backgrounds here in Boston. 'Somebody's starting point in life,' said Ben from the podium, 'should never dictate where they finish. No limits. No barriers. Only dreams and the means to make them come true.' And when the means that the Stanton Foundation was willing to donate in order to make them come true were announced, even the waiters fringing the room burst into cheers.

Even the man with the hooded eyes.

'That was *so* Bruce Wayne, Ben,' Cally grinned after he'd returned to their table and the meal at last was being served. 'Why didn't you *tell* me . . .?'

'And spoil the big moment?' Ben laughed. 'No way. But what I am going to tell you, Cal, is that the Stanton Foundation's generosity is down to you.'

'What do you mean?'

'Without you, I doubt I'd have thought of suggesting the educational fund to my father. And one of our first projects is going to be to fully restore Mac Luther's old refuge, turn it into a place where street kids can go and learn with state-of-the-art computer equipment. Get some competition for you, Cal.'

'I can live with it.' Cally thought fondly of her former mentor, Mac Luther. He was dead now, but he'd have approved of Ben's gesture. So did she. She reached out, grabbed him by the bow tie – 'No, not the tie, Cal. If it comes undone I'll never . . .' – and pulled him towards her. Their lips met just above the candles. 'Thank you,' she said, and she meant it. 'You don't know how this makes me feel, but you will. I promise.' Cally's eyes gleamed suggestively.

'Maybe we can cut straight to mints and coffee,' said Ben.

It seemed not. 'Excuse me, please.' They were forced to resume their seats while a waiter slopped out their soup.

'Hey, careful.' Ben jerked back as the hot liquid splashed. 'I didn't bring a change of shirt with me.'

'So sorry,' said the waiter, in a tone that implied the opposite.

Ben looked at the man critically. Maybe he shouldn't be surprised he had almost missed the bowl. With eyelids drooping like that, it was a miracle he could even see the table. But there was something else, something more dangerous than incompetence. The way the man had clenched his teeth at Ben's protest, the way he avoided his gaze. That was hatred. That was contempt, barely controlled. Ben had come top of the year in the Body Language Analysis and Evaluation Module at Spy High. He decided to keep an eye on their not-so-friendly waiter.

'Chill, Ben,' said Cally, observing her boyfriend tracking the man's every move. 'So the guy needs more practice with a ladle. Who doesn't? Maybe he's nervous. Maybe he's new. Forget it. Stare at him much longer and you might make me jealous.'

'Something's not right,' Ben mused. 'Look at his mannerisms with all the other diners. It's like he can hardly stand being close to them. And he keeps passing these meaningful kinds of glances to some of the other waiters. Not all of them. Some. Like they're in something together. And he keeps looking at his watch.'

'And here he comes to clear away the soup plates,' noted Cally. 'You're not going to accuse him of being a Diluvian in disguise, are you, Ben?'

'Don't worry,' Ben said. He was going to be more subtle than that. 'Where's Silvio tonight?' he asked genially, as the man with hooded eyes removed their plates. 'You must know Silvio. He's waited here for years. Big guy. Can't miss him. Said he was going to be on duty tonight.'

'Silvio,' said the man with hooded eyes. 'He's sick.'

'Is he? That's a shame.' As well as being taught how to deduce other people's inner feelings from their body language, Spy High students were instructed in techniques to obscure their own. They came in handy for Ben just then.

'Who's Silvio?' said Cally as the waiter departed.

'As far as I know, nobody. Which means,' Ben pursued grimly, 'either I've just been involved in the biggest coincidence of all time, or I was right in the first place and our evening is about to take a turn for the worse.'

The waiters with whom their own had been silently communicating were clustered by two covered trolleys on either side of the Liffey Room. By the main entrance and the kitchen entrance, Ben realised. To stop people leaving, maybe. The man with the hooded eyes was ignoring an irate diner and heading for the group by the main entrance. That would make four on each side.

'What are you wearing, Cal?' Ben said.

'Sleepshot bracelets. I never leave home without them. Why?'

A sudden, startling howl of rage from the man with the hooded eyes. Covers torn from the trolleys. Not food beneath. Pulse rifles. Seized and fired above the heads of the assembly.

'That's why,' gritted Ben. 'Get down!'

Screams of terror and shrieks of fear as close to a hundred of the wealthiest and, in many cases, most out-of-condition members of Boston's citizenry dived inelegantly for cover. Crystal glasses shattered. Wedgwood plates smashed. Vintage wine gurgled freely from bottles sent flying in the panic, over virgin tablecloths, over thousand-dollar dresses, splattering to the floor like blood. Middle-aged men crawled for shelter under tables. Middle-aged women beat them to it.

Only Ben and Cally crouched, poised and purposeful.

'Yes! Yes! That's it!' They couldn't really hear Hooded-Eyes' voice over the rattle of the pulse rifles, but they could read his lips accurately enough. 'On your knees, you pampered pieces of filth, where you belong! Grovel! Beg for mercy! Not a cent of your riches can save you now!'

'Ransom's out, then,' Cally muttered.

'Oh, yes. This guy's lost it big-time,' Ben judged. 'But they're not shooting *at* us yet, which means they've got something to say first. Gives us time.'

'Odds of four to one?' said Cally. 'And a hundred innocent bystanders besides?'

'They won't be standing,' Ben pointed out, 'but you're right, we'll need an edge. You got access to radar vision?'

'Glasses. In my bag.'

'Excellent. Put 'em on. Maybe we should leave these guys in the dark.' Ben slipped out of his jacket and began to pull off his bow tie. 'This thing was never me, anyway.'

Hooded-Eyes had climbed on to the platform while his companions held their positions around the perimeter of the Liffey Room, weapons pointing inwards. The firing had stopped. The clamour of the captive diners had subsided to moans and sobs and the occasional abject squeal. Hooded-Eyes raised his hands for silence and even that was stilled.

'You're wondering who we are,' he shouted, his voice as venomous as a cobra's fangs. 'We are your ultimate nightmare. We are the impoverished, the dispossessed. We are those you cringe from behind your high walls and your security shields in the temporary safety of your mansions. We are the anger and the hate of those who have nothing. We are their burning need for revenge.'

'Keep talking, sucker,' Ben urged under his breath. He was tying a new knot in what had been his bow tie so that now it looked more like a blindfold. Cally had donned a pair of rimless spectacles: nobody had noticed.

'You're wondering more precisely what we want,' Hooded-Eyes was continuing. 'We want to prove to you, once and for all, to you and the masses beyond this building, that there can *never* be community between the rich and the poor, between those who support this iniquitous social system and those who are its victims.'

'That's right,' Ben snorted. 'Everyone's a victim.'

'Your pathetic masquerade of charity does not deceive us. A scrap volunteered from a table is still a scrap. But some who are too gullible to know better *may* be deceived, may see potential friends where they should see only implacable enemies. Some may even start to believe the old lie that society can change through co-operation, tolerance and mutual understanding. They and everyone else must be reminded that society can only change through revolution. What we accomplish here tonight will be a lesson for us all.' He reached into his pocket and withdrew a small, glittering spherical object. 'Behold, our teacher!'

'Not good,' groaned Cally. 'Detonator. This joker is wired for more than sound.'

Ben had bared his right forearm. A sleepshot wrist-band had been hidden beneath his shirt. He fiddled with the cufflink on his left sleeve as if it was a radio receiver. 'We're gonna need to keep it snappy,' he said.

'When I press this button, we will all die,' announced Hooded-Eyes with a blend of pride, defiance and even a little excitement. An aghast wail from the cowering diners, silenced by another salutary burst of pulse rifle fire. Death now was even less preferable to death a minute from now. 'We will be consumed together in the flames of explosion and light the touchpaper for inevitable revolution.'

'Okay,' said Ben. 'You take the four on the kitchen side. I'll take the other three and Mr Would-Be-Suicide Bomber. And Cal, no mistakes.'

'Don't worry,' Cally replied, determined. 'There won't be.'

'You will be forgotten.' Hooded-Eyes just didn't let up. 'But I will live on for ever. In the ghettos. In the slums. In the children of the poor.'

'In your dreams, scumbag,' said Ben. And twisted his cufflink hard.

The Lenehan Hotel plunged into darkness.

Because no cufflink belonging to a graduate of Spy High was ever simply a cufflink. They always came equipped with certain properties that might prove useful in a mission situation, such as the ability, once activated, to disrupt the electricity supply for a range of one hundred yards and for a time period of five minutes.

As the terrorists instinctively opened fire with their pulse rifles, Ben and Cally would need to eliminate them in less than one.

Chaos and confusion in the dark. But not for the former members of Bond Team. Cally's spectacles were treated for infra-red vision. Ben's bow tie was woven with nano-chips that, once he'd tugged the material over his eyes, provided him with the same capability. The two of them could see as well as ever.

And after countless hours on the sleepshot range, their aim was impeccable. It was certainly good enough to shoot the detonator from Hooded-Eyes' hand. Now Ben had won himself and Cally some time.

'Stay down! Stay down!' Ben yelled as he bounded over fallen chairs and quaking bodies, whittling his opponents down as he charged.

Cally quickly halved the number of terrorists on her side of the room. The force of the sleepshot shells spun them round or slammed them into the wall, bringing instant unconsciousness. But even one foe left standing now could be a casualty disaster. They were shooting wildly, indiscriminately, no longer able above the renewed eruption of shouts and screams to hear instructions from Hooded-Eyes, even if he was still barking them. Cally's concentration had to be absolute. *Third man down. Fourth.* And it was.

Ben too had finished off his original opponents. Now only Hooded-Eyes himself remained. Ben smiled humourlessly as he saw the man on his knees, groping blindly for the fallen detonator. He wasn't going to be blowing anybody up for at least four minutes. Shooting them *down*, however, might be a different matter. Hooded-Eyes leapt to his feet in disgust and let loose with his pulse rifle. No firing harmlessly into the air now. Raking the Liffey Room with deadly sparks. If he couldn't murder everyone, he'd make do with a percentage.

'Over here! Hey, big guy! Over here!' Ben hurtled towards him, hoped the sound of his voice might draw his fire. It did. Only too well. He had to leap forward before the barrage of pulse blasts punched holes in his best dress shirt. (Spy High issue, of course, so it *was* reinforced with Kevlar.) Ben sprawled on the floor, outside the actual dining area. No protection from Hooded-Eyes' continued attack. The pulse rifle's blasts were dazzling his infra-red vision, difficult to focus on a shot. *If* he wanted to hit the terrorist directly.

In the field, an agent had to remember that there were always alternatives.

Sleepshot spat from Ben's wristband like a gesture of scorn.

The chandelier above Hooded-Eyes' head found its cable to the ceiling severed. It did the only thing an unsupported weight *could* do under the circumstances.

Ben and Cally arrived on the platform simultaneously. By the time the terrorist recovered from the impact of the chandelier, there'd be plenty of cops around to escort him into custody.

'Ben?' said Cally. 'Do you think he saw the light?'

Her partner grinned. 'As long as *they* didn't see *us*,' he said, indicating the scramble of diners stampeding for the doors now that the guns had stopped firing. Nobody seemed to have been badly hurt. 'That's a lot of people to mind-wipe if they did, and all with access to very good legal representation.'

'I reckon they'd volunteer to have the entire evening erased from their memories,' said Cally, 'but I won't. It was special what you did earlier, Ben, this thing with the Stanton Foundation. I'll never forget it.'

Ben waved her gratitude aside. 'Now, about this moonlit walk you mentioned . . .'

The moon-hopper was aptly named. It didn't so much fly above the lunar surface as travel in great cushioned leaps, propelled by powerful jets of air that took full advantage of the lack of gravity. Thus, the vehicle, which Tolly always thought resembled a modernist sculpture of an oversized frog, could cover significant distances without placing any real strain on the Moon Colony's limited energy resources.

For a hopper to reach the area from which the surface probe had mysteriously ceased transmissions would not be a problem.

'But what about this power source?' Chief of Security Brankovic twitched. 'If it could short out the probe, couldn't it do the same to the hopper?'

'Possibly,' admitted Professor Robertson. 'We'll just have to hope that it disrupts energies only operating on certain frequencies, won't we, low levels like the probe. Of course, Chief Brankovic, if you'd sooner *not* accompany us, I'll understand. The emphasis of this excursion *is* on science rather than security.'

Chief Brankovic evidently wasn't so sure. He came anyway, and he brought another security officer with him. Added to Tolly, Robertson, a third scientist called Shabuki, who was always rubbing his hands together as if they were cold, and a specialist hopper pilot, that made six adventurers in total. The vehicle could carry twice as many.

They were nearing the crater. All around them, the desolate, interminable greyness of the Moon was pocked and scarred with innumerable pits and chasms, like the rock had developed a bad case of acne millennia ago. And the stillness, the utter silence and lifelessness out there, in a world grey like tombstone, grey like impending snow. When Tolly had first arrived on the Moon, it had struck him that before the coming of man nothing had moved on the entire grey globe for countless centuries, not even a wind. The footprints of the first astronauts had still been perfectly visible when the earliest colony buildings had been constructed, as if they'd only been made that morning (not that, disorientatingly, day and night held any meaning on the Moon). No life before man; no sign of life since.

At least, not until now, perhaps.

The hopper came gently to rest on the surface. Its passengers crowded on to the bridge. 'Crater's up ahead,' the pilot informed them. Magnification on the viewing screen showed them the probe, as still and as lifeless as its surroundings, but kind of half turned towards them, as if waiting patiently for its human masters to catch up. 'Next leap'll take us over the wall and into it. Navigator can compute a safe landing if you want to proceed.'

'Why would we *not* want to proceed?' challenged Professor Robertson. 'Energy data, Tolly?'

'The same readings emanating from the crater as before,' Tolly said. 'And so far, no interference with the hopper's systems. That makes us green for go as far as I'm concerned.' He hadn't come all the way out here for nothing. If they didn't learn what was in the crater, he'd miss his chance to get in touch with Deveraux.

'Very well, then,' decided Professor Robertson. 'Take us in, pilot.'

'Yes, ma'am.'

Silent bursts of air, perfectly placed, launched the hopper into the sky. It vaulted the rising ground towards the crater's rim.

Aliens, Tolly was repeating in his mind, over and over again. Aliens. Aliens. Aliens.

Dr Shabuki's hands were creating sufficient friction to light a fire. Chief Brankovic's security officer had lowered automatically to his shock blaster. Professor Robertson was muttering words to herself that Tolly could not hear.

They were at the rim. The ground fell steeply away. The crater was deep. The crater was wide.

Everyone pressed forward to see. A collective gasp rose within the hopper.

Tolly's eyes widened with wonder. Whatever he'd expected to find, it hadn't been *this* . . .

ONE

Naturally, parental visits to the Deveraux College ('Educating for Achievement') during term-time were discouraged. Independence and self-sufficiency were among the core qualities that the school strove to develop in its students, and neither was helped if Mum and Dad just happened to drop by every other weekend. On certain set-piece occasions, of course – graduation, the annual prize-giving ceremony – parents were more than welcome, but as a rule it was best for all concerned if otherwise they simply stayed away.

If fussy or over-protective relatives *did* turn up on the sprawling Deveraux estate unexpectedly, however, this was what they'd see. As they approached the imposing and slightly intimidating gothic façade of the college itself, a football game on the sports fields that never seemed to end and that was played in total silence; athletes circling the track relentlessly who never seemed to tire. In the reception area, a secretary, Violet Crabtree, who appeared well past retirement age but who could kill them with her bare hands should the inclination take her, which happily so far it never had. In the corridors, more students, dutifully trooping from one lesson to another but never entering a classroom, largely because holograms came already programmed and therefore did not require conventional education. If this was all the visiting parents saw before Mrs Crabtree could summon their offspring or a flesh-and-blood member of staff to fool them further, then all was normally well. If not, there was the unpleasant but necessary business of the mind-wiping to go through.

There are some things about their children that parents should certainly *not* know.

Applied to the Deveraux College, such things included its nickname, Spy High, which rather eloquently described the establishment's true purpose: to provide an education in espionage, classes in covert activity, semesters for secret agents. They included the fact that the Jonathan Deveraux who'd founded the institution had actually died years back, and that the Jonathan Deveraux who now resided on the top floor of the main building was all that remained of him, his computerised and digitalised brain (small wonder he was notoriously reclusive). They included the study elevators, book-lined rooms with desks that transported their occupants far below ground to the kind of accommodation not routinely available for use by minors; the holo-gym, the virtual reality chamber replete with state-of-the-art cyber-cradles; the Gun Run; the enspyronments.

The Intelligence Gathering Centre.

The IGC had never been Ben's favourite part of Spy High. As a student here, he'd always preferred the more physical and more competitive elements of the training, and had tended to spend his spare time in the holo-gym or reducing the world's population of virtual terrorists on one of the shooting ranges. Now that he'd graduated, however, things were different.

Now that he was no longer simply Benjamin T. Stanton Jr, but Benjamin White besides.

'Computer, Region White,' he said, reclining in the leather chair, his cyber-helmet secured. Immediately, his mind was bombarded with images of everything from politics to pop music, from statesmen to sport, from art to armed conflict. This was what the Intelligence Gathering Centre did: it plugged in to every news broadcast on the planet and downloaded them to Spy High for analysis and evaluation; it classified, categorised and cross-referenced. Jonathan Deveraux believed that for the organisation he'd founded to succeed in its avowed aim, to keep the world safe for tomorrow, it should never only *react* to events: it had to anticipate them as well, and for that intelligence was critical. Expert threat analysts scrutinised the IGC's data twenty-four hours a day in order to identify the next likely global flashpoint where Spy High intervention might be required.

Ben didn't have to involve himself with any of that – which for his own sanity was just as well – but he did feel beholden to keep up to date with the latest from his assigned area of operation. Region White extended from the eastern borders of Europa, including many of the former Soviet satellites from the last century, right across the nations of the Russian Tsarist Federation to the shores of the Pacific Ocean. That was a lot of square miles, and something seemed to have been happening in every one. Ben had intended this only to be a fleeting visit to Deveraux, between his eventful evening in Boston with Cally and his return to New Moscow. If he wasn't careful, he'd still be in the IGC next week.

'Computer, refine data,' he said. The computer didn't notice, not having eyes, but Ben's expression became stern before he spoke again: 'Focus on Wallachia.'

He scarcely needed the IGC to alert him to the volatile political situation that was on everyone's lips, but at least here he got graphics. A map formed in his mind. A helpful newscaster pointed out the tiny country of Wallachia almost crushed between the Corpornation of Romania and the eastern edge of Europa where once had been Hungary. Cue stock footage of proud mountains and plunging valleys, dense, dark forests, all-singing, all-dancing peasants with nothing on their feet and probably nothing in their bellies either, Ben thought. He doubted that Vlad cared much for the feeding of commoners. And it had to be stock footage, of course, officially released via a spokesperson for the Tepesch government. Outlanders were not allowed to trespass on hallowed Wallachian soil.

Cut to a journalist outside the United Nations building in Cairo. 'Tension between the western powers and Wallachia continues to grow,' she said, 'with little hope for compromise in sight. The isolated and little-known kingdom of Wallachia has been ruled by the Tepesch family for generations and has always, it seems, revelled in its reputation as a maverick, fiercely independent sovereign state. It appeared, when President Vlad Tepesch approached the United States to bid for corpornation status some three years ago, that its international exile might finally be coming to an end, and that Wallachia

was ready at last to enter the modern age. Such did not
prove to be the case.' Visuals of a tall, dark, heavily robed
figure being bundled by swarthy and bearded security
men into a hover-limo. Ben didn't require a clear view of
the man's face to recognise him. The features of Vlad
Tepesch were burned on to his memory as with a brand-
ing iron. His hands were fists. 'Indeed,' the journalist
continued, 'rumours persist that while in America and
under the protection of diplomatic immunity, President
Tepesch was actively involved in certain illegal activities,
including the manufacture and sale of drugs . . .'

'You can say that again, baby,' snarled Ben. 'If you
only *knew*. Computer, fast forward thirty seconds.'

The journalist jumped in time with nary a hair out of
place. 'The accusations of both the United States and
Europa that the Tepesch regime is in possession of
weapons of mass destruction have received a combative
denial from Dracholtz.'

Ben recognised the spokesperson as well, the man like
a heavily whiskered bull. Boris had once saved their lives
back in the days of Bond Team. Of course, he'd also tried
to kill them. *Never trust a Wallachian*, Ben reminded
himself.

'It is a lie,' Boris was claiming defiantly. 'We have no
weapons. We Wallachians are a peaceful people who
love our liberty and wish to be left alone. The charges
brought against us by the Americans and the Europans
are entirely and absolutely false. This talk of weapons of
mass destruction is nothing but a smokescreen, a deception to mask the true agenda of the outlanders. Regime
change. These decadent so-called democracies look envi-
ously to Wallachia and see a country they have yet to

dominate, a leader in President Tepesch they have yet to intimidate, a people they have yet to cow. No, we will not submit to their outrageous demands for weapons inspectors to be allowed entry within our borders. We will not submit to *anything* that compromises the sovereignty and authority of the Wallachian state. Our land is inviolable, and we will defend it by whatever means necessary.'

'I bet you will, Boris,' muttered Ben. 'I bet old Vlad is just gagging for an excuse to go to war.'

That was Ben's interpretation of the Wallachian's darkly threatening 'whatever means necessary'. It was the journalist's, too, as the IGC brought her back to life, *and* the opinion of the five permanent members of the UN Security Council, though India didn't seem entirely convinced. Whatever small differences of thinking remained, however, one conclusion seemed inarguable. The Wallachian situation was swiftly escalating into crisis.

Ben let his mind drift while the journalist talked. Inevitable, too, he thought. It had been bound to happen. Not necessarily conflict between Wallachia and the west, no, but confrontation between himself and Vlad Tepesch. After the Serpent Scenario three years ago. After the turf war between the Serpent gang and the Wallachians, muscling in on the streets with their poisonous drug, Drac. After Bond Team had been caught in the middle. After Jennifer had been killed, a team-mate, a friend.

After Tepesch had got away.

But not again. Not next time. And there *was* going to be a next time, Ben sensed. Soon. The present unrest demanded it. Wallachia was White. *He* was White. His next assignment would be to Vlad's homeland, he was certain, and he'd be taking it professionally, sure. But more than that. He'd be taking it *personally*.

As if he was suddenly psychic, Ben's cyber-helmet cut out, the IGC program over-ridden by a voice that requested 'Benjamin White to Briefing Room One, please. Benjamin White to Briefing Room One.'

Here it was already. His mission to Wallachia.

He was wrong by about 384,000 km.

Dr Fredo Franco groaned in his bed. He seemed to remember the bleeper sounding for the end of his rest period long minutes ago, but he was unable to move. His limbs, they had no strength in them, as if his muscles had turned to liquid during his sleep and leaked away. He felt as feeble as an old man on the last day of life.

And thirsty? His throat seemed caked with a Saharan dryness. He had to drink. He had to drink or he'd die.

Dr Fredo Franco lurched painfully into a sitting position. A lance of agony bolted through his brain, causing him to gasp. He couldn't get up. He couldn't do it. Movement hurt too much.

He wasn't well.

He looked down at his hands. He could just about make them out, even though his vision was thick and rheumy, like a window smeared with filth. His hands seemed paler than they should be, almost as if his skin had been peeled back like cellophane to expose the bone. And he thought he'd cut his fingernails only recently.

He was sick. Clearly, sickness had seized him as he'd slept. Given the quality of his dreams, he wasn't surprised. On a grey Moon, Dr Fredo Franco had dreamed of red. Deep red, and everything drowning in it.

He had to get up. There was work to do. Especially after what they'd found in the crater. Moon Colony Armstrong didn't run itself.

And he had to drink. He had to drink or he'd die.

He was on the floor. Somehow, at some point, he'd fallen. His tongue was like a stone in his mouth. A drink. A long, cold guzzle of purified water and he'd be fine. He remembered being fine, once.

And he was in the bathroom, by the sink. And someone else was in there with him. Someone in the mirror. Because that couldn't be Dr Fredo Franco staring out at him, the ghostly white face, the burning red eyes, the mouth a gaping black hole. And the *teeth* . . .

He had to drink. He had to drink or . . .

But it was no good. It was no good. A lost wail from deep within him, the fear of a child sleeping alone in his room for the first time. The water, no matter how much gushed down his throat, no matter how much he gulped and glugged, it didn't relieve the desert dryness that parched him. It couldn't slake his thirst.

He needed something else for that. Something stronger. Something sweeter.

From his red dreams, Dr Fredo Franco remembered what it was.

'Fredo?' A voice from the corridor, conveyed into his quarters by the intercom. 'It's Marianne. Hope you don't think I'm being intrusive, but do you know you're late? Shuttle's on its approach path now. Are you all right?'

Dr Fredo Franco's eyes narrowed craftily. 'Computer,' he croaked, 'open door.'

The door dutifully slid open. Marianne Laporte took the hint and stepped inside. Didn't see her colleague, but guessed he was in the bathroom. Could hear the sound of water running. 'They're sending someone from some hush-hush government agency to look at our find. He's supposed to be aboard.'

'Computer,' Dr Fredo Franco said, 'close door.'

And Marianne Laporte started at the guttural tone of his voice. 'Fredo?' she ventured. 'Is something wrong? What are you doing in there?'

He had to drink. And he knew now what it was he had to drink.

Marianne Laporte screamed as her former colleague leaped at her from the bathroom, as he bore her down and snarled and growled more like an animal than a human being, as his clawed hands tore at her collar and his skeleton face thrust closer.

As his lips parted. As his fangs were bared.

There was only one liquid, bubbling and crimson and hot, that could save Dr Fredo Franco.

In a place where everything existed but nothing lived, Ben and Tolly Porter shook hands. They were two of only three intrusions in an otherwise perfect and illimitable cyberscape of white. The third was the head of Jonathan Deveraux, appearing as usual as if it had been cast in iron, austere and determined, the size of a man's body and suspended in the nothingness like a sun. Or a god.

'I know who *you* are, Ben,' Tolly was saying, with an awe usually reserved for pop stars or sporting heroes. 'How could anyone who's been to Deveraux *not*? Ben Stanton. Highest aggregate score of any Spy High student ever. Even when training, found time to fight and foil CHAOS, Nemesis, the Diluvians, Dr Frankenstein – twice. I was really sorry when you lost the leadership of Bond Team, Ben, and when you split up with Lori Angel, and that unfortunate business with your Uncle Alex . . .'

'Have I died?' Ben interrupted. 'Is this my whole life flashing before me or what?'

'Sorry. Sorry.' Tolly coloured. 'I just . . . I always used to . . . I was at Spy High the same time as you, Ben, well, the year below actually, but I went into EXIST. Kind of low profile. I don't suppose you remember me.'

'Sure I do,' said Ben, even though he didn't. His days of gratuitously hurting other people's feelings were behind him. 'Tolly Parker, right?' *Largely* behind him.

'*Porter*, actually,' Tolly corrected shyly. 'Tolly Porter.'

'That would have been my next guess. And hey, what's a vowel and a consonant between friends?'

Friends. Tolly grinned. Ben Stanton had said *friends*. Porter, Parker or whatever they wanted to call him, Tolly was on the up.

'Perhaps,' said Jonathan Deveraux, 'as you've taken the trouble to establish this virtual link, Agent Porter, you could show us the crater.' Whatever he'd been like as a man, as a computer program the founder of Spy High had no time for small talk.

'Oh. Sorry, sir. Of course. At once,' Tolly said.

And the virtual reality reconfigured itself around them. Ben's physical form might have been stationary in his cyber-cradle at Deveraux, but thanks to the marvels of modern science his cyber-self was walking on the Moon. Or would have been, had the sight before him not stunned him into motionlessness.

Clearly, a battle had once raged in the crater, a battle fought by giants. What it had concerned, who its combatants were, these were questions at the moment imponderable, but that the conflict had occurred was beyond dispute. Its casualties remained. Bodies lay strewn on the lunar surface, bodies in armoured space suits, clasping weapons with unguessable functions in centuries-dead fingers, bodies that were arched and twisted, preserved in death throes that had endured since the Romans, since the Greeks. Bodies that seemed to Ben to be twelve feet tall.

'That's right,' Tolly said to this estimate. 'We haven't moved any of them yet, but we've started analysis. Twice the height of a human being. And if you're thinking could they be statues, they might look like it now, but no. Preliminary bio-scans reveal internal organs similar to our own. They might be freeze-dried now, but once they were living, breathing beings.'

'It's amazing,' Ben marvelled. He leaned over one of the sprawling giants, peered through the visor of his helmet. A face could just about be discerned, grey and ghostly and fixed in an eternal scream, a face like a man's but with the features less distinct, less *finished*, somehow, as if the god who had created this particular race had grown bored with the task halfway through and abandoned it.

'How many are there?' Ben asked Tolly.

'One hundred and twelve. The markings on their armour, their suits, all seem to have certain symbols in common, so we're assuming they were on the same side. The bodies are all in this segment of the crater, which is about a mile in diameter and a perfect circle,

Ben,' Tolly seemed to think this significant, 'a *perfect* circle, so I reckon they were either making a last stand or mounting a charge against something. I'm betting it was the stone.'

'The what?'

'The starstone.'

Tolly beckoned towards the centre of the crater and the ground shifted obediently beneath the teenagers' virtual feet. An object moved towards them that was slightly taller than the alien giants, the same measurement across. It took the shape of a multi-pointed star flung wide to embrace the furthest reaches of space. It was clearly an artefact, not a naturally occurring body, and it seemed to be made of a substance not unlike marble, smooth and grey tinged with green and miraculously unblemished after possibly a thousand lifetimes standing lonely sentinel here in the crater. The star was anchored by a base of the same material, while into its precise centre was set a display of panels, control panels, Ben imagined, a profusion of flashing, flickering buttons and lights amid scribbles of incomprehensible and ever-changing notation.

'We call it the starstone, for want of a better name.' Tolly laughed lamely. 'I guess you can see why.'

'It's active.' Ben sounded more startled than he'd intended. 'These panels. It's still operational.'

'That's right,' said Tolly. 'The starstone is the source of the energy readings that the probe first identified. They told you about the probe in your original briefing, didn't they?'

'What does it do, Tolly?' Ben seemed less than interested in the probe. 'Your starstone. What's it for?'

'At the moment,' Tolly reluctantly admitted, 'we have no idea. That's not to say we don't have theories, however. At least, *I* have a theory.' He paused almost coyly.

'Well, don't keep us in suspense,' Ben chided.

'Right. Sorry.' Tolly wasn't sure he was making the secret-agent-in-waiting impression he was looking for. 'Well, I don't think it's a coincidence that the starstone stands *exactly* in the middle of the crater,' he said, 'a crater that's, as I mentioned, perfectly circular. I think the starstone *caused* the crater. I think it killed the giants. Ben, I think the starstone is a weapon of some kind.'

'A functioning alien device,' summarised Jonathan Deveraux, 'of a technology potentially capable of untold carnage and devastation. The starstone must not be permitted to fall into the wrong hands, Agent Stanton.'

'No, sir.'

'Further investigation into its nature, purpose and capabilities must be carried out as a matter of urgency.'

'Yes, sir.'

'Your cover story has already been established. You will pose as a member of a government agency affiliated to NASA. By the time the authorities officially involve themselves, the Deveraux organisation should already have ascertained how dangerous this starstone might be.'

'You're sending me to Armstrong, sir?' Ben had still harboured faint hopes for Wallachia. 'But I'm no scientist. I don't know —'

'Your experience with the Diluvians may prove useful, Agent Stanton,' said Deveraux. 'EXIST Agent Porter will carry out all necessary scientific researches. You will ensure that he can do so *safely*.'

Ben regarded EXIST Agent Porter without enthusiasm.

'It's going to be a real privilege working with you,
Ben,' grinned Tolly.

So here he was, the only passenger aboard the Moon
Colony's supply shuttle, which was coming in to land
exactly on schedule. The milky, featureless rings of
Armstrong's buildings grew larger beneath him as he
gazed from the window. It didn't look like a happening
venue. The starstone and the aliens in the crater gen-
uinely intrigued him, sure, and it was a Spy High maxim
that any mission was a good mission, but Ben still felt
that another agent might have been better suited for this
assignment, someone who *liked* sitting around in labs and
doing analysis.

'Entering our final approach now,' announced the
pilot. 'Please remain seated until the umbilical has connected and the door safely opened.'

Course, it wouldn't have been so bad if Deveraux had
sent Cal with him, and not just because of their personal
relationship (though he wouldn't have said no to some
literally out-of-this-world lip action about now). Cally
possessed a brilliant computer mind, the best. Ben guar-
anteed she could have made something of the alien
technology. Instead, he was lumbered with this Tolly
Porter guy who, okay, probably knew his stuff all right,
and okay again, he shouldn't rush to judgements on first
impressions, that was something the old, unrehabili-
tated Ben Stanton had used to do, often to his cost, but if
he was honest, bottom line, the guy *did* look like he'd
majored in Nerd.

Ben sighed as he watched the umbilical corridor extend across the landing pad and lock on to the shuttle's door.

'Welcome to Moon Colony Armstrong,' greeted a cheery female voice. 'We hope your visit here is a pleasant one.'

Yep, Ben bolstered himself. There was always hope. But the reality was that the next few days were likely to be long on talk, short on action.

Then the woman started screaming.

'My God, what was that?' the pilot fretted, possibly considering an immediate return to Earth.

Ben had unbuckled his safety belt and was leaping to his feet. Whatever planet you were on, screams meant trouble, and trouble was the lifeblood of Spy High. 'Open the door!' he barked commandingly. The pilot did.

Ben pounded down the umbilical corridor and into the Colony proper. The woman who'd screamed had been guiding them in. Chances were good she was in the command centre. Ben had never been to Armstrong before, but he'd memorised its geography as part of his mission briefing. He raced in the appropriate direction as unhesitatingly as if he was its architect. Besides, he wasn't alone. Clusters of colonists, techs, scientists, security officers with blasters held in uncertain hands, all seemed to be heading towards the command centre, anxious, confused. The alarm was sounding and in the corridors red lights flashed.

An emergency door had been closed to seal off the final metres of corridor leading to the command centre. Several members of security were waving their blasters as if to suggest that they were in control of the situation, yes, honestly, and that the best their fellow colonists now pressing before them and crowding them with questions could do was to back off and let them do their job.

'Who's in charge here?' Ben's voice was impressive with authority. The colonists instinctively parted to let the newcomer through.

'Who are you?' one of the security officers parried.

'That wasn't what I asked.'

'I guess . . . we're still waiting for Chief Brankovic . . .'

'What's happening?

'I don't . . .' The security officer was *going* to say something like 'I don't have to answer to teenagers', but there was a quality in the blond boy's intense blue stare, a confidence, a leadership, that changed his mind and made him give way before the stranger's demand. 'One of our scientists, Dr Franco, something's *changed* him . . . He's gone mad, killed two people. He's in the command centre. We've cordoned it off until Chief Brankovic —'

'Are there any personnel still in there?'

'There might be . . .'

'Open the door,' Ben ordered. 'I'm going in.'

The security officer baulked. 'You can't . . . it's . . . hadn't we better wait for Chief Brankovic?'

'Do as he says, Milgrom!'

Ben and the security officer both looked round. Tolly Porter had joined the assembly.

'Tolly,' acknowledged Ben. 'You heard him' – to Milgrom – 'we don't have time to wait for instructions from your boss. I'm going in.' He punched the emergency door release himself.

'I'm coming with you,' piped up EXIST Agent Porter.

'No you're not,' stated Ben. 'You're staying here. Milgrom, see to it.' He raced forward.

'Don't you want a blaster?' the security officer called after him.

Ben didn't respond. His own was still aboard the shuttle with the rest of his luggage, but he was wearing sleepshot wristbands. They'd do.

'Isn't he just *so* cool,' admired Tolly.

Ben hadn't heard his fellow Deveraux graduate's final remark, but even if he had, and even if he agreed with it, which was likely, only one characteristic was of any consequence to him now. Discipline. The discipline forged from four years of training since the day he'd first entered Spy High's gates.

The discipline that would allow him to cope with the kind of nightmare scene that confronted him in the command centre.

Victims: three. A woman, spreadeagled on the floor and sticky with her own blood, beyond help. Another woman and a man, hurt, bleeding, but conscious. Alive. Groping painfully across the floor in glazed retreat from the figure that twitched and jerked among the computer consoles as if an electric current was being passed through him. The pale, cadaverous figure splashed with red as if children had been hurling buckets of paint at him in a fairground sideshow. But of course, it wasn't paint.

Dr Fredo Franco's senses were sharp. He wheeled to face the new intruder at once. He showed him his fangs, sharp and white where they weren't already stained with scarlet. His thirst, assuaged by the dead woman only temporarily, though for long enough to keep her erst-while colleagues alive, was returning with a vengeance. Ben was drink.

He was also, for a second, shocked. Discipline should have taken over and Ben should have fired his sleepshot and ended the threat in a heartbeat. But he'd seen a sickness like Franco's before and he hadn't expected to see it again. Not here. Not on the Moon.

So he was indisciplined. He paused. Just for a second. Just for a second Ben Stanton reacted like an average human being rather than a highly trained professional secret agent.

And the second almost killed him.

Franco was missile-fast. He launched himself clawing and ravening at Ben. Fingers tore for his throat. Their quarters were too close for sleepshot. But the spy was back. Ben didn't resist the impact of Franco's attack but rolled with it, used judo to throw the deranged scientist off him. Scrambled to his feet. Could get a shot in now.

But no. Franco recovered just as quickly, was seizing Ben's arm, clamping, squeezing. Sleepshot astray. His other hand, a vice at the teenager's throat. Ben pummelling, punching, but the madman seemed oblivious to pain, oblivious to everything but his craving, his vampire thirst. Ben was forced backwards, down, across the console.

Maybe he should have listened to Milgrom and waited. It was a long way to have come just to die.

The shuttle on the landing pad. He could still see it, through the command centre's window, the reinforced glass of its emergency airlock.

Its emergency airlock.

Desperate times, thought Ben. 'Hold on to something!' he managed to shout for the benefit of the two survivors. Fending Franco off with one forearm, with the other Ben aimed his sleepshot. Painfully twisted his neck in the lunatic's grasp for the best possible view of his target. If he missed, the snapping teeth wouldn't allow him a second chance.

He fired. At the airlock's controls. He didn't miss. The airlock sprang open.

All of a sudden the atmosphere inside the command centre had somewhere to go, and it seemed keen to get there. Breath was ripped from the lungs. A gusting rush of escaping oxygen filled the ears. Everything not bolted down was plucked from its place and sucked spiralling out on to the surface of the Moon.

The depressurisation yanked at Franco and Ben like a rope. But Ben knew it was coming. His crazed assailant did not. The teenager grabbed for a handhold on the console, found one. And now it wasn't so bad that Franco had forced him on to his back. It made it easier for him to lift his legs, to kick at the blood-spattered body on top of him. With his hand, one final, shuddering blow. 'Sorry, pal,' gritted Ben, 'seems you've got to fly.'

With a howl of anguish, the creature that had been Dr Fredo Franco lost his grip on Ben, was snatched up by the irresistible vortex of the depressurisation. He vanished flailing through the gaping airlock, out into the vacuum.

Ben didn't fancy going the same way. A second, equally accurate burst of sleepshot ensured he wouldn't. The airlock door resealed itself. The atmosphere stabilised. Air pressure returned to normal.

Life on Moon Colony Armstrong was unlikely to follow suit any time soon, Ben feared. The situation was more serious than even Jonathan Deveraux could have imagined. It seemed he'd have plenty to keep him occupied after all.

TWO

From *The Secret Agent's Guide to the World* by E. J. Grant

APPENDIX ONE: THE FINAL FRONTIER
(a) THE MOON

Had the Deveraux College been training secret agents thirty years ago, its graduates might well have found themselves on assignment to Earth's only natural satellite. The 2030s was the time of the Moon Rush. It was a period when the nations of the world were gradually recovering from the social and political upheavals caused by the Great Contamination of the previous decade, when stability and even prosperity were slowly returning, and when people were beginning to look to the future with renewed hope, with aspiration and ambition.

The Moon became a symbol of this new era.

Small, isolated scientific bases had been established on the lunar surface since 2019, fifty years after the original Moon landing, but now colonisation on a much wider scale was suddenly envisaged.

It was as if recent disasters earthside had made the prospect of a life beyond our atmosphere an altogether more attractive proposition. Sadly, however, the human race was to take with it into space not only those qualities that have helped to create the great civilisations of the past – courage, ingenuity, resourcefulness and sacrifice – but those that too often contributed to their destruction – suspicion, selfishness, aggression and greed. There followed a grab for land the like of which had not been seen since the European powers carved Africa up between them in the nineteenth century. In short, the Moon Rush.

The results were depressingly predictable, and dishearteningly familiar. Individual countries seized upon what they considered to be the most advantageous sites for their own colonies by whatever means necessary. Confrontation and conflict rather than cooperation and collaboration were the order of the day. There was sabotage. There was terrorism. There was loss of life. There was everything a Deveraux agent is trained to tackle.

But time passed, and times changed.

By the end of the thirties it became apparent that the vast majority of the Moon's colonies were simply unsustainable, not least because governments on Earth had seriously underestimated the financial costs of maintaining them. Economic reality meant that the Moon *Rush* soon turned into a Moon *Retreat*. Finally, at the Apollo-Soyuz Conference in 2041 it was decided between those nations that still preserved a presence on the Moon that their efforts should be rationalised and combined, that the few remaining colonies should become one, an international scientific and research facility named after the first man to set foot on the lunar surface. Thus was born Moon Colony Armstrong.

The Moon Rush and its sequel provide further evidence to support one of Mr Deveraux's most fervently held beliefs: though human beings seem by their nature inclined towards conflict and violence, they *are* capable of working and coexisting peacefully together when conditions permit them no other choice.

This is why now, at the time of writing in the mid-sixties, Spy High operatives are increasingly unlikely to visit the Moon during the course of their active duties. For twenty years Moon Colony Armstrong has been a shining example of concord and harmony. It seems improbable that circumstances will change in the foreseeable future.

What was left of Dr Fredo Franco lay on the medtable (and bearing in mind the effect on the body of subjection to a vacuum without a space suit, that wasn't too much). There was no need for restraints.

Autopsies in 2066 were at least less bloody than they'd used to be. Saws and scalpels had long ago been replaced by the medscan, which, fixed to the table, flashing lights in a range of colours and humming to itself as if engaging positively with its work, passed up and down above the remains of the hapless scientist like a magic wand. In any case, most of the small gathering clustered around the medtable like mourners around a coffin had seen deceased persons before. Dr Adebe, of course, and Ben and Chief of Security Brankovic, no doubt. Almost certainly Professor Robertson, too. Only Tolly looked as if passing time in the company of corpses was new to him. His colour was as grey as the landscape outside, his lips pressed tightly closed, largely to prevent his lunch from making a run for it, and if it wouldn't have disgraced him beyond redemption to have done so in front of Ben Stanton, he would have quite liked to have fainted.

To make matters worse, 'None of this is necessary,' Ben was claiming. 'Your instruments are only going to confirm what I've already told you. Franco's been infected with Drac. I've seen it before.'

'So you say, Mr Stanton,' sniffed Chief Brankovic. 'A drug that attacks the bloodstream and induces a violent craving *for* blood in the victim. A drug that turns you into a twenty-first-century version of a vampire. Perhaps you read a lot of fiction in this government agency you work for and which none of us have heard of, Mr Stanton. At the very least, perhaps you'll allow us to verify the condition ourselves before we go any further.'

Tolly felt like he ought to protest. Who was Brankovic to doubt Ben Stanton? Didn't he know what the Spy High agent had *done* over the past few years? But of course he didn't, and neither could he. Best to keep his mouth shut and secrets unspoken. Should help to reduce the risk of regurgitation as well.

Besides, Ben could evidently fight his own battles. 'Fine. We'll do it your way,' he was saying. 'You're the chief of security around here, Brankovic, though maybe if you'd been around here a little sooner when Dr Franco was on his rampage you might not be needing quite as many body bags.'

'I was outside the Colony buildings checking the new installations,' Brankovic retorted. 'I arrived on the scene as quickly as I could. My men were right to wait for my instructions.'

'Yeah? Tell that to . . . what are the names of the dead again?'

'Please,' intervened Professor Robertson, 'arguments are not conducive to progress. Dr Adebe?'

Who was examining the medscan's data and nodding her head thoughtfully. 'Seems you're right, Mr Stanton,' she accepted. 'Readings confirm a blood infection, a massive reduction in Dr Franco's red corpuscles. Extreme anaemia, accounting for the pallor of the skin. The fangs, physical mutation caused by the infection —'

'And leading the victim to try to heal himself by consuming, *drinking*, the uncorrupted blood of others. Your space-age vampire, Brankovic. It's Drac.' Ben frowned. While he hadn't gone to Wallachia after all, it seemed that Wallachia had followed him here. 'How many people live in the Colony, Professor Robertson?'

'Fifty,' came the answer. 'Fifty before our casualties, I should say . . .'

'Is the condition contagious?' Dr Adebe asked.

'If you're bitten and survive it is. Luckily, the late Dr Franco didn't get as far as sinking his teeth into the survivors from the command centre, though I still think they should be kept in isolation and under observation for the time being.'

'Taken care of,' said Chief of Security Brankovic. 'I've also signalled our condition to Earth and initiated a state of emergency quarantine. No more shuttles to or fro until our situation is resolved. We're on our own.'

'That was a little premature, wasn't it, Chief Brankovic?' Professor Robertson turned to him curiously. 'As leader of the scientific task force on Armstrong, shouldn't I have been consulted first?'

'With respect, Professor,' said Brankovic, 'in a security emergency, decisions are mine to make, and I thought that time was of the essence.'

'Agreed,' said Ben, 'so let's not waste it. Chief Brankovic, I suggest that your men carry out a complete and thorough search of the entire facility. Dr Franco didn't just wake up with Drac infection for no reason. Someone on Armstrong *gave* him the drug, slipped it into his food, his drink, something. Someone on the Moon isn't who he – or she – seems to be.'

'That's impossible,' declared Professor Robertson. 'Our personnel undergo the most stringent checks . . .'

'Professor,' Ben indicated the grisly remains of Dr Fredo Franco, 'I'm afraid it's not only possible, it's *certain*.'

'I'll order a search immediately,' said Brankovic.

'And I'll need a moon-hopper prepared for flight right now,' Ben said.

'Will you indeed?' The Chief of Security seemed to wonder why.

'I need to get to the crater and the starstone as soon as I can. That's why I'm here. My, ah, agency is extremely interested in your discovery, and I don't think we're the only ones.' Ben regarded his companions grimly. 'Alien artefacts one day and Drac in the colony the next. Coincidence? No way. I realise this is not what you want to hear, but every one of us is in deadly danger.'

Deadly danger? Tolly thought. *Fantastic*.

He'd drawn the short straw and no mistake, reflected Security Officer Milgrom gloomily. Search details were dull enough at the best of times, but he might at least have managed to stave off total boredom if he'd been allocated one of the more inspiring parts of the Colony to scour. That medtech Candy Carson's private quarters, for example – he wouldn't mind spending a few minutes going through *her* drawers – or the recreational areas, where maybe he could pause now and again for refreshment. Instead, here he was loitering rather unprofessionally in the Colony's storage chambers, surrounded by nothing but unwanted equipment and piles of steel containers that reached almost to the ceiling.

It was the blond kid's fault, that Ben Stanton or whatever he was called. Who did he think he was anyway, appearing on Armstrong like that, like some kind of superhero wannabe, throwing his weight around, giving orders? Making Milgrom look stupid. Okay, so he'd maybe saved the lives of two of the command centre's techs, and he'd sure put an end to that Dr Franco, but so what? He, Milgrom, could have done the same. *Would* have done the same if he hadn't been following orders and awaiting the arrival of Chief of Security Brankovic. It wasn't fair. It wasn't right. He'd noticed Candy Carson gazing at Stanton after they'd recovered Franco's body for an autopsy with the kind of expression he'd dreamed she might one day reserve for him. Seemed dreaming was all it would be.

And now Brankovic had completed his misery by condemning him to storage, so to speak. And that was Blondie's fault as well. His quick action had impressed the Colony at large and reflected badly on the Chief of Security. Brankovic, while maintaining in public that Milgrom and his colleagues who'd cordoned off the command centre had done the right thing, privately seemed to believe the opposite. Their duties since had not been the kind that earned promotion. Milgrom was not going to unearth a stack of this Drac drug or whatever it was called *here*. No chance of *him* saving the day. There was nothing here but himself and a load of useless containers.

So what was that then? That scrabbling sound.

What scrabbling sound? Milgrom listened more attentively. To nothing. He must have imagined it. A sound like mice scratching behind skirting-boards (though mice and skirting-boards were both in short supply on Moon Colony Armstrong) or fingernails scraping against a surface. *Long* fingernails, Milgrom judged, and a *metal* surface.

There it was again. He definitely heard it this time. Like someone trying to claw their way into something.

Or out.

Maybe this was his chance, Security Officer Milgrom's big opportunity to earn Brankovic's respect, put the blond kid in his place and turn Candy Carson's pretty little head in his direction, all at once. He listened more alertly still.

The scratching, it was close. It was coming from one

of the containers that had just been unloaded from the shuttle, the shuttle that had brought Stanton. Was this something to do with him?

Cautiously, Milgrom crossed to where the containers were lined up neatly in a row, as if only too eager for inspection.

His eyes flickered left to right, surveying them. A dozen identical steel caskets, fresh from Earth, like coffins, he found himself thinking, like metal coffins. Except that you tended only to place what was dead in a coffin. And inside at least one of these containers, something was alive.

But how could it be?

It didn't matter. It *was*. And in more than one. The scratching, the clawing, like sinister echoes, now from several, now from all of the caskets, all twelve. Gaining in strength, in animation, agitation.

As if his approach had awakened whatever lay inside.

With one of the final rational thoughts of his life, Milgrom considered contacting his chief of security and requesting advice before attempting to open any of the caskets. Perhaps, if waiting for a superior's instructions hadn't in his estimation shamed him before, he would have done so.

But he didn't.

Instead, he leaned across the gleaming steel casket nearest to him, the one from which the fingernail sound had first issued. He leaned across it to reach the panel release mechanism on the other side. He didn't get that far. He didn't need to.

The casket opened from the inside.

And something living *was* contained within. Some*one*.

Security Officer Milgrom would have screamed then. If he'd been given the chance.

'So tell me again,' enthused Tolly. 'Dr Franco's got his hands around your throat and there's no way you can shake him off, and then you think airlock door and—'

'Tolly, Tolly,' calmed Ben, 'can we not do this right now? I just put my training into practice, that's all.'

'That's *all*?' Tolly suspected undue modesty. 'We never got that kind of training in EXIST. Basic physical stuff in the first term and that was it. Hey, you couldn't teach me a few moves before you go back to Earth, could you?'

'Maybe,' Ben conceded. 'Sure. If you like.' He was uncertain whether having such an ardent fan alongside him was flattering or irritating. Or, indeed, both. It might have helped make up his mind if the fan had been female, gorgeous, and . . . But no. He only had eyes for Cally. 'But listen, Tolly, first things first. Something else I learned at Deveraux: yesterday and tomorrow only distract you from today. Your turn to tell *me* something. Update me on what's been happening at the crater.'

They were in a moon-hopper heading across the terrae towards it. Robertson, Brankovic and one of the security officer guys he'd encountered before were up front with the pilot, but Ben had directed Tolly to the passenger seating at the rear of the bridge. That way it meant they could talk business without having to whisper or pretend that they didn't both belong to the same covert organisation.

'We've already set up a temporary base,' Tolly said, 'inside the crater itself. Dr Shabuki and a team of three other scientists are working there full-time. We've moved one of the aliens into the analysis bay, started a more detailed and sophisticated bio-scan, begun trying to date the armour, that kind of thing. Haven't even attempted to shift the starstone itself, though. Professor Robertson thinks it might be safer if we worked on it where it is for the time being, at least until we've got a clearer idea of its actual purpose.'

'She might be right,' agreed Ben.

'I can take you out to it, though,' Tolly promised, 'when we get there.'

'That'd be great, Tolly,' said Ben. 'Thanks.'

'Ben? Can I tell you something else?'

'Sure.' Ben's heart slowly sank. There was the hint of imminently-to-be-shared confidences in Tolly's earnest and bespectacled gaze.

'My name. I don't like many people knowing, but Tolly's only an abbreviation.'

'Is that right?'

'My full name is Tolkien.'

Straight face, Ben commanded himself. Whatever you do, keep a straight face.

'After the guy who wrote the *Lord of the Rings* books back in the twentieth century. My dad was a real fan. My middle name is Aragorn.'

'Is that right?' Could have been worse, Ben thought. Could have been Gollum.

'I guess my dad thought that if I had names connected with adventure, I might have an adventurous kind of life. I think that's what he would have wanted. He was an accountant.'

'*Was*, Tolly?'

'He died. About a month before I was selected for Deveraux. If only he'd lived to have seen me . . . but I guess he couldn't have done anyway, could he? We can't tell anybody what we really do.' He pondered. 'Do you find that difficult sometimes, Ben?'

'All the time,' Ben admitted, more friendly now. 'But there's no alternative.'

'I guess not.' Tolly pushed his glasses higher up the bridge of his nose. 'So anyway, I just wanted to say, this is kind of like my *first* real taste of adventure, Ben, and I know you've been on lots of missions already and sur-vived certain death lots of times – well, you've done it once since you've *been* here – and I know being lum-bered with me as a partner – first name on the nerd team-sheet, Tolkien Aragorn Porter – I realise that must have come as a bit of a disappointment to you, especially as you're used to hanging with hot chicks like Lori Angel and Cally Cross, but I just wanted to say, Ben, I won't let you down. This is my chance to prove that I deserved to be at Deveraux. You can rely on me.'

'I know I can, Tolly,' Ben said. (Straight face.) They shook hands and he was glad. For a moment he thought Tolly might be going for the hug.

'Just . . . can you not tell anyone else my full name?'

'No worries,' Ben promised. 'Other things on my mind.' He felt it might be wise to return attention to the business at hand. 'Like how much longer is it going to take us to get to the crater?'

'At present forward velocity, thirty-three minutes and twenty seconds,' Tolly calculated. 'Approximately. I don't know, we seem really slow today. Like the air-jets aren't operating at full capacity or we're carrying extra weight or something.'

Ben doubted the latter. He glanced towards their quartet of co-travellers, a total well within the moon-hopper's advised limits. For a second the security officer was staring back at him and smiling rather disconcertingly. Then he'd turned to face the window. 'What did you say that guy's name was again?' Ben asked his companion, indicating.

'Oh, him,' said Tolly. 'That's Milgrom.'

The crater base was a series of simple, square accommodation and scientific units that could be added to and therefore extended with ease. Ben didn't linger. Long enough to be introduced to Dr Shabuki and his colleagues. Long enough to be given a brief tour, focusing on the petrified alien giant. Long enough to make a call to Armstrong, which established that no trace of Drac had yet been found, though neither, so far, had there occurred any new case of infection. Then he and Tolly donned space suits to venture out to the starstone.

The suits were of the newest design. Advances in insulation and life-support systems made them much less bulky, lighter to wear; helmets now were a single piece of transparent plasteel mounded to the shape of an average human head, contoured for eyes and nose and chin, like placing a hollow skull over your own. Fashion-conscious citizens of Earth were still unlikely to be seen stepping out in the season's latest line of spacewear, but if you happened to find yourself on the Moon and in need of mobility, you could hardly do better.

What with the suits and the reduced gravity on the lunar surface, the Deveraux agents made quick progress to the starstone.

'Your moon-walking technique is excellent, Ben,' complimented Tolly over their comlink.

Ben thanked him and assured him that his was pretty cool, too. Which, when he thought about it, was true. Even though he, Ben, had been subjected to various gravitational conditions as part of his Altered States Module at Spy High, there was no substitute for real experience in the field. Tolly must have walked the Moon many times. Maybe that fact would come in useful at some point. It was just a little odd to see him without his spectacles. Tolly's space helmet was personalised, the plasteel manufactured to the same specifications as his glasses. But anybody would have to be half-blind not to be aware of the starstone.

It loomed at the heart of the crater. It rose up powerfully, dominatingly, ominously. It was a jagged mouth raging in silence at the cosmos. It was a detonation, an explosion frozen in the act of destruction. It was something at which Ben could only guess. Somehow, he felt that before its mysterious mass he ought to speak only in whispers. How many eons had it stood here amidst this desolate greyness? And why did the reality of it now, so close he could reach out and touch it, and he did, why did the starstone fill him with a premonition of impending disaster?

The marble, the rock, whatever it was, it was warm – Ben could feel it through the temperature-sensitive pads of his gloves – warm as if heated by an inner flame.

'I know.' Tolly guessed what Ben was thinking. 'The only thing is, the heat doesn't register on any of our instruments. The only readings we're getting are of the unknown energy that's locked up in the starstone and that drew us here in the first place. We're going to need more sophisticated equipment, I think, if we're going to do better. Either that or find a language genius to decode these symbols for us.' Tolly gestured to the continually altering notation on the likely control panels. 'I haven't got anywhere even with my Babel chip.'

'Babel chip didn't help with Diluvian, either,' Ben said. 'It can only translate Earth languages. But all your star-stone data's with Deveraux, isn't it, visuals and everything? Maybe the langtechs'll get lucky. Either way, our immediate priority isn't divining the thing's secrets, it's ensuring we keep hold of it.'

'What? You think someone might try to steal it?' Tolly blinked disbelievingly as if he still wore his glasses. 'The starstone? From the *Moon*?'

'That's exactly what I think,' said Ben, 'and I've got a pretty good idea who.'

'Who?' pressed Tolly urgently.

'Come on, let's get back. This is something everyone needs to hear.'

'Wallachia?' grunted Chief of Security Brankovic. 'Never heard of it.'

'Then you obviously don't keep abreast of the news earthside, Chief Brankovic,' chided Professor Robertson. 'At the present moment there is what we might call tension between Wallachia and the western world, is there not, Mr Stanton?'

Ben acknowledged that there was indeed.

'Even so,' said Dr Shabuki, 'Earth politics are not supposed to interfere with the work or operation of this colony. Armstrong is an *international* facility. We have a treaty guaranteeing our independence.'

'President Tepesch doesn't do treaties,' said Ben. 'He'll take what he wants and he won't care about casualties. Look what happened with your Dr Franco.'

'But even if you're right,' worried Professor Robertson, 'and some Wallachian agent *is* responsible for the outbreak of Drac, I still find it difficult to believe that a tiny country like Wallachia can possess the kind of technology that would be required to remove the starstone.'

'When my agency encountered Tepesch before,' Ben countered, 'he was in the market for technology, weapons technology in particular. Who knows what he might have got hold of from other unscrupulous governments.'

'Ben's right,' Tolly blurted out, unable to keep quiet any longer. 'Why don't you all just *listen* to him?'

The ten-strong personnel of the crater base were gathered in the control room to do precisely that. After returning from the starstone, Ben had called them together, explained who he suspected of being behind the Drac infection and why. And to be fair, whether they seemed to accept his word or not, the group were granting him their complete attention. With one exception.

Security Officer Milgrom placed himself at the very fringe of the assembly, his face turned away from the others, as if he didn't want to see them, or them to see him. He couldn't contribute, his mouth was too dry. He couldn't follow what was being said anyway, even understand the words. He couldn't understand where he was or what he was supposed to be doing. Only one thought occupied his mind. *Thirst*.

The person closest to him, the moon-hopper's pilot, realised that something was wrong. 'Milgrom?' he enquired. 'Are you sick?'

Not sick. Thirsty.

Milgrom's mouth gaped wide and seemed to the pilot full of blades, shiny white blades. He screamed. He recoiled from the infected man. Not far enough. Not fast enough. Milgrom fell on him and drank.

A gout of shouts and cries. People leaping to their feet, scattering in fear and disarray. Ben's voice alone making sense, resisting panic. 'Get behind Brankovic or me. We can take Milgrom out if we can get a clear shot.' The Chief of Security's blaster. His own sleepshot. One or the other would halt the infected Milgrom in his tracks. 'No, out of the way!' A terrified scientist collided with him, blocked his aim. 'Brankovic!'

But Brankovic was running, fleeing, darting through the door and into the further reaches of the base. So that was why he'd taken so long to arrive at the command centre before. Moon Colony Armstrong had a coward for a Chief of Security.

Forget Brankovic, Ben prioritised. Save Shabuki first. But it was going to be difficult. The scientist was struggling, shrieking. Milgrom was using him almost like a shield. Ben couldn't get a shot. Everyone else was clinging to the sides of the room like they were welded in place, like their brains and their legs had both turned to mush. 'Tolly,' Ben yelled, 'get them *out* of here!'

Tolly nodded. 'Let's move! Let's *move*!'

He was doing it. Ben felt a kind of pride. He allowed his eyes to stray from Milgrom to Tolly for the merest moment, was punished for it.

Drac might ultimately destroy its victims, but in the meantime it bestowed great strength upon them. Strength sufficient for Milgrom to lift and hurl the bleeding body of Dr Shabuki at Ben, to knock him backwards, to make him momentarily vulnerable.

The infected man was at his throat.

'Not . . . *again* . . .' cursed Ben, grappling. 'Déjà vu I can do . . . without . . .'

And this time no emergency airlock to come to the rescue.

Ben had to make do with Tolly. 'Ben! No! Get *off* him!' Tolly pounding double-fisted on Milgrom's back, his head, making little impact. If only EXIST agents were trained to target the disabling pressure points on an enemy. If he survived to report back to Deveraux, Ben would suggest it for the future.

'Tol . . . ly . . .' But first things first. Yesterday and tomorrow only distract you from today. 'Ears . . .' As the strangling pressure around his throat squeezed darkness into his vision. 'His . . . ears . . .'

'Gotcha.' And Tolly slammed both fists against the sides of Milgrom's head.

The infected man felt the pain now. A vampire howl. His hands leaving Ben's throat to grasp at his injured ears. Ben thumping him to the floor, bringing his sleepshot to bear, Tolly flushed and expectant beside him. 'Now, Ben!'

But somebody got there first.

Milgrom's chest exploded as the shock blast struck it squarely. The shock blast from the doorway. Where Chief of Security Brankovic was standing.

'I wouldn't move if I were you, Stanton,' he advised, with the smile Ben recognised as routinely belonging to someone who thinks they're in control, 'or any of you snivelling weaklings either, except to raise your hands and place them on your heads, nice and slowly.'

'Ben?' Tolly looked to his partner for advice.

The shock blaster was pointing directly at him. Ben was lightning with sleepshot, but even so, to take such a risk as the true enemy, he assumed, was revealing himself was perhaps a little reckless. 'Do as he says, Tolly,' Ben muttered. 'For now.'

'Pity,' said Brankovic. 'I'd hoped you were going to play the hero again. Then I could have shot you with impunity.'

'You could have tried.'

'Oh, well, perhaps later.' Brankovic entered further into the control room.

'One gun to cover seven people?' Ben observed. 'What's to stop us rushing you?'

'Oh, my friends will do that,' supplied Brankovic, 'the friends I've just informed that they can come out now and stretch their legs. Milgrom's violent little diversion has served its purpose.'

There were shadows in the doorway, figures shuffling forward. The surviving scientists instinctively moved closer to Ben. Tolly blinked big behind his glasses.

'You didn't know you had travelling companions with you on the shuttle, did you, Stanton?' said Brankovic. 'Or, indeed, on the moon-hopper here. *Wallachian* companions.

Well, they did keep themselves very much to themselves in their life-capsules in the cargo hold, but they're quite keen to meet you now.'

Flanking Brankovic, bringing with them the stench of darkness and death.

'Agent Stanton, my former colleagues,' said the traitor, 'the Draculesti.'

THREE

They looked like lurkers from a graveyard. They looked like apparitions from the darkest nightmare. Black suits that clung to them like night. Hands and faces pale as fear. Hair curling long and inky to their shoulders, in the case of the females to their waists. Talons and fangs and lips of blood. But worst of all, most disturbing of all, were the eyes, pitiless, penetrating and as black as murder.

Involuntary moans rose in several of the scientists' throats, the sound of the condemned on first sight of the hangman. But Ben had to resist an emotional response. He could only afford to think in terms of numbers. Twelve new enemies, four of them the kind of women you wouldn't dare take home to your parents. Twelve plus Brankovic.

It was as well Ben wasn't superstitious.

'I see you shrink from the Draculesti,' approved the former Chief of Security. 'So you should. So you should. Cringe and squirm in the presence of my master's elite breed of warrior-assassins.'

They were demonstrating all the physical symptoms of Drac addiction, Ben noted, but they seemed entirely in control of their condition. More vampire than human, the Drac equivalent of body-builders on steroids. There was no doubt about it. He was in trouble.

'And so I claim the starstone in the name of his Royal Majesty Vlad Tepesch, Prince of Wallachia, in whose service—'

'Be silent, Brankovic.' One of the female Draculesti spoke, her voice sibilant with menace, flickering from her lips like a serpent's tongue.

'Yes, Modrussa.' Brankovic was quick to oblige.

'Stanton, boy, come forward.' The Draculesti's eyes glittered at Ben. She knew him. She'd singled him out.

Ben had no choice. His hands still on his head, he edged towards her. 'If you're going to ask me for a date, I'm afraid you're not my type.'

Lips peeled back in a hollow parody of a smile. Fangs protruded. 'I am Modrussa, Benjamin Stanton,' the Draculesti said. 'In my beloved homeland of Wallachia I am my prince's chief assassin.'

'Just as well we're on the Moon, then.'

'My prince has told me all about you,' Modrussa revealed, 'you and your little secret agent friends. I am disappointed to see none of them with you this time. Fortunate for the absentees, not fortunate for you. My prince instructed me to deliver you a message, Benjamin Stanton.'

'Couldn't he have used e-mail like everyone else?' But the Draculesti seemed impervious to distraction by one-liners. Another bad sign.

'My prince wants you to know that he remembers you

well, and the inconvenience you caused him in your United States. He wants you to know that he has waited patiently for three years to exact from you the payment in pain that you owe for the temerity of opposing him.' Modrussa's blank eyes gleamed. 'But now his waiting is over.'

Ben didn't see the blow coming. He felt it, though. The coppery taste of blood was in his mouth as he crashed to the floor. His least favourite flavour, too: his own.

'Ben!' And here was Tolly starting forward only for a male Draculesti to stab a shock blaster warningly in his face. But Tolly might still have tried something. He seemed to be eyeing up the Draculesti's ears.

'Tolly, no!' Ben cried. 'You, leave him al—' The remainder throttled by Modrussa's steel grip.

'We have no interest in your friend,' she placated, 'but *you*, on the other hand . . . We could hardly believe our good fortune when Brankovic reported your presence on the Moon. Once our primary task here is completed, you and I will become better acquainted, Benjamin Stanton. You are as pleasing to the eye as your reputation suggests. I may decide to *indulge* myself a little with you. Before you die.'

Modrussa released him and Ben dropped again to the floor. He felt cold hands removing his sleepshot wristbands. The Draculesti began herding the scientists towards the door.

'Ben, are you okay?' Tolly, his bespectacled features fraught with concern.

'I'll live,' he coughed. '*We'll* live.'

'Brankovic' – the chain of command was clear now – 'dismantle their vehicle and destroy all communications systems. There must be no possibility of contact with the rest of the Colony while we remain here.'

'Yes, Modrussa.'

'And then, comrades, we must be about our prince's work. Within the hour the ship will be here and the starstone will be ours.'

Within the hour. So the clock was already ticking for him to break out of the lab where they'd been incarcerated, Draculesti posted outside the door, overpower all twelve of them (plus Brankovic) *and* prevent the abduction of the starstone by a Wallachian spaceship. You couldn't *write* this stuff, Ben thought, or if you could, at least you might know how to resolve it.

He wasn't going to get much help from the scientists. They were whimpering, huddling together. The injured Dr Shabuki was shuddering as if about to go into shock. That had been Ben's first ploy, the 'this man/woman needs urgent medical attention' routine, which in Shabuki's case happened to be true. Ethics in Espionage: was taking advantage of somebody's wounds, maybe life-threatening wounds, was that morally acceptable if it advanced the mission? Irrelevant, anyway. The Draculesti on guard didn't care whether the captives lived or died. The door was not opened.

'Looks like it's you and me, then,' said Tolly. 'I'm ready. Let's go.'

'Go where?' Ben's enforced powerlessness was making him irritable. It was a hangover from the old, less mature Ben Stanton, when things weren't going his way to snap at somebody else. 'Even I can't conjure up an escape route out of thin air, Tolly. Only one door, locked and guarded. No space suits, so trying to smash the window's out.'

'We don't have to go outside.' Tolly grinned helpfully. He pointed upwards. 'In the ceiling. There's a space between the inner and the outer skins of each unit to improve insulation. I know. I designed these units for a science project when I was at school.'

'Why didn't you say so?'

'I *am* saying so. I know what they budgeted for as well. These overhead panels should be really easy to get off.'

They were. Ben and Tolly clambered on to one of the lab's benches and quickly exposed an enclosure certainly large enough to crawl through.

'Okay,' Ben said. 'I'll take out the Draculesti on the door as a priority, then we'll at least have some numbers on our side. Professor Robertson, does the base have any kind of armoury, weapons?'

'Why would a scientific research installation need an armoury?' Robertson replied.

So I can save your life, Ben almost retorted, but not quite. Professor Robertson was not Violet Crabtree. He should make allowances. 'Okay, so I'll see what I can do.'

'Ben?' Tolly. 'What's with the *I'll*? Don't you mean *we'll*?'

'No, Tol.' More diplomacy needed. Never his strength. 'I appreciate your help so far, I really do, but I need you to stay here and, ah, look after the others.' In a lower voice: 'You said yourself your EXIST combat training was minimal. This is too dangerous.'

'It's dangerous out there. It's dangerous in here,' Tolly protested. 'And we haven't got much time. And I know my way around this base better than you do, Ben. It makes *sense* to let me go with you. You know it does.'

Tolly's blinking eyes and absurd Christian names aside, Ben had to concede that he knew it did. 'All right, then,' resignedly, 'but you do what I say, when I say it.' Tolly wouldn't want it any other way. 'Let's move.' Ben just hoped that neither of them would regret it.

They hauled themselves up into the loft-like enclosure, Ben easily, Tolly, with less muscle in his arms, requiring some assistance. Steel struts stitching the outer and inner skins of the crater base together obstructed their passage. The heat that constantly circulated drenched them with sweat. Ben didn't mind that. You were a long time cold when you were dead.

'I've got an idea about something to fight with as well,' he said. 'Can we access the analysis bay from here?'

'Sure,' said Tolly. 'Just give me a moment to work out where it should be relative to our present position.'

Ben smiled as he watched his younger companion's brow furrow with concentration. It wasn't a mocking or a condescending smile; it wasn't 'let's humour the nerd'. Tolly was doing well. Concentration before action was good. It kept you alive.

'Fifty metres,' Tolly announced, '*that* way.'

Fifty metres *that* way later and the Deveraux agents were lowering themselves into the analysis bay, a variation on the theme of a lab and thankfully unoccupied by anything but the long-dead body of the alien giant. This was lying in a kind of bath that in fact contained delicate scientific measuring instruments rather than taps and a plug-hole. Scanners and screens crowded the figure like cameras around a celebrity. Ben ignored the giant. It was his weapon he wanted.

'I don't think that's going to work, Ben,' Tolly said gingerly as the blond boy lifted the metre-long object from a table alongside the alien. 'Whatever it might have fired once, the mechanism's totally fused now, useless.'

Ben weighed it in his hands. It was like a chunk from a girder. 'So you're saying all we've got is a great hunk of metal that can't shoot anything, is that right, Tolly?' Tolly shrugged that it was. Ben wielded the weapon like a club. 'Sounds good enough to me.'

The Draculesti guarding the prisoners didn't want to be there. He wanted to be on the surface of the Moon with Modrussa when the spaceship came. He'd have been just as happy to have slaughtered the outlanders and be done with it. They'd ensured they were going to die anyway. But nobody, not her fellow Draculesti, perhaps not even Vlad Tepesch himself, openly contradicted Modrussa.

So it was more than a shock when he saw the bespectacled boy dart across the corridor in the distance; it was an opportunity to *do* something. His clawed fingers itched. He'd deal with this the traditional way, the *proper* way. Draculesti should never have to resort to firearms, though he understood why they'd had to bring them into space. He'd tear the poor wretch open with his bare and practised hands.

He was anticipating it now, relishing the prospect as he moved lithely after the boy, his talons digging deep into the helpless flesh like dough, and rending, and the blood hot and slippery. And that wasn't even the best part. The best, most intoxicating part came when—

Ben smashed the alien gun directly into the pale and bloodless face. Perhaps not *quite* so bloodless now. The Draculesti went down. Didn't stir.

'I wonder how much dentists cost in Wallachia,' Ben grinned to Tolly, 'especially for a mouthful like that.'

'Wow.' Tolly admired his partner's work. 'Talk about timing. *Wham*. Straight in the kisser. And I lured him in. We're making a great team, Ben, aren't we?'

'Sure we are,' said Ben, almost with conviction. But he was also thinking about the eleven Draculesti still at large. He doubted he'd be able to club them all.

'Shall we free the others now?'

'Not yet. I want to see what's happening in the control room first. Here, hold this.' He passed the alien weapon to Tolly while he knelt by the fallen Draculesti and relieved him of his shock blaster, reset it.

'What are you doing?' Tolly asked.

'Switching it to stun. One of those annoyingly moral rules Spy High agents have to live by. We don't kill unless it's absolutely unavoidable, not even Draculesti.'

'Otherwise that'd make us as bad as them, right?'

'I don't think anything could make us as bad as *them*, Tolly,' said Ben, 'not even a makeover in evil.'

'Can you get a makeover in evil?'

'These days you can get anything. Come on. Control room. Where?'

Tolly led Ben swiftly to it. Unlike the analysis bay, this *was* occupied by Draculesti, but only two of them, one male, one female, and both had their backs turned to the door, were transfixed by what was occurring in the crater. Ben didn't waste time. Or shock blasts. Perhaps incongruously, Spy High had no rule against shooting your enemies in the back.

'More guns for us,' grinned Tolly. 'Ben? Ah, what about Milgrom's?'

Neither the body of the unfortunate security officer nor that of the even unluckier pilot had been moved.

'Take it. He's not going to need it, is he?' Ben spoke tersely. He was at the window and could see what had been engrossing the now unconscious Draculesti.

A spaceship was manoeuvring into position above the crater, above the starstone. Its shadow turned the grey landscape a darker, more sinister hue. Ben didn't need to spot the ship's insignia of red crosses on a white background to know which country it served.

He increased the magnification of the viewscreen, counted. Ten space-suited figures around the starstone, the remaining Draculesti and Brankovic. At least that meant no further dangers in the base itself.

'What are we waiting for?' Tolly prompted. 'We've got firepower. Let's get out there and show them who's boss.'

'No, Tolly.' Unexpectedly, Ben had begun to like Tolkien Aragorn Porter. He wasn't going to get him killed. 'Not this time. *I'm* going out there. *You're* freeing the others. Then your next job's to get the moon-hopper operational again. Modrussa gave orders to put it out of action and I doubt they were ignored. Tell the others to watch our sleeping beauties and try to fix communications with Armstrong. Understand, Tolly?'

'But Ben,' came the inevitable protest, 'I can . . .'

'*Understand*, Tolly?'

Ben's eyes were stern with authority. There was no standing up to them. Tolly glanced groundward defeatedly. 'I understand.'

'Okay. Good. But hey' – Ben clapped him on the shoulder – 'don't look so down. I couldn't have got this far without you but you just don't have the combat skills to face the Draculesti. Get the hopper functioning, Tolly. We need it, and with the pilot dead you're the only one who can.'

'Yes, Ben,' said Tolly, feeling better, confidence restored. Ben Stanton couldn't have got this far without him. Ben *Stanton*. 'You can rely on me. I promise. And Ben?' As his companion sprinted for a space suit. 'Good luck.'

Ben activated the airlock and stepped out on to the surface of the Moon. To still be breathing after the next few minutes he'd need something more in the realm of miracles. These kinds of odds were so ridiculous they didn't even feature on the training scenarios. But he had maybe one thing going for him. The lunar environment itself. The lack of oxygen condemned the Draculesti as well as everyone else to space suits, which drew their teeth a little, so to speak, effectively neutralising their fangs and talons as weapons. Not even Modrussa could tear his throat out through a plasteel helmet. Was probably why she and her grisly comrades had come equipped with shock blasters. And then there was the reduction in the satellite's gravitational pull compared to Earth. Here you could move further, faster. And Ben imagined he'd spent longer practising under similar conditions than the Draculesti. He had to be able to exploit them more tellingly.

He'd soon find out.

Clasping his own blaster firmly in his gloved hand, Ben made one giant leap for secret agent kind.

The Wallachian ship was hovering above the crater. Lights blazed down from its fuselage, brilliant, blinding white, as if the crater was a stage and a show was ready to begin. If the Draculesti were the performers, Ben thought, then he was going to heckle. He was within striking distance. They were bewitched by the starstone.

Time to prove he was as good as Tolly *thought* he was.

First shot and a Draculesti pitched forward. Second shot the same, both bodies falling in slow motion, crashing silently into the dust like an out-take from a Peckinpah movie. The Wallachians switched attention, from starstone to lone assailant. Ben anticipated their move, took advantage of minimal gravity and sprung high. The shock blasts scorched beneath him.

Three and four, slow to take evasive action.

Somebody, swift to move on to the offensive, bounding towards him, shock blasts stabbing. Modrussa. It had to be her. Almost swooping, a white flame in the light from the ship. She was as quick as him, as deft and agile in her movements. Ben imagined her lips peeling back from her hacksaw teeth. He couldn't get a shot. Neither could she.

Ben braced himself.

The Draculesti rammed into him and her momentum lifted and carried them back more than a dozen metres, their bodies wrestling together. It *was* Modrussa. Her face seemed distorted through the plasteel, animal, insane, jaws snapping vainly. Each of the combatants grappled with the other's gun arm. Ben's back struck the lunar surface, which was fine. He brought his feet up and thrust his boots into Modrussa's belly and propelled her from him. It was a move he was finding extremely useful since he'd arrived on the Moon.

But he didn't have time for self-congratulation. The doors to the Wallachian ship's cargo hold were opening. A distinctive blue light sparkled from within.

Tractor beam.

Ben was on his feet and vaulting forward like some kind of manic hurdler. Eyes not on the Draculesti now but on the spacecraft. Blaster set to Materials. He had to disrupt the tractor beam before it fully energised.

Modrussa wasn't going to let him. She battered into him from behind, the unexpected impact spilling the blaster from his grasp. It seemed she'd voluntarily abandoned hers. Both arms were clenched around his neck, fingers fumbling for his helmet release control. Not friendly. Ben lunged forwards, threw her over his back this time.

He spun to retrieve his blaster. Which was no longer there.

'Are you looking for this?' Former Chief of Security Brankovic's comlink was operating on the same frequency as Ben's, even if the Draculesti's evidently were not. He was also in possession of the teenager's shock blaster as well as his own.

Ben clenched his teeth. Two blasters jabbing at him virtually point blank. Modrussa joining Brankovic, her ghost's face creased with silent, mocking laughter. The tractor beam now flashing from the spacecraft and bathing the ancient alien rock in ethereal blue, immediately causing it to tremble, to vibrate, to move for the first time in centuries. It was game over.

'Any last words, Stanton?' enquired Brankovic.

'None you'd want to hear,' said Ben.

'No? Then shall I put him out of his misery, Modrussa?'

Ben tensed. He'd have to try *something*, even if he knew he couldn't elude a shock blast at this range. But he wasn't going to die standing still. As soon as Modrussa nodded, he'd throw himself at Brankovic and hope for that miracle.

The chief assassin of the Draculesti shook her head.

'You want me to simply keep him helpless like this?' Disappointedly.

Now the nod. Ironic, Ben thought grimly. Modrussa had just saved his life.

Or maybe it was the starstone, the tractor beam. The artefact was rising now into space, tremulously, uncertainly, but drawn inexorably towards the bowels of the Wallachian ship. Modrussa's fellow Draculesti were ascending with it, tending it like nurses with a patient, ensuring that nothing went wrong with the transfer. The seizure of the starstone was the primary purpose of their mission. Modrussa had to oversee its final stages. Not even the death of Benjamin Stanton superseded that.

'A pleasure deferred, I think,' said Brankovic as the assassin left them for the starstone. 'You have a little more time to pray, Stanton.'

'It isn't me who ought to be praying, Brankovic,' Ben said. When you couldn't out*fight* an enemy, out*wit* them. 'Can't you see what's going on here?'

The starstone floating upwards, its vast mass rendered

weightless. Space suited Draculesti in congregation around it. Modrussa among them.

That was what Brankovic saw, and he told Ben so.

Ben had been more observant still. 'The Dracs I stunned,' he pointed out, 'they've tractor-beamed them aboard already.'

'Your meaning?' snapped Brankovic. 'The ship is how we intend to return to Earth.'

'And you think Modrussa's coming back for you?' Ben snorted cynically. 'You're not even a Draculesti. Why would they put themselves out for you?'

'You underestimate the loyalty of Wallachians, out-lander.' But there was doubt in Brankovic's tone.

'Yeah? So why is the cargo hold closing?'

And Brankovic glanced. It wasn't closing. The star-stone was only half inside. But he didn't get a chance to tell Ben that. The teenager was already barrelling into him, karate chops to both arms. Through the material of the space suit the limbs would not be entirely incapaci-tated, but deadened enough for Ben's purpose.

He wrested the shock blasters from Brankovic's twitching grasp, fired them instantly at the spaceship. One of them was still set to Materials.

An explosion rocked the spacecraft as the fuselage flared. Another. The tractor beam shook like a spray of water. The starstone lurched but did not fall. It passed beyond view into the ship's interior, the last of the Draculesti with it. Too little, cursed Ben inwardly, too little and too late. A shock blaster was only ever going to inflict minor damage on a spaceship from this distance. The doors to the cargo hold did indeed now close. The stone was the Wallachians'.

But maybe he'd managed to foul up some important systems after all. The ship was wasting no time in increasing its height, lifting away from the crater.

'What did I tell you, Brankovic?' Ben reminded him. 'You want to revise your opinion of Wallachian so-called loyalty?'

Ben's attack had knocked Brankovic to his knees. He remained on them now and hung his head and moaned. 'You fool, Stanton. Don't you know what you've done? You've killed us both. And your friends. You've killed all of us.'

'What are you talking about?' Ben's heart clutched with fear. What had he missed?

In a sudden spout of flame, the crater base erupted.

FOUR

There wasn't any point searching the wreckage for survivors. There could be none. If the blast hadn't killed everybody instantly, which judging by its magnitude was unlikely, the sudden exposure to the vacuum would have finished them off. Why Ben had troubled himself to return to the ruined base as quickly as possible was difficult to determine.

Professor Robertson, Dr Shabuki, their colleagues, even the three Draculesti he'd defeated, all of them dead. *And Tolly?*

Maybe that was why he'd hastened, in a slim and desperate hope, not to sift through the tangle of twisted steel that once had built a base but to reach the moon-hopper, which lay on its side like a wounded whale, its hull gashed. But not utterly destroyed, not obliterated. He'd told Tolly to try to fix the craft. If he'd followed orders, if he'd been in there when the bomb went off . . .

'This wasn't supposed to happen.' Brankovic was still despairing. He hadn't yet risen from his knees, not even to secure the shock blasters that after the horror of the explosion Ben had dropped. There was no appetite in either of them to continue fighting. 'I was supposed to go with Modrussa. I was supposed to be safe before they detonated the bombs. Only the outlanders were supposed—'

'Let's suppose you shut up, Brankovic,' snapped Ben. 'I'm finding your whining nearly as offensive as your actions. Just be thankful I've got more important—'

'Ben? Ben, is that you?'

'Tolly!' Over the comlink. Tolly, alive and suited up. 'Where are you?'

'In the hopper. Am I glad to hear your voice, Ben.'

'Yeah, and you know what? The feeling's mutual.'

Tolly had been working on the moon-hopper's sabotaged propulsion systems when the blast came. Evidently, no explosives had been placed aboard the vehicle, the Draculesti believing they'd already put it beyond use, and though the hull had ruptured, the subsequent slow depressurisation had still allowed Tolly time to scramble into a space suit before his air supply expired. 'I tried to think clearly,' he explained. 'I tried to keep calm and do what an agent in the field *should* do, what I guessed *you'd* do, Ben.'

'You did well, Tolly,' nodded Ben. The clap on the shoulder was getting to be a habit.

Brankovic's laughter rung hollowly, metallically in their ears. 'All you've *done*, Porter,' he scorned bitterly, 'is delay the inevitable, even made it *worse*.' The former Chief of Security had finally forced himself to move, and all three survivors were surveying the pitiful remains of the base. Without oxygen, of course, the initial fires had been swiftly extinguished: the destruction here might have happened as long ago as the death of the giants. 'You've swapped a quick and sudden death for a long, lingering one, that's what *you've* achieved. Well done. Well done.'

Tolly looked nervously to Ben. 'What does he mean?' From necessity, he'd kept his glasses on this time, and his eyes through the plasteel helmet seemed large with unease.

'I assume our resident Mr Cheerful is referring to the fact that the oxygen packs in our suits don't contain an unlimited amount.' The thought had already occurred to Ben, but he hadn't wanted to share it with Tolly.

'And less every second,' Brankovic added cruelly.

'So why don't you start conserving yours by keeping your mouth shut?' said Ben.

'What are we going to do?' Tolly's determination to keep calm and think clearly seemed to be slipping. 'Ben, what are we going to do?'

'Check our oxygen gauges first, see how much time we've got.'

As with the space suits themselves, the oxygen packs employed at Moon Colony Armstrong had been slimmed and streamlined until they appeared across the shoulders more like a soldier's epaulettes, a fashion accessory rather than a crucial means of sustaining life. A fully charged set of packs provided sufficient oxygen for twelve hours. Tolly and Ben had an eight-hour supply left, Brankovic ten.

If he couldn't save himself – and Tolly, too – in eight hours, Ben thought, he didn't deserve to be a Deveraux agent.

'How long until we can expect Armstrong to send a team out here to the crater?'

'Communications aren't always good at the best of times, Ben,' Tolly admitted. 'Armstrong won't have any idea what's happened with the Draculesti. They'll assume the loss of contact is a systems problem and temporary. It'll take them a while to get worried enough to send another hopper.'

'Even in a state of emergency after the outbreak of Drac?' Ben frowned.

'I'm afraid you don't understand the mentality of the colonists, Stanton,' said Brankovic. 'They prefer research to real life. If there was sand on the Moon, they'd bury their heads in it on a daily basis. It's why they were so easy to betray.'

'But they'll have seen the Wallachian ship on the scanners, won't they?'

'My country is in proud possession of stealth technology,' Brankovic revealed. 'In short, therefore, Stanton, no.'

'Okay. So it takes about six hours to reach here from Armstrong depending on the weight in the hopper, right, Tolly? And we can't guarantee them making any kind of move for several hours yet. *We* can't get in touch with *them*.'

'Not even from the hopper,' Tolly said. 'Everything's useless. Our suit communicators are strictly short range.'

There was silence while everyone did the maths. Brankovic's ironic chuckle and Tolly's look of anxious appeal suggested that they'd reached the same inescapable conclusion as Ben. Sitting around and waiting for a rescue team was not an option.

'*Maybe* they've set off already,' Tolly suggested optimistically. 'Maybe there's a hopper on its way right now.'

The lunar landscape seemed bleak and unmerciful to Ben. He shook his head. 'Sorry, Tolly, we have to assume the worst.' That was how he'd been trained. In mission situations, proceed on the basis of worst-case scenarios: anything else then becomes a bonus. 'Are there any spare oxygen packs on the hopper?'

'Of course!' Tolly slapped a hand against his helmet. 'I'm an idiot. Of course there are, a whole stack of them in storage.' He dared a grin. 'Looks like the worst might be over after all, Ben.'

But it wasn't. It was probably only beginning, Ben anticipated grimly. The hopper *did* contain a store of oxygen packs, but they were kept along the side of the craft that had taken the full brunt of the bombs. The packs were damaged, unusable.

Tolly couldn't conceal his dismay. 'Ben?'

'Yes, Ben,' mocked Brankovic, 'secret agent supreme, what's your big idea now? *Walk* all the way back to Armstrong?'

'Actually, Brankovic, that's exactly right. We walk.'

'But Ben, that's impossible. To make it on foot back to Armstrong . . .' Tolly shook his head dejectedly. 'It can't be done.'

'Not all the way,' qualified Ben, 'but we have to use the oxygen time we've got to reduce the distance between us and any moon-hopper that *is* finally sent out. The further we travel, the quicker they'll find us.' He gazed earnestly at Tolly. 'It's our only hope, Tolly. If we stay here we're dead for sure.'

'Well don't expect me to join you on your suicide stroll,' scoffed Brankovic. 'I have more air than either of you. I'll take my chances here.'

'Feel free, Brankovic,' said Ben. 'The sooner I don't have to look at you the better. But if you're thinking your Wallachian comrades might still come back for you, you're even more stupid than you look, and let me tell you, that'd be difficult.' He returned his attention to his fellow Spy High graduate. 'Tolly?'

Uncertainty. 'Ben, I don't know. A lot of the terrae is uncharted territory. I . . .' And then the sudden gleam in the eyes, the dawning of a wild hope. 'Wait. Maybe it *is* possible. Ben, listen. During the Moon Rush some expeditions *were* mounted to this part of the Moon. They didn't get as far as the crater, obviously, but if I remember rightly' – he furrowed his brow and racked his brain to ensure that he did – 'if I remember rightly, one of them came fairly close. I learned all the details when I joined Armstrong, you know, dates, distances . . .'

'Sounds like Porter would be more useful in a quiz rather than a survival situation, don't you think, Stanton?' jibed Brankovic.

'If you insist on reminding me of your presence, scumbag,' threatened Ben, 'I might also recall your involvement in the deaths of a lot of good people and be tempted to save the state the expense of a cell for the next thirty years.' Though he secretly had to admit that he too was failing to see how Tolly's history lesson could help their present predicament. Maybe the strain was beginning to tell.

'That's it! That's it!' In normal gravity, Tolly might have jumped for joy.

'That's *what*, Tol?'

'The Danby-Smythe Expedition of 2038.' As if the answer had been glaringly obvious all along. 'Its final depot was set up at the foot of the Selene Ridge. That's about eight hours from here by foot. I've done the calculations. We can reach it. We *have* to, Ben.'

'Depot?'

'A camp. With provisions. Like the Antarctic explorers used to leave. Captain Scott and all that heroic sacrifice stuff. Only Danby-Smythe will have stored a distress beacon. And fully charged oxygen packs.'

Ben grinned, laughed. Who'd ever doubted Tolkien Aragorn Porter? Not him. 'You'd better lead the way then, Tolly,' he said. 'Time's wasting.'

'Lead the way?' Tolly flushed with pride. He felt this to be the finest moment of his life. 'Sure, Ben.'

'Brankovic?'

'Place my life in the hands of a boy who's learned all he knows from a textbook?' Brankovic scoffed. 'When the rescue team arrives, I'll point out the direction you took so they can recover your bodies.'

'You're all heart, Brankovic,' said Ben.

Later, when they'd scaled the crater wall, the Wallachian spy could still be seen circling the ruins of the camp like an insect, the only moving figure in a moonscape filled with death. Ben and Tolly paused briefly to gaze down upon him, but *only* briefly. Their air supply was too precious to squander on former Chief of Security Brankovic.

Or on conversation, either. 'We're going to need all our strength for walking,' Ben advised early on. 'And no stopping to admire the scenery, either,' he grinned.

There was little chance of that. For the first hour of their long walk, perhaps even the second as well, the teenagers would certainly have had to concede that the lunar environment was staggeringly impressive, with a stark, almost brutal beauty of its own, uncompromising and elemental. The deep pits of the craters, the chasms and crevices that opened up abruptly and often forced them to divert from the route Tolly's memory of the Danby-Smythe Expedition told him they should take, these were dramatic, awe-inspiring. The silence, the proud desolation, the wheeling stars in the endless blackness above: Tolly's earlier reference to Antarctica wasn't far wrong, Ben thought at one point, except that grey rather than white was the hue of the wilderness here, and arid dust plumed about their feet instead of them sinking into deep drifts of snow. By the end of the third and fourth hours, however, any novelty value the moonscape might have had for either of the Deveraux agents had long worn off. Their surroundings became something not to appreciate but to overcome, not a thing of beauty but an enemy, sullenly and implacably hostile. The rise and fall of the surface seemed designed to slow them down and delay them; the way the jolting, unyielding rock drained the strength from their legs, the same. The terrae was punishing those foolish enough to set foot in its silent territory. And the interminable greyness, by the fifth hour, was confusing the sight and making it appear as if they'd never moved, made no progress towards life at all, but were immobilised in a wasteland of timelessness and death. It would engulf them, the thought occurred even to Ben, the eternal greyness would wash over them like an ancient sea and their bones would slowly bleach like those of perished adventurers in deserts on Earth.

They had to push on. Six hours they'd trudged. They had to keep going, despite the hunger, despite the thirst, the numbing weariness of the body, the exhaustion of the mind.

'Ben, I need . . . I need to rest.' Tolly's voice was wan and distant.

'No time. No time.' Ben knew that if they stopped now, they'd never move again. It would be the end. He wasn't going to let it be the end. 'We have to keep on, Tolly. You're doing well. You're doing really well. Swing your legs from the hips. Avoid bending them as much as you can. It'll help.' But the pain still shot through his own limbs, and nobody could ever accuse Ben Stanton of not being a fine physical specimen. Tolly, with his awkward, ungainly physique, he must be in agony. 'Hold on,' Ben encouraged with all the vigour he could muster. 'We've come too far to fail.'

And the seventh hour came and went.

The moonscape seemed to swirl and blur around them. Nothing but grey, overpowering and all-consuming grey. Ben tried to visualise green or yellow or orange. Couldn't do it. The Moon was erasing his concept of colour. Soon it would erase himself and Tolly. Where was the hopper? Where was it? They *had* to have sent one by now. If they hadn't soon, they needn't at all.

'. . . can't . . .' Tolly had stumbled to his knees.

Ben halted, felt himself swaying as if he too were likely to fall. 'You *can*,' he urged. He reached down, helped his companion to his feet again. 'Put your arm . . . lean on me. We're going to make it and we're going to do it together. You and me, Tolly.'

'I don't know . . . I'm not sure where we are any more. I can't remember which way to go. We should have stayed at the base. We should have stayed with Brankovic.'

'If we'd stayed where we were we'd *die*, Tolly.' Ben tried to force the younger boy to look at him. 'We did the right thing. Staying at the base we'd have been giving up. You *never* give up, Tolly. *Never.*'

Their oxygen gauges flashed in unison. Only minutes of supply remaining.

'Ben, I want to tell you . . .'

'No you don't. Tolly, look at me. We don't have time for this. All I want to hear from you is the location of the depot. Where's the depot, Tolly? We've got to be close. We can reach it if you *think*, Tolly.'

'I . . .' He couldn't focus, even with his glasses. Everything looked the same and he only wanted to sleep, to sleep and dream of gadgets and girls and of not being on the Moon and suffocating slowly but of maybe lounging in a casino somewhere, dinner-jacketed and cocktail in hand, and it was a sweetly tempting dream as well, but Ben was shouting at him and he couldn't let Ben down, not Ben. He had to concentrate first. He had to think, even if he could hardly breathe.

One last time.

'The Selene Ridge,' Tolly gasped. 'That's what we want. The Selene Ridge.'

'Where, though, Tolly?' Ben demanded, all too aware of the increasing inaudibility of his companion's voice.

'There.' Tolly pointed weakly, smiled just as feebly. It was in front of them, higher ground less than a mile away. 'That's it. The Selene Ridge. It was there all the time.'

'Good, Tolly,' Ben encouraged. 'Now no more talking. We're going to get there. Just hold on and help me as best you can.'

Because he was the hero, wasn't he? He was the one in the peak of condition. He should be able to bear Tolly's weight, to climb to the top of the ridge without faltering or fumbling or falling by the way. And though each arduous, agonising step almost had him crying out in pain, though Tolly seemed to grow heavier the further he was hauled, though he was gasping for breath and dizzy, drunk with fatigue, he was Ben Stanton, he was Benjamin White. He would not surrender. He would not submit. He would save himself. He would save Tolly. No lesser outcome was acceptable.

And Ben teetered on the summit of the ridge and below him, on the other side, was the bright red square of the depot.

'It's there. I see it!' he whooped, unable to contain himself, despite the strain on his remaining reserves of oxygen and strength. 'Tolly, you did it!'

Tolkien Aragorn Porter smiled faintly, as sleepers do when dreaming. 'I told you,' he said, 'I wouldn't let you down.'

'So you did,' acknowledged Ben. 'And I won't let *you* down, either.'

And he really thought he hadn't. Not after he'd dragged himself and Tolly the final tortured metres to the depot. Not after they'd spilled inside, their oxygen gauges desperately signalling empty. Especially not after he'd swapped the spent packs for fresh ones, rewarded at once by a renewed and reviving flow of air pumping into his helmet. Only when Tolly showed no sign of recovery, even with the new packs fitted, only then did Ben realise the truth.

'Tolly?'

When the moon-hopper finally arrived and returned them to Armstrong, Ben was made to undergo a full medical examination. For Tolly, the same level of attention was not necessary.

Dracholtz, the capital city of Wallachia, stands on the Krasnova River, and seems more out of place with each passing decade. From a distance, the city walls of stone, its jumbles of buildings, like crowds flocking to market, its winding, labyrinthine streets and archaic, flagstoned squares, the red-tiled roofs of its houses, the ornate towers of its churches, suggest a centuries-past era of warriors and priests, of chivalry and swords. This impression is confirmed by the appearance of the citadel that flanks the river and rises taller than any other construction in Dracholtz, as if by right, as if in architectural testament to the greatness of the Tepesch family who have ruled this land since the Middle Ages and resided in the citadel for nearly as long. It is the castle of a king, turreted, crenellated and gaunt, standing as ready to resist siege now as at any other point in its history. It seems to exist to remind Wallachians of the old days, and more, to assure them, whether they like it or not, that nothing in this remote nation will ever change.

But approach more closely, enter the city through iron gates forged by craftsmen generations in their graves, and a visitor will note that the twenty-first century has in fact reached Wallachia. The guardsmen who patrol the streets wear armour, but armour webbed with complex circuitry, with plasteel visors granting infra-red vision. Their weapons are pulse rifles, shock blasters. They travel on discs that hover ten metres in the air. There are carts drawn by livestock, true, but some of the transport owned by the wealthier Wallachians is magnetically powered, and the beasts hitched to it are animates. Technology is not absent from the country of Vlad Tepesch, but like commodities such as happiness, freedom and human rights, it is not available to all.

The whirring of a helicopter's rotor blades is therefore still an unusual sound for many Wallachians to hear. It might be thought, today, when the approaching drone comes in stereo, that the novelty of such a noise might invite the people of Dracholtz to lift their heads, to look up, to witness the arrival of something not seen on the whole of Earth before, let alone in the backwater of Wallachia. But they do not. They fix their eyes on the cobbles of the street and their minds on their families and how they'd quite like to see them again. Whatever is being shipped to the citadel is President Tepesch's business, not theirs.

So the starstone passes above them virtually unnoticed.

The same is not true of the small group waiting on the ramparts of the citadel. Dominating it, the wind whipping at his long black cloak, is Vlad Tepesch, Prince of Wallachia, president and undisputed leader of his country. A tall man, imposing, black of beard and hair and eye, the latter like the Draculesti, his assassins, and equally white of skin. Around his neck he wears the golden chain of his forefathers but without need; there radiates from Vlad Tepesch an aura of power that requires no trinket to assert its authority. Clustered about him are his advisers, though the fawning attitude and the sycophantic smile of the first man, the balding man, might lead one to suspect that he views agreement and advice as one and the same thing. The second man seems more confident, more independent, as if he can stand up for himself. He is heavily whiskered and boasts the physique of a bull, so perhaps he can. Both men wear the ceremonial black robes of the Wallachian aristocracy. The woman, the fourth and final member of the party, does not. But nobody is likely to tell Modrussa, chief assassin of the Draculesti, that she is inappropriately attired.

Even though she appears to be in apologetic mood at the moment. 'I am sorry, my prince. I should have attended to the boy personally. I underestimated him.'

'It matters little, Modrussa,' says Vlad Tepesch magnanimously. 'What you did not accomplish by hand, your explosives no doubt achieved at a distance. I know how difficult it is to eliminate these secret agent whelps. Stanton frustrated me before.'

'Surely not, my prince,' sympathises the balding man.

'It would have been a pleasure to hear the details of his death from his killer's own lips, but in the end, his death was all that was required. Your priority was the stone, Modrussa,' Tepesch says with satisfaction, 'and there you succeeded admirably.'

'Thank you, my prince.' Modrussa bends low to kiss his hand. She lingers there.

'My prince, behold!' Exultantly, the balding man points aloft.

Twin helicopters fly in parallel. Between and beneath them, locked in the light of diagonal stasis beams, hangs the starstone.

'Is all prepared, Craniescu?' demands Vlad Tepesch.

'Everything, my prince,' the balding man is quick to respond. 'Everything is in place. Security in the tower is absolute, you have my personal guarantee.'

'As you are my Head of Internal Security, Craniescu,' observes Tepesch, 'your personal guarantee is the least of my hopes.'

A glance is exchanged between the Prince of Wallachia and the whiskered man, an amused glance with Craniescu the source of the amusement. Craniescu's own obsequious smile does not falter for a second, but his loathing for Tepesch's favourite rages within him more fiercely than ever. One day, he vows, one day there will be a reckoning. One day he will prove to his prince that it is he, Craniescu, who should be foremost among his advisers in Wallachia.

The helicopters hover above the citadel's central tower. Another technological secret is revealed. The tower splits apart and opens up like the uncurling fingers of a fist. Within, glimpses of a high-tech scientific laboratory, a place already cleared for its latest occupant. The starstone is lowered into the lab.

'What do you think, Boris?' prompts Tepesch.

'As ever,' says the bull-like man, 'I can only speak as a loyal patriot, my prince. My sole interest lies in the preservation of our nation's culture and traditions. If this starstone is going to help us resist the western outlanders, then I offer nothing but praise. But I also counsel caution. To harbour such an alien object in the heart of Wallachia makes me feel uneasy.'

'The fears of a child, Boris,' scoffs Craniescu. He knows how jealously Vlad Tepesch covets the starstone. 'The stone can only contribute to our greatness.'

'Exactly,' concurs the President. 'Wisely spoken, Craniescu. Our seizure of the starstone from under the noses of the so-called international community is a coup. It shows that we are strong. It will make our western enemies think again before they dare to move against us. And if it transpires that the artefact is indeed a weapon, then I will have no hesitation in deploying it.' Vlad Tepesch's lips peel back. His fangs display themselves, sharp and white and predatory. 'Once and for all, the world will learn what it means to oppose Wallachia.'

```
IGC DATA-FEED: REGION WHITE
SUB-SECTION: WALLACHIA (FILE XL924)
```

A stormy session of the General Assembly of the United Nations in Cairo today came to a controversial end when the Wallachian delegate walked out. The dramatic moment occurred during a debate concerning Wallachia's refusal to allow UN-administered teams of weapons inspectors on to its territory to search for its alleged stockpiles of weapons of mass destruction. The issue has been at the forefront of diplomatic activity lately amid accusations from the United States and Europa that Wallachia has accrued from an unnamed source a new and potentially devastating form of weapons technology.

'President Tepesch can end this crisis any time he likes,' an American spokeswoman said. 'All he has to do is come clean on his weapons programmes. We *know* what he's hiding. He must admit to it and surrender it or the United States government and our allies will have no choice but to employ any and all sanctions within our power.' When asked whether those sanctions included military action, 'At this stage we rule nothing out,' said the spokeswoman.

The Wallachian delegate to the United Nations, however, saw the situation somewhat differently: 'America and its lackeys can end this crisis any time they like. All they have to do is acknowledge the Wallachian people's right to self-determination within their borders. They must cease at once their persecution of President Tepesch and my nation, they must stop this bullying masquerading as diplomacy, or they will find that Wallachia is prepared to defend itself vigorously against any attempted impositions from the west.' When asked whether this defence might include military action, 'We are a peaceful people but we will *not* be dictated to,' said the delegate.

Support has been expressed for the Wallachian stance by a number of smaller African and Pan-Asian states. It seems that some admire President Vlad Tepesch for his robust defiance of the west's wishes. Whether right or wrong, the President's leadership is seen as giving hope to other, poorer nations who see themselves as being pressurised by more powerful countries into ceding vital areas of sovereignty.

'Why do we bother?'

Cally, assuming this to be a rhetorical question, did not reply. She chose instead to watch the footballers repeating their plays as she and Ben stood on the side-lines in the grounds of Spy High.

'I mean, why? Tepesch is a tyrant, a dictator, a full-time scumbag. There he is, exploiting and abusing his own people, poisoning as many countries as he can with Drac, responsible for the deaths of who knows how many good people, innocent people, like the scientists on Armstrong, like Tolly, and there are some lunatics out there, tinpot countries, actively encouraging him, cheering him on, as if he'd think twice about crushing any of *them* under his boot if they ever got in his way. And these are the guys we're pledged to protect, the guys we risk our lives to defend. They don't deserve us, Cal. Sometimes I think that. Sometimes I think, why do we bother?'

'I know you're hurting right now, Ben.' Cally could only tolerate rhetorical for so long, and besides, she felt for her boyfriend deeply. She'd put her arms around him if she could. 'But you mustn't be bitter. Losing a friend is a risk in what we do. Everyone who signs up for Spy High knows it. We lost Jennifer and it was hard but we recovered, didn't we? We moved on. That's what we had to do. In time it'll be the same with Tolly, Ben, though I know that probably doesn't sound like much of a consolation now.'

'No, no,' sighed Ben, also gazing at the footballers and their endless contest. 'You're right, Cal. Of course you are. But *knowing* what's right and accepting it isn't always the same thing. Besides, there is one difference between Jennifer's . . . loss and Tolly's. I wasn't there to help Jen, but Tolly, I ought to have saved him. He relied on me, he looked up to me, and I let him down.'

'You did everything you could, Ben,' Cally protested. 'You couldn't have done more.'

'You can always do more,' Ben grunted in response. 'And I *should* have. At least Brankovic didn't survive either. That *would* have been the pits, Tolly dying and the traitor responsible picked up hale and hearty . . .'

'Ben!' Cally recoiled. 'You mustn't talk like that.'

'No.' In sullen apology. 'Guess not.'

'Look at me, Ben. Look at me.' Ben did. 'You're a good secret agent. You know you are. Maybe the best. But not even Benjamin White is superhuman. Nobody is. And to blame yourself for something you couldn't have prevented and to wallow in it isn't going to help you. It's self-pitying indulgence, Ben.'

He winced and smiled thinly. 'Is this your day for being right or what, Cal?'

'Your girlfriend is *always* right.'

'You know, I was just thinking.'

'Dangerous.'

'These guys playing football. They were playing exactly the same game the day we joined Spy High, they're playing the same game now four years later, and they'll probably *still* be playing the same game long after we've retired and are, I don't know, settling down, maybe, patter of tiny —'

'Don't go there, Ben,' warned Cally playfully. 'Don't even *think* of going there. Keep to the point. The footballers, please.'

'Yeah.' Ben considered. 'They never grow. They never adapt. They never learn from the past. But we do, or at least, we *can*. I guess that's the difference between holograms and human beings.'

'Very profound, Ben. If I had a pen and paper I'd write that down.'

'It's something I'm going to take with me to Wallachia, Cal.' Ben's expression steeled into greater seriousness again. 'I've learned. Twice now I've encountered Wallachians. Each time a partner's died. But that's not going to happen again. Mr Deveraux's assigned me to learn how far Vlad's techs have progressed with the star-stone, to neutralise it before war breaks out, and I'll be on my own. Next time, it's just going to be me and Vlad.' He returned his gaze to the footballers. 'And things are gonna change.'

Cally felt a chill along her spine, though technically, of course, she could feel nothing at all. 'Ben, you're going to be careful, though, aren't you?'

'Sure I am.' A broad, blue-eyed smile was back. 'I'll be fine. 'Cause you were wrong before, Cal.'

'Wrong?'

'When you said I was a good secret agent, *maybe* the best. No doubt about it. I'll be in and out of Wallachia before you know it. And when I come back, I want to see the *real* you.'

Cally grinned, Ben's restored swagger ending her fears. 'Hmm,' she mused. 'I'm sure that can be arranged.'

'I'd better go get my final briefing,' Ben said. 'Thanks for being here, though, Cal. Our little talk's meant a lot. See you soon.' He began to press buttons on the control panel he held.

'Not even a parting kiss?' Cally complained.

'What? With all those guys watching?' Ben grinned.

'Those guys are holograms, Ben.'

'Yep. And sadly, Cal, so are you. 'Bye.'

And Cally vanished into thin air, or rather, her holographic image dissipated while the flesh-and-blood Cally Cross remained three thousand miles away in her own operational region. It was as well she did. If Ben's attitude had produced a chill in her before, his expression now that he was alone, his aspect darkened with thoughts of Tolly and Drac and Modrussa and Vlad Tepesch himself, would have turned her to ice.

FIVE

From *The Secret Agent's Guide to the World* by E. J. Grant

EUROPEAN CONTINENT: WALLACHIA

Among the few facts we do know is that the drug commonly called Drac is refined from the seeds of the dracul or dragul flower, native to Wallachia. The bloom can be identified by its white petals and crimson seeds, colours adopted by the Wallachians for their national flag. Apparently, its by-products can be beneficial as well as destructive. According to intelligence gleaned from those Wallachians who have managed to defect to the west from Tepesch's regime and to avoid subsequent assassination, the dracul flower contains healing properties and can bestow great strength upon those who consume its seeds carefully, in a manner consistent with prepa-rations and treatments developed over hundreds of years. This may be so, but it is the more lethal appli-cation of the bloom with which a Deveraux agent is likely to be concerned.

In the last century, in the days of the Cold War, it was said that an Iron Curtain separated the democracies of the west from the communist states of the east. The latter have long since vanished, but there still exists an unbreakable barrier between those who love freedom and those unfortunate souls languishing under the tyranny of Tepesch. The Wallachian Curtain has scarcely been parted by Deveraux. Tepesch's gothtech resources scramble the signals from our surveillance satellites, while his secret police and the unquestioning loyalty that he does unfortunately inspire in some of his less rational people have made it virtually impossible for our agents to penetrate Wallachia for any useful length of time.

The Deveraux organisation will continue to oppose Vlad Tepesch, however, for as long as he constitutes a threat. Any agent assigned to Wallachia must obviously proceed with extreme caution.

It was when the members of the Resistance got to their knees to kiss the holy soil of their homeland that Ben knew he could be *deep* in it. They just threw their guns down and knelt and bent forward to kind of nuzzle at the grass, and anybody lurking in the surrounding forest and intent on ambush would have had a field day. Ben noted that Kuritsyn at least kept hold of his pulse rifle, but as far as Blescu and the others were concerned, they might as well have come with targets hanging round their necks. The Wallachians probably had a word for it. Ben certainly did. *Unprofessional.*

He'd had his doubts from the first. He'd rendezvoused as arranged with the Resistance yesterday, close to the eastern borders of Europa in steep, mountainous territory that had once belonged to Hungary. The Resistance were to escort him to their stronghold in Karinthia, a town located in the most remote and inaccessible region of the mighty Wallachian forest of Nocnitsa. From Karinthia, Ben was to strike out for Dracholtz and the starstone. That was the plan. He wore light khaki fatigues of a synthetic fabric woven with Kevlar, was armed with a shock blaster, his sleepshot wristbands and the various goodies hiding in the pouches of his mission-belt, and he carried a slimline pack containing a chameleon suit and various helpful items of computer hardware. In other words, Ben had come prepared.

The half-dozen Resistance men looked like they'd recently completed a ten-stretch for armed robbery. Unkempt. Slovenly. Indisciplined. And that designer stubble look was *so* late-twentieth-century-sensitive-singer-songwriter. Corporal Keene, Ben and his team-mates' instructor back at Spy High, would not have tolerated such slackness. But they weren't at Spy High now, and Ben needed to keep on side with the Resistance, at least for the time being.

They don't deserve us, Cal. Sometimes I think that.

'My name is Blescu,' their swarthy, bearded leader had introduced himself, clasping Ben's palm with a heavily scarred hand. 'It may be a little premature just now, but let me say it anyway. Welcome to Wallachia, Agent Stanton. And may the devil Tepesch be taken in the night.'

Ben heard that traditional Wallachian curse often during the rest of the day. And well into the night. The Resistance seemed to enjoy their food, meat in greasy, scarcely cooked hunks, and their drink, cheap ale frothing in tankards and jugs, and the tavern where they were staying had plentiful supplies of both. They seemed to enjoy singing the folk songs of their homeland, loudly and tunelessly but with mawkish sentimentality. And they seemed to have forgotten that their trek across the border was due to commence before dawn.

It was the first time that Ben had sensed that Kuritsyn was different from the rest. He appeared the same, but he ate little, drank less, and mouthed the words of the songs silently while staring into the flickering flames of the fire. Kuritsyn, Ben decided even then, was a man he could trust.

And maybe he'd been too harsh on the others. In the end they departed on time. They deftly avoided any border patrols belonging to either Europa or Wallachia, entering the realm of Tepesch among towering peaks, plunging valleys and narrow, winding mountain passes. The forests, largely of pine, prickled the terrain like the spines of a porcupine. Yes, Ben had thought at this point. Maybe he'd misjudged Blescu and his comrades, been too quick to impose his own way of doing things on them – it wouldn't have been the first time. Maybe there were many roads to professionalism.

But dropping your weapons to smooch with the ground was one heck of a detour.

Ben drew his blaster, crouched as if expecting immediate attack. 'I don't want to sound pushy, but have we got time for this?'

Blescu chuckled as he retrieved his gun and got to his feet. 'Ah, you are not Wallachian, young Ben,' he remarked, as if that was a source of personal sadness to him. 'If you were, you would understand. For a Wallachian there is always time to express his love for his land. It is from this good soil that each one of us sprung, and it is to the same soil that we will one day be returned. But *not*, I trust, until the devil Tepesch has gone before us, yes?' He boomed with laughter and embraced Ben like a brother.

Such robustly physical expressions of male solidarity did not always endear themselves to Ben. And that laugh: it probably could be heard for a ten-mile radius. With Resistance like this, no wonder Vlad was still in power.

Perhaps Blescu saw those thoughts in Ben's eyes. 'But you are right. When a man is Wallachian, his home can be a dangerous place. We must push on.'

Through woodland where the trees were packed so densely together, perhaps for moral support in a treacherous world, that they blacked out the morning then the afternoon sun and made their way like night. Out again into splashes of brilliant light where the ground dipped and fell to crashing, frantic rivers far below, where the senses reeled at such stupendous drops. Then higher still, and stonier soil, the exposed roots of plants and trees clinging to the slope like desperate fingers. The vistas of valley and forest and mountain and stream. And throughout their long and gruelling march, no sign of any other human being.

'Our country stirs the soul, yes?' said Blescu.

'It certainly strains the tendons,' Ben returned. 'No, it's cool. It's a painting.'

'Wallachia is like its people,' Blescu continued. 'It is rugged, proud, untamed. Difficult. And its beauty and its abundant riches rightly belong to all.'

Ben felt a party political broadcast on behalf of the Wallachian Resistance in the offing. He wasn't wrong. There was a lot about what the Resistance was going to do when the devil Tepesch was swept from power, a lot about how it was going to enfranchise the peasants and guarantee freedom and equal shares in the country's wealth for every true-born Wallachian. Ben observed Blescu's expression as the man waxed lyrical about the future utopia that would bless his homeland when the devil Tepesch was swept from power. It was serene, blissful, visionary. And fatally flawed. Because there was one rather important snippet of information missing from Blescu's dreaming. The devil Tepesch. Sweeping him from power. How, exactly?

There was more of the same after they'd pitched camp for the night. Blescu estimated that they should reach Karinthia before dark on the morrow and, as even Kuritsyn grudgingly concurred, his spirits were high. Around the blazing campfire his conversation turned to the past as well as the future. The fire had been something of an issue itself. Both Ben – politely – and Kuritsyn – less so – had suggested that such an obvious sign of human presence might not be a good idea. There was always the possibility that prying eyes loyal to the devil Tepesch might spot it and make unwelcome assumptions about those who had lit it. Blescu had dismissed such fears. 'The night before the Battle of Our Salvation,' he'd said, 'Kresniki's army lit a thousand bonfires in full view of the enemy, yet who triumphed when daylight dawned?'

It was this recollection that began Blescu's nostalgia. 'Have you heard of Kresniki, Ben?' he asked. 'Of course you haven't. But to the people of Wallachia he is a hero, the greatest warrior in our history. Without him, Wallachia might have ceased to exist five centuries ago.'

Ben noticed that while the mere mention of Kresniki's name produced a gaze of rapt adoration on the faces of most of the Resistance, like a spell, Kuritsyn seemed immune. He scowled, drew back from the fire to conceal himself in shadow.

'To understand Wallachia, Ben,' said Blescu, 'you must understand Kresniki. There was a time when our borders were under constant attack from the Magyars to the west. The Magyar king saw our homeland as weak and divided and ripe for conquest. He gathered an army more mighty than any that had been seen since the days of the Mongol hordes, and he pointed that army at Wallachia.

'Well, in our moment of gravest crisis, the feuding noble families of our nation put aside their petty squabbles and grievances and joined together against a common foe. Kresniki was given charge of our forces. He pledged not simply to repel the Magyars but to crush them so absolutely that no outlander would ever dare attempt an invasion on Wallachian soil again. Outnumbered massively though he was, Kresniki also knew that he had two advantages over the enemy. One was the potion made from the scarlet seeds of the dracul flower, a drink which he and his soldiers imbibed and which turned their limbs to steel and filled them with a warrior rage and a ferocity in battle that could not be matched. The second was the site where he would choose to engage the Magyar army. A narrow pass above the Krasnova River whose original name has long been lost but which is now known gloriously as the Kresniki Pass.'

No surprise there, thought Ben. He could guess what was coming next.

'The Magyars were arrogant, vain. They believed that their strength would allow them to sweep over Kresniki's forces and on to Dracholtz itself. They learned otherwise. As they entered the pass their vast numbers quickly became a hindrance rather than a help, crushing men together and making them easy targets for our archers. Their much-vaunted cavalry was rendered useless in such steep and enclosed terrain. They fought bravely, which is good – for what glory can come from a victory against cowards? – but after hours of battle and blood, after deaths too many to count, it was not the Magyars who stood triumphant on the field but the Wallachians, with the scant and broken remnants of a once-proud army in full and abject retreat. It is said that so many Magyar bodies had plunged into the Krasnova, so much Magyar blood had been spilled, that the river flowed red through the city of Dracholtz the next day, and that the peopled dipped cloths into the scarlet stream to keep as mementos of the greatest moment in Wallachian history. For Kresniki had achieved precisely what he had promised. No more did the humbled Magyars trouble our borders. Our nation lived, and it lived on its own terms.

'And *that* is what you must understand, Ben,' Blescu concluded. 'Now, as then, we Wallachians are an independent people. We value our ancient customs and traditions and we do not appreciate interference from outlanders.' He laughed, the sound like cannon fire in the night. 'Unless, of course, it is to help us secure the downfall of the devil Tepesch!'

'I'm pleased to hear that,' said Ben. He thought it impolite to mention that his mission was more about the incapacitation of the starstone than the removal of Vlad.

'The Kresniki Pass is only a little out of our way,' it occurred to Blescu. 'Perhaps we should divert there first thing tomorrow. We'll still reach Karinthia by nightfall and you should see the monument where Kresniki himself is buried, Ben, his bones guarding the pass in death as he did in life. It is a place of pilgrimage for all true-born Wallachians.'

'Ah . . .' Ben was searching for a form of words that recommended they move on without delay but which avoided offence in doing so. He suspected he'd need more than a Babel chip to get through to the Resistance man.

Kuritsyn was unhindered by diplomacy. 'Stanton isn't a tourist,' he ridiculed. 'This isn't a sightseeing trip.' He leaned forward once more and the fire blazed in his eyes. 'Blescu, Kresniki has been dead for five hundred years. He's dust. He can't help us now and we don't have time to squander on the ghosts of the past. We must move to Karinthia as swiftly as possible before we find the Draculesti barring our way. Can't you see that?'

'Mind your tongue, Kuritsyn,' snapped Blescu, physically bridling at the outburst. 'I command here, not you, and what I can see is a man whose evident contempt for Wallachia's heroes might lead *some* to question where his loyalties truly lie.'

'If you think *that*, Blescu,' snorted an unfazed Kuritsyn, 'then you are even more of a fool than I imagined.' He rose abruptly to his feet and stalked into the forest. 'I've listened to enough of your idle chatter for one night.'

'Where's he going?' Kuritsyn was the last person Ben wanted to leave.

'Somewhere. Anywhere.' Not so Blescu. 'Let him go, Ben. He'll be here again before dawn. He always is. A good fighter, Kuritsyn, but good company, never.'

'No, I'd better . . .' Ben jumped up to follow him. 'I'll be back.' But not until he'd had a private talk with the man called Kuritsyn.

And Blescu was undoubtedly right about one thing. Kuritsyn's prowess in battle was likely to be exceptional if his ability to move through the night in stealthy silence was anything to go by. His hand was on Ben's shoulder in the darkness before even Deveraux-trained hearing could detect his approach.

'What do you want, Agent Stanton?' Uninvitingly.

'Don't worry,' said Ben. 'I don't want to *bond* or anything. I just want to ask you a question.'

'Not about Kresniki or any other of Wallachia's glorious dead, I trust.'

'Not quite. You and Blescu. Both Resistance but not exactly blood brothers. How come?'

'Isn't it obvious?' Kuritsyn's distaste was visible even in the forest shadows. 'Blescu is deluded, a fantasist. Like many a Wallachian, he has been weaned on the myths of the past, and though his mind is full of plans for a future free of Vlad Tepesch, in reality he has as little idea of how to achieve them as he does of how to raise the dead. You know this to be true, Agent Stanton. I have seen your

expression when you look at him sometimes. I am familiar with doubt.'

'Maybe,' Ben conceded. 'So why is Blescu leader?'

'He says what others want to hear. He makes promises. And he is brave, that I do *not* doubt, but animals too
have courage. He is an easy man to follow.'

'But what?' Ben probed further. 'You think the
Resistance might be following Blescu to disaster?'

'I think you would be wise to keep your wits about
you, Agent Stanton.'

Already on it, Ben thought. 'So what about you,
Kuritsyn? If the Resistance is so hopeless, why are you
still here?'

'The devil Tepesch is a curse on our land,' he said. 'I
have no choice but to make my stand. Besides, in
Wallachia no cause is ever truly hopeless.' He smiled
ironically. 'Has not the story of Kresniki taught you that,
Agent Stanton?'

Blescu had his way. The early light was still grey and
cold when the small party left their campsite and struck
out for the Kresniki Pass.

'My father first brought me here before I could walk,'
the Resistance leader reminisced to Ben. 'I have never
forgotten it. I think, even then . . .' As Blescu continued
his monologue, Ben did not dare catch Kuritsyn's eye.
He would betray himself.

He was only too grateful when they reached the pass.
Wooded hillsides on both sides of the valley sloped pre-
cipitously to stony trails worn by centuries of feet and
hoofs. Beyond these, the final vertical plummet to the
deep, fast-flowing torrents of the Krasnova River. Ben

could appreciate Kresniki's eagerness to engage the Magyar army here. It was a place designed for massacre. He stood on the brink of the cliff and gazed down. The river churned and foamed. It was a long drop, with or without a Wallachian arrow or axe-head between your shoulder blades. He was glad he hadn't been born a Magyar.

'Come, Ben,' urged Blescu. 'The monument. We must pay our respects and then make haste to Karinthia.' As if now, too late, even Blescu had realised the inadvisability of their excursion.

But the monument was striking. A larger-than-life statue of a man in full armour, no doubt Kresniki himself, keeping eternal watch in the direction of Europa atop a tomb which also no doubt contained the earthly remains of the hero of the Battle of Our Salvation. The size thing was probably symbolic, Ben thought.

'Kresniki,' breathed Blescu, like he was mouthing a prayer.

'Impressive,' admitted Ben.

And they did it again. The Resistance men cast their weapons aside and knelt to pay homage to their nation's saviour. This time, while he didn't kneel, even Ben allowed his guard to relax. Which only proved that indiscipline, like the common cold, was catching.

A sudden droning in the air, like wasps or bees, insects that sting. From behind the monument, from where Kresniki's proud figure had to this point concealed them, a trio of spinning steel balls, spiked like the head of a mace and larger than the head of a man, rose startlingly into sight.

'Border globes!' cried Kuritsyn.

Which Ben assumed was bad.

'Stay. Where. You. Are.' They had voices, rasping, metallic, unfriendly.

The Resistance men grabbed for their guns and opened fire at once. The globes flitted out of the way like flies evading a swatter.

They fired laser bolts as well. One of them speared through a Resistance fighter and he fell backwards, rolled down the slope and did not move again.

The tips of the spikes crackled with electricity. 'Visual. Scanning. Engaged. Subject. Identified. Matthias. Blescu. Resistance. Leader.'

'Get out of here!' Ben thought that Blescu was yelling to him, but it could have been to any of his comrades.

The Resistance men were scattering, making no attempt to mount an organised defence. 'Stand! Stand!' Except Kuritsyn, of course. 'Stand or die!' Because the globes could fly faster than the men could run, and they swooped down like steel birds of prey on the hapless Wallachians fleeing for the cover of the forest. And they fired their laser bolts. And they didn't miss.

'Subject. Identified. Pavel. Kuritsyn. Resistance. Member.'

A globe honed in on Kuritsyn. Ben knew what it wanted. He couldn't let his ally perish. Not like Tolly. *Now* he went down on one knee, clasped the handle of his shock blaster, set to Materials, with both hands. Scanned the path of the border globe. Estimated its trajectory.

Fired.

The globe was a burning comet, careering wildly through the air. It crashed into the statue of Kresniki. It sliced off the dead warrior's head.

'No! *No!*' Blescu probably found that mutilation harder to accept than his own demise as the globe's surviving partners focused on him simultaneously. Pierced by twin lasers, he pitched against the tomb. One last reason to be thankful before the darkness claimed him. Blescu's laser wounds were instantly cauterised. He would not bleed over the resting place of his hero.

And so it was down to Ben and Kuritsyn. Neither was surprised. Sustained fire from them both kept the globes at a distance, but the laser bolts were flashing closer all the time, scorching at their feet, sizzling the soil. One lanced through Ben's left sleeve, scalded the flesh of his arm. He didn't think it necessary to indulge himself with an expression of pain. It wouldn't deter the globes.

'Subject. Identified. Benjamin. Stanton. Enemy. Of. Wallachia.'

'No!' denied Kuritsyn. '*Friend* of Wallachia. Friend of mine.' The globes circled and struck. Ben's thigh, a minor injury. Kuritsyn's right knee, a disastrous one. 'You must go, Ben.' He battled through the agony. He *endured*. 'One chance of escape. The river. Leap into the Krasnova. Let it take you to Tepesch.'

'Eliminate. The. Enemies. Of. Wallachia.'

Ben and Kuritsyn stumbled, scrambled down the slope, leaving the monument and Blescu behind.

'We can both do it. We can both make it.' It was the Moon again, Benjamin White blowing it again.

'No. *You.*' Kuritsyn's eyes bored into him. 'Be our hope. Go.' And he pushed Ben away, and Ben was sliding further down the mountainside towards the trail, towards the river. 'I'll hold them back!'

Kuritsyn's choice. Ben had to respect it. Kuritsyn's sacrifice. He would never forget it. (*They don't deserve us, Cal.*) And he mustn't waste it, either. Ben hurtled towards the cliff, scarcely able to control his speed, the slope was so steep. He had a mission to complete. He'd do it. He wouldn't let Kuritsyn down as he'd done Tolly.

Behind him, an explosion of shattered steel and circuits. Kuritsyn had got lucky.

Before him, the yawning, plunging chasm to the Krasnova. Ben did not pause.

Behind him, a strangled cry as the inevitable laser bolt found its mark.

Before him, the lip of the precipice, the river raging like distant lions.

The final border globe closing in. The searing stab of the lasers.

Ben filled his lungs with air. He braced the muscles of his legs. The last of the land dropped vertically away.

Ben jumped.

SIX

A man might have made assumptions. A man might have peered over the vertiginous ledge from which Ben had just leaped and decided that nobody could possibly have survived such a fall, that the absence of a body didn't make the diver any less drowned, and that it was a waste of his time to clamber down the perilous cliff-face to check. The border globe, however, was mechanical rather than human, and it had been programmed to accept nothing less than incontrovertible evidence before making decisions.

It also didn't need to negotiate the cliffside. It glided low to the river, hovered above the flood at a height sufficient to avoid getting wet, and its scanners probed for the presence of a body in the dark waters. Nothing immediately. The globe was not discouraged, disappointment being another inapplicable human trait. It contented itself with following the course of the current, slowly, methodically, analysing the Krasnova every metre of the way.

Surprise was not an attribute with which its programmers had equipped the globe, either, but if they had, about now would have been the moment for its expression. Just as the scanners seemed to detect a suspiciously human shape directly below . . .

The shock blast lashed out with the suddenness of lightning. The border globe had no opportunity even to register its own destruction. It dropped into the waters like a flaming stone.

Ben fought to surface. The threats to his life were reduced by one, but the Krasnova maybe didn't need help to finish him off. He'd managed to fit his belt-breather so that he'd been able to lurk underwater and lure the globe to him, but still his senses now seemed to be slipping away. His bones ached and his muscles screamed for rest. His body was on fire from its impact with the river. And the current was grasping him, securing him like chains, reluctant to release him. Ben thrashed in its icy and pitiless grip.

His blaster was useless to him now. He let that go. His pack too he struggled to shrug from his back. He battled to steady himself, to control his motion, to swim, but the Krasnova swirled inexorably, relentlessly around him, and his ebbing strength was nothing to the rushing might of the river.

He felt himself dragged deeper. He felt himself colder. His belt-breather would keep him alive for minutes more but it couldn't prevent unconsciousness.

Ben's final thought was a bleak one. He wondered briefly if his body would drift in the Krasnova as far as Dracholtz. He wondered whether Vlad would find him. He imagined so. As the darkness flooded in, Ben could already hear him laughing.

❋

Vlad Tepesch, Prince of Wallachia, was not a man who feared technology. No, he embraced it, when it helped to kill his enemies, when it reinforced his own position. But his taste when it came to his private apartments in the citadel was unapologetically traditional. The room in which he lounged now, the torches blazing on stone walls, the hanging tapestries and exotic carpets, the silk cushions on stiff-backed chairs of oak and gold, all decorated with scenes of pageantry and war, this chamber could have been plucked intact from the sixteenth century. The Wallachians of that period, however, had possibly encountered no one quite like the woman who reclined at Tepesch's feet, like a loyal pet: Modrussa, foremost assassin of the Draculesti.

'Will you take some refreshment, my dear?' invited Vlad. And as an invitation from the President was identical to an instruction, Modrussa obeyed. She accepted the goblet of thick red liquid that Tepesch poured for her. He was sipping the same. 'Freshly pressed from my own strain of dracul seeds. My biochemists are refining the potion's quality all the time. Our powers will never wane. We shall only grow stronger.'

'Yes, my prince.' She drank.

'And when the secrets of the starstone are uncovered, a new order will rise in the world with Wallachia at its heart.'

'And with *you*, my prince, at the heart of Wallachia,' smiled the assassin.

'Indeed, my dear Modrussa.' Tepesch's fingers stroked the black and cobweb hair of the Draculesti. 'In matters of the heart you are always most perceptive.' He condescended to lean down towards her.

A guard appeared at the door. Chief of Internal Security Craniescu craved an audience with the President on a matter of the utmost importance. Tepesch didn't need to be told the latter. Not even *Boris* would dare to interrupt him when he was with Modrussa for anything less.

'We have a situation, my prince,' said Craniescu, his lowly bow to his liege including the Draculesti as well, just to be on the safe side. 'A breach of our borders.'

'Where?' Vlad enquired, though he seemed hardly concerned.

'At the Kresniki Pass. It was yet another example of your wisdom and foresight to place border globes at the monument, my prince. They relayed data back to my control centre immediately. Six Resistance identified and eliminated, including Blescu.'

'Why, this is good news, Craniescu,' gloated Tepesch. 'The Resistance are predictably sentimental. Memorials to our past draw them like moths to a flame.' His eyes narrowed. 'But you said a breach of our borders, Craniescu. The Resistance, though it pains me to concede the fact, are Wallachians.'

'They were not ... alone, my prince,' ventured Craniescu. 'A single outlander was with them. The globes' data-banks identified him too.'

'Who was it?' Tepesch sat forward.

'According to the globes,' Craniescu qualified, reluctant to take responsibility for the name, 'it was Benjamin Stanton.'

'Hah!' Tepesch's cry sounded as if this was intelligence he'd half expected.

'Impossible!' protested Modrussa.

'No. No, my dear. Only *too* possible.' Tepesch rose and prowled the chamber like a wild beast roused to defend its territory. 'It seems Stanton survived your bombs on the Moon and has followed the starstone to Wallachia. Did he also survive the border globes?'

'I'm afraid the globes were destroyed, my prince,' Craniescu admitted. 'But the final transmission showed Stanton beneath the waters of the Krasnova. The current is strong. He was already injured. He has surely drowned, my prince.'

'I expect so, Craniescu, I expect so.' Vlad Tepesch nodded in exaggerated agreement. Then his brow darkened and his lips sneered and his voice became thunder. 'Stanton has surely drowned in the Krasnova, has he? Just as surely as he was blown to pieces on the surface of the Moon! How many times must you underestimate him? This boy has more lives than a cat. He is alive now. Until I can see his corpse with my own eyes, until I can take his cold wrist into my hands and feel no pulse, Stanton is alive. And he must be found.'

'Yes, my prince.' Craniescu was only too eager to begin. Anything to avoid Vlad Tepesch as his anger grew.

'Search every inch of the Krasnova from the Kresniki Pass to Dracholtz itself if necessary. Scour its depths. Sweep its banks. Ransack every town and every village in Wallachia. Arrest all suspected dissidents who might have information. And their families. Do whatever you must, Craniescu, but do not fail to find him. And when you have him, bring him to me. Alive would be entertaining, but dead, dead would be equally acceptable.' Tepesch's black eyes glittered with hatred. 'Benjamin Stanton has been a thorn in my side for long enough. But

Wallachia is mine. Daring to come here is a mistake, and this Vlad Tepesch vows, it is a mistake Stanton will soon be made to regret.'

He was alive. His pain told him that. In some ways, Ben knew, pain was good. All the while you could feel it you weren't dead. And this was a better pain now than when he'd lost consciousness, duller, more distant. Manageable.

He guessed he'd better get up then.

Eyes open. He was in a bed, a rough woollen blanket covering him. The bed was in a room, primitive, wooden walls and floor and ceiling, dark with a single window and a curtain drawn, only himself as occupant. The room was in a house or a hut and the house or a hut had to be in Wallachia, but that didn't narrow his location down sufficiently to satisfy Ben. And it didn't let him know whether whoever must have found him in the Krasnova, or washed to the shore, and brought him here – and stripped him to his boxers and bandaged his wounds besides – was on his side or Vlad's.

First rule of spycraft: never wait around long enough to find out.

Ben swung himself out of bed and on to his feet. The room spun around him like a carousel at a fair. His gorge rose and his legs all but gave way. Fitness rating out of ten only just into single figures. Ben steadied himself against the wall. His clothes and more importantly his mission-belt were nowhere to be seen, but they'd left his wristbands on, obviously unaware of sleepshot. Could be a good sign. If his captors were loyal to Tepesch, surely they'd *know*.

Ben parted the curtain a sliver and peeped outside. A

peasant village, it seemed, a scattering of one-storey wooden houses and forest all around. He saw bearded men in leather leggings and jackets, black-haired women in long floral skirts going about their business. They reminded him that however sick he felt, he'd better be going about his.

The door opened. A girl. He registered raven curls, flashing green eyes and laughing white teeth. 'And where do you think you're going dressed like that?'

'Out of my way.' He jabbed his arm at her, though why did she keep *swaying* like that? 'Don't . . . try to stop me . . .'

He lurched for the door, pushed past the girl.

'Don't be stupid. You won't get far in that condition.' Her laughter followed him. 'Put some clothes on. You'll give Widow Weezak a heart attack!'

Ben stumbled out of the hut, into dappled forest light. The ground seemed more uneven than it should. These Wallachians, they should invest in proper roads. Now, which way to Tepesch? The girl was behind him, calling someone's name. It didn't *sound* like Vlad. He could get away and rest up. If he could make the trees . . .

A man who seemed more oak than human blocked his path, a man grey-haired and bearded. Ben's first thought was that it was Boris sent by Vlad to fetch him, but Boris didn't have a beard, only those absurd whiskers. 'Leaving so soon, young one?' the man said. 'I think you'd better enjoy our hospitality a little longer yet, don't you?'

'Out . . .' began Ben, trying to lift his arm to fire sleepshot, 'of my . . . way . . .'

'I don't think so,' said the man. 'Here, young one, let

me help you.' He held out both of his arms easily.

And caught Ben as he fell.

'I knew you were coming.' The voice drifted in and out of his dreams. 'The spirits showed me. They told me you would come.' An old woman's voice. 'We have been waiting for you. To lead us against the devil Tepesch.'

Over the next couple of days, Ben's condition improved steadily. His strength grew, as did his understanding of where he was and who was tending him.

He was in the home of the Vukic family in the village of Nostravista, deep within the sacred forest of the Nocnitsa. He'd been found floating half-dead in the Krasnova. '*I* found you,' the raven-haired girl was quick to inform him. 'I go to the Krasnova to bathe. If it wasn't for me . . .'

The girl's name was Natalia. Natalia Strepescu. She seemed to be in the room with him a lot during the days of his recovery, and though she never personally dressed his laser wounds or administered the restorative cordial that he was coaxed into drinking, Ben was always glad when she was there, and felt more vigorous still, and when she was gone it was like dusk in daylight.

His actual nurse was Lyvia Vukic, a crone with skin as scaled as a reptile's, a back as arched as a bow, and with an apparently constitutional inability to lift her feet from the floor as she walked. But her eyes, they shone with the zest of someone fifty years younger, and Ben soon learned from Natalia that old Lyvia was a vital and venerated member of the Nostravistan community. It seemed she was not only a healer, but a seer too, and conversed with the spirits on a regular basis. Ben realised that it was the voice of Lyvia Vukic that had haunted his dreams.

There was a third Wallachian he came to know during his recuperation, the man who'd stood in his way during his abortive and misguided attempt to escape. This house was *his* house. He was Vissarion Vukic, Lyvia's son. 'And a great soldier in his youth, Ben,' Natalia revealed. 'But of course, what man of conscience – or woman of conscience, too – could serve the devil Tepesch, may he be taken in the night? None. So many years ago Vissarion returned here, to Nostravista, the home of his forefathers, and to a different way of life. But like all of us, he longs for the day when the devil Tepesch will be overthrown. And now, with your coming, Ben, that day is near.'

Natalia expressed similar sentiments on several occasions. While Ben did nothing to stop her, largely because when she grew excited she had a habit of shaking her head a little from side to side which made her cascading black curls dance most enticingly, in the end he thought he'd better put the record straight. On the third evening of his enforced incarceration at Nostravista, he asked to speak to Natalia and both Vukics together.

'I think it's time we sorted one or two things out,' he said. 'I haven't yet told you exactly who I am or what I'm doing in Wallachia, and so far you've been patient enough not to push it. But I already owe you a lot – life included – so I reckon I owe you the truth, too. You've probably guessed most of it. I'm a spy. I work for a secret organisation based in the United States but which has agents operating worldwide. And right now, we're what you might call concerned about your president.' Keeping details to a minimum, Ben told the Wallachians about the starstone, about his confrontation with the Draculesti on the Moon, about the deaths of Kuritsyn, Blescu and the others at the Kresniki Memorial.

'We have heard of this strange alien artefact in Tepesch's possession,' said Vissarion. 'We have heard that its power, once unleashed, will be incalculable. Already there are stories of mysterious lights filling the skies above the citadel in Dracholtz as the dictator's scientists work to master it.' He scowled. 'It is another scar on Wallachia's back.'

'So you can understand why my organisation's so keen to see the starstone put out of commission before Tepesch can do any real damage with it. Right now, the way things are going in the outside world, there's every chance of war between the west and Wallachia, and I don't need to tell you what *that'll* mean.'

'Many of our people who despise Tepesch would still support him in any battle between Wallachia and outlanders,' Vissarion predicted with certainty. 'It would be for them a matter of priorities. To protect the homeland against the invader is a patriotic duty.'

'Yeah,' said Ben ruefully. 'I've already had my history lesson in Kresniki.'

'You waste words,' Lyvia interrupted. 'There will be no war. There will be no *need*. Ben will lead us to victory over the devil Tepesch before armies can be mustered.'

'Yeah, well, I know you've kind of got to *thinking* that,' he ventured, 'but I've got to tell you, and I'm sorry, I really am, but that's not quite what I'm here for.'

'The spirits say differently,' remarked the old woman.

'The spirits don't set my mission parameters,' said Ben, though in some cultures maybe the digitalised consciousness of Jonathan Deveraux would qualify as a spirit. 'This is about the starstone, not regime change. Now I've got reason to despise Tepesch the same as you—'

'The same?' Lyvia crackled. 'I doubt it. You see my strong, good son here, Benjamin? I had another son once, Vissarion's brother. He was taken from us many years ago. By Vlad Tepesch. And now, not even the spirits speak of him. For a mother to lose a son, stranger, is a pain that cannot be healed.'

'I'm sorry,' said Ben. He didn't mention Jennifer or Tolly.

'We suffer every day,' said Vissarion. 'Craniescu's secret police. The cursed Draculesti. No one lives in Wallachia without fear. The yoke of tyranny remains tight about the neck no matter how many years it has been worn. There are men who would follow you, Ben, if you were to lead.'

'Yeah. Six of them are already dead getting me *this* far.' He frowned, thinking of Kuritsyn. (*Be our hope.*) 'No. This is what I wanted to make clear, *now*, so nobody's under any illusions. Like I said, I appreciate everything you've done for me, but I'm not here to take Vlad down. And if that's not what you wanted to hear, then again, I'm sorry. I'm fit enough now. I'll leave in the morning.'

'You can't leave!' cried Natalia. 'There's so much I want you to tell me! He's not well enough to leave, Lyvia. You can't let him.'

Lyvia calmed the younger girl with a gnarled but gentle hand on her shoulder. 'There will be no need for hasty departures,' she said. 'In three days more you will be fully restored, Benjamin. Stay with us until then. And believe me, the plans of men are as leaves tossed in the wind, but the design of the spirits is the wind itself. Tepesch will fall, and you will help us.'

The following evening Natalia brought him a present. A traditional Wallachian peasant outfit, faded and well-worn, complete with leather leggings and jacket and even a shapeless leather cap. 'They belonged to Janos Mirescu,' she grinned. 'I won them last night in a card game. He's *almost* your size.'

'That's very nice of you,' said Ben. 'But shouldn't presents come wrapped?'

'No time,' Natalia laughed. 'Put them on. Let me see how you look as a Wallachian. I think you're well enough to go out now and your own clothes set you too much apart.'

Ben couldn't disagree with that. 'I do feel better,' he said, dressing quickly and aware of Natalia's gaze upon him.

'You *look* better,' she said with relish.

'If Lyvia could patent that medicine she's been dosing me with and sell it on the international market she'd make a fortune.'

'Oh, she couldn't do that,' said Natalia. 'The dracul flower must be used strictly for the benefit of Wallachians. And our guests, of course.'

'What?' Ben started. 'That stuff I've been drinking, it's made from *Drac*?' He instinctively ran his tongue along the line of his upper teeth. No sharper or more pointed than usual.

'Drac?' frowned Natalia. 'I don't know what you mean. The dracul flower grows only in the Nocnitsa and its seeds have many wonderful applications. Lyvia knows more about them than anyone, but the dracul is important to us all. Nostravista would not exist without it. We make our living by cultivating and harvesting the flower.'

'Say again?' A second shock. Ben wondered briefly if he might be having a relapse. Here was Natalia, young, vibrant, beautiful (maybe not in Cally's ball park, but she was certainly at the turnstiles), and how she and her family earned their bread was essentially no different from the great drug producers in the poppy-growing regions of Colombia or Afghanistan. Pretty flowers here; not so pretty drug addicts there. And Ben knew from experience that Drac was even more lethal than heroin.

'Are you all right, Ben?' Natalia said curiously.

'Sure, sure. I'm fine.' Should he tell her about Drac? If so, now probably wasn't the moment. He forced a smile instead. 'I think I've just been in bed too long.'

'Well, next time,' Natalia flirted, 'maybe you should ask for some company.'

Maybe the priority was to tell the girl about *Cally*. 'Did someone mention going out?' he said.

The village was small. It didn't take them long to walk its entire length. Ben was the subject of many inquisitive stares, especially from the children, though he received one or two surprises himself. The wheelless carts with their very 2060s magnetic engines parked outside wooden huts that still had smoke rising from chimneys. The meeting hall, after the church the largest building in Nostravista, with its banks of computers and giant videscreen inside, oxen grazing lazily outside. The traditional and the technological coexisting in apparent harmony.

'You see,' teased Natalia, twining her arm around him as if he wouldn't notice, 'we're not as backward as you might think.'

'You're not backward at all, Natalia,' observed Ben.

They sauntered away from the village and towards the Krasnova. It was broad and placid here, a stark contrast to the boiling torrent at the pass.

'I'm not sure I want to stay in Nostravista for the rest of my life, though,' Natalia pouted, 'or even Wallachia. Even when the devil Tepesch is replaced and we win our freedom. A Wallachian's horizons are limited, Ben. It's the mountains. I'd love to travel, to go places I've only read about or seen on videvision, and Craniescu's secret police even censor *that*. Europa. America. Japan.' Her green eyes half closed in blissful daydream. 'I expect you've been everywhere, haven't you, Ben?'

'Not exactly everywhere,' he said. 'A few places.'

'You're too modest,' Natalia accused playfully. 'I want you to tell me everything, where you've been, what you've done. I want you to tell me everything I'm missing trapped here in a backwater country most civilised people probably can't even pronounce.'

'*Where* you live really isn't all that important, Natalia,' said Ben. 'It's *how* you live that counts.'

'Says a boy who's walked the surface of the Moon!' admired Natalia. 'What was that like, Ben?'

He turned to the river but seemed to be seeing beyond it. 'Oh, great. Unless you happen to be walking it for eight hours with a friend dying by your side.'

Natalia's face fell. 'Oh, Ben, I didn't know.' The eyes that had sparkled with high good humour now misted with instant compassion. 'I didn't know. I'm sorry.'

He frowned. 'No. *I'm* sorry, Natalia. It was unfair of me just to come out with that. I shouldn't have said it.' Why had he? The girl hadn't meant any harm. He should have answered her superficially or changed the subject. Instead, he'd indulged in the worst kind of emotional indiscipline in the field. It was a very un-Ben-Stanton-like thing to have done. Maybe the mission was getting to him. Or maybe Natalia was.

'Did it really happen, though?' Natalia asked.

'Yeah. It really happened.'

'Then I'm glad you told me. I've seen friends die too, Ben,' she confided. 'A Resistance fighter came here once, on the run after an assassination attempt on Vlad Tepesch had failed. He had family in Nostravista and they sheltered him. The Shukhovs. They had two daughters I played with, Daria and Dunia. Daria and I were best friends. We were perhaps ten, eleven years old then. But that didn't matter to the Draculesti who hunted the Resistance man down. They were all executed, the entire Shukhov family – I can still hear Daria squealing sometimes – and their house was razed to the ground. I'll show you the site, if you like. It's never been built on since. The Draculesti responsible said that the Shukhovs' fate should serve as an example to all those who dared to challenge the rule of Vlad Tepesch and that we should learn from it. I think we did learn, Ben, but not necessarily the lesson the Draculesti wanted. I can see her evil face now, bone-white, her cruel fangs, her *eyes* . . .'

'Modrussa,' said Ben.

'I used to feel guilty, Ben,' confessed Natalia, 'that I was alive and Daria and Dunia were dead. And I used to worry that one day, or one *night*, the Draculesti would come for *me*. But that was wrong and foolish. In the end, you can't let your fear consume your life, can you? Or grief. Or regret. You have to live, Ben, make the most of every minute, take every opportunity.' Her fingers toyed in exploratory fashion with the buttons of his shirt. Her green-eyed gaze permitted no escape. 'That's what I want. I want to *live*. And when I see something good, I go after it.'

'We'd better be getting back,' said Ben, with greater reluctance than he'd hoped. 'I think it's time I got in touch with my organisation.'

Unlike his shock blaster and pack, Ben's mission-belt hadn't been lost in the Krasnova, simply put aside by Lyvia Vukic for safekeeping. He suspected it was the gadgets in the belt's pouches rather than the perceptive voice of the spirits that had led the old woman to identify his line of work and to miscast him in the role of Wallachia's saviour.

His communicator was damaged but salvageable. He worked on it at the Vukic house with tools borrowed from the meeting hall. Lyvia herself preserved a haughty disdain for technological means of communication and left Ben alone. Leaving Ben alone, however, was not an attractive proposition for Natalia, even if watching him fiddling with wires and computer chips was a less than riveting pastime.

'Are you nearly finished, Ben?' she asked hopefully at last.

'Nope. Not nearly.' Ben winked. 'I *am* finished. As good as new. And now for the bad news. I'm going to need some privacy while I contact my base. I don't want to sound rude, Natalia, but could you . . .' He glanced meaningfully towards the door. 'Just for a minute?'

'If I do, Ben, I want you to know,' Natalia said, 'you're the first boy who's ever asked me to leave. I'll wait outside while you swap passwords with Z or X or P or whoever.'

'Appreciate it,' said Ben.

And in fact he got Cally.

'I've been seconded to the starstone mission,' she said. 'The langtechs are still studying the data that Tolly downloaded and the latest thinking is that the notation on the stone's control panels is in some kind of *computer* language. My area of speciality. So I'm back at Deveraux for the duration. What's the status with you?'

Ben told her as succinctly as he could, which conveniently meant avoiding any mention of Natalia.

Cally sounded concerned enough, in any case. 'Ben, you've got to abort the mission. I'll patch you through to Jonathan Deveraux. If your Resistance contacts are dead, you can't be expected to continue alone.'

'The people who fished me out of the river'll help me, Cal,' Ben responded. 'They may not be official Resistance but they hate Vlad just as much, believe me. I can't abort, not now. You can see that, can't you? Mission's gone too far. There's too much at stake.' Silence over the communicator. 'Cal?' Maybe his repairs hadn't been so effective after all.

But Cally's reticence had nothing to do with faulty communications. 'You're right, Ben. Of course you are.'

With a sense of wishing otherwise. 'Do you need anything from us?'

Ben needed a replacement pack. A chameleon suit in particular was likely to prove useful. Cally had located Nostravista on a holo-map of Wallachia. 'We can try a drop,' she said, 'but you're in the middle of thick forest. I'm not sure where would be best, away from the village just in *case* we get tracked.'

'Don't worry, Cal,' said Ben. 'There's someone here who'll know. Keep the channel open. Natalia!'

She thrust her head round the door. Her hair was swept back exposing one pretty, gold-ringed ear, almost as if the organ had recently been pressed against something. 'I knew you couldn't do without me for long. Who's Cally?'

She asked the same question again after a drop-zone some miles north of Nostravista and a time tomorrow for it to take place had been decided. Cally had told Ben there'd be a little something extra in the pack, a holographic communicator attachment for his wristbands, then she'd signed off with a 'take care' that seemed to go beyond the merely professional.

Ben didn't deny it. 'Cally's my girlfriend, Natalia.'

'Of course she is,' Natalia said, as if it was obvious. 'I expect you have lots of girlfriends, don't you, Ben?'

'Only the one,' Ben said. 'And she's the *only* one. Sorry to disappoint you.'

'Disappoint me? Who's disappointed? I don't know what you mean.' But the sudden colour rising to Natalia Strepescu's cheeks suggested that she did, only too well.

Which perhaps explained why, later that evening, the Wallachian girl was conspicuously in the company of a

Wallachian boy when Ben and the Vukics, like the rest of the village, attended the meeting hall.

'Ben, this is Janos Mirescu,' Natalia presented.

Ben nodded. Janos Mirescu had a bit of a swagger and pride about him, was Ben's build and height but was black-haired like Natalia, the locks almost as curly and almost as long. His features were strong and perfectly proportioned, like a leader's ready to be sculpted. 'Janos,' said Ben. 'I think I'm in your clothes.'

'Ben,' returned the Wallachian. 'I think you are.'

'Janos has said he'll come with us tomorrow to your drop-zone,' informed Natalia. 'We'll need all the eyes we can muster to spot your equipment and Janos' sight is an eagle's.'

Ben regarded her disapprovingly. 'You told him about the drop?'

'Why not?' shrugged Natalia. 'Janos is one of us. A Wallachian, I mean.'

Ben might have pursued the matter, but if Janos' presence wasn't obstruction enough, at that point the nightly broadcast to his people by Vlad Tepesch, Prince and President of Wallachia, commenced, and all eyes turned to the videscreen.

He had a matter of the gravest concern to share with them tonight, it seemed. It appeared that the enemies of Wallachia were mobilising against them. The despised outlanders, with the collusion and collaboration of known traitors, had already penetrated the sanctity of Wallachia's borders, were already placing their polluted feet on holy Wallachian soil. The threat posed to every loyal Wallachian's freedom and happiness and way of life was real, but the people were not to fear and never to despair. He, Vlad Tepesch, would protect them from corrupting influences and defend them from outlander invasion, as the great Kresniki had once done heroic centuries before. In tones of outraged benevolence, the President revealed that steps were already being taken to counter and eliminate the danger to the homeland. Those who would betray their noble heritage were already being rounded up. Hotbeds of dissension and disloyalty such as Karinthia were even now being purged by the righteous wrath of the Draculesti, the state security forces, and other friends of the people. The dungeons beneath Dracholtz were filling. Therefore, patriotic Wallachians everywhere should rejoice and be glad. The crisis would soon be over. The grace and wisdom of Tepesch would make it so. But vigilance, eternal vigilance had still to be maintained. If strangers were seen, even if they appeared to be no more than innocent travellers, their whereabouts should be reported immediately. It was the duty of every loyal and right-minded Wallachian . . .

There'd been hoots of derision and howls of fury from the Nostravistans from the moment of Vlad's first utterance. Now, though, the cruel, vampiric figure could no longer be heard above the jeers and the catcalls and the rage. It seemed that at least one village in the Nocnitsa was inhabited solely by *disloyal* and *wrong*-minded Wallachians. Who looked now to Ben for a sign of hope.

'The spirits have brought you here to do their bidding, Benjamin Stanton,' cackled old Lyvia, who was somehow at his shoulder.

Ben gazed up at the cold, sadistic visage of Vlad Tepesch. How he'd like to wipe that arrogant sneer from

the Prince of Wallachia's lips. But the successful com-
pletion of his mission alone would have to do that. And
the next stage was to get to the drop-zone.

Ben didn't like the way Janos Mirescu looked at him. It
wasn't overtly hostile, not a provocatively confronta-
tional 'you lookin' at *me*?' or anything like that, but it was
hardly a happy-clappy let's-all-be-friends-and-welcome-
to-Wallachia-beam, either. It was kind of sullen, kind of
suspicious. Ben knew why. *Natalia*. Yet another variation
on the theme of the eternal triangle. Not desirable at the
best of times, but in a mission situation potentially disastrous. He almost wished that Natalia had been closer to
Lyvia in age – almost, but he couldn't *quite* make it.

At least he doubted much could go wrong en route to
the drop-zone.

The three of them had set off in the slate-grey light of
dawn – it was no good training to be a secret agent if you
couldn't handle early starts – and even now, several
hours later, the rising sun lacked the power to penetrate
the dark green foliage above their heads. Mist hung
between the trees like phantom washing. Natalia led the
way, her arm around Janos' waist as if one or the other
of them needed support.

'You keeping up all right?' Janos glanced back at the
recent invalid. 'We can go slower if you'd like.'

'No, I'm fine,' said Ben. 'Thanks.' And I'm not aiming
to steal your girl off you either, he considered adding.

'We're here anyway,' announced Natalia, 'the general
area we settled with – what was her name again, Ben?'
Ben reminded her. 'Oh, that's right. Must be short for
something, is it? Well, perhaps we'd better split up and

search. If they've already dropped your equipment it could still take some finding. Janos knows his way around. Ben, maybe I'd better partner you.'

Ben tried to pre-empt the Mirescu scowl. 'No need.' He consulted the chronometer inlaid in his wristband. 'Cal said they'd drop at nine and it's coming up to that now. And we won't have to search, either. The pilot'll lock on to our heat signatures. All we need to do is stand and wait.'

'Standing and waiting,' Natalia said grudgingly. 'And here was I thinking secret agents led *exciting* lives.'

'Not all the time,' conceded Ben with a smile, 'but we're always punctual.'

The roar of a jet overhead. Everybody snapped their attention upwards. In time to see a gleaming square metal object descending towards them, suspended from a parachute. Weights brought it crashing through the tree-tops and thudding to rest not twenty metres away. Ben's replacement pack.

'Any more accurate and it might have had your head off,' said Janos, as if that might have been something worth the price of admission.

Ben made no comment. He was detaching the pack from the parachute and weights, burying the latter beneath topsoil and leaves. Natalia helped, and if her fingers happened to touch Ben's during the course of their work, it probably couldn't be avoided. Even if an aloof Janos clearly thought otherwise.

When they'd done, 'Let's go,' said Ben briskly. Natalia was playing games, and while it was flattering that she should find him attractive, they were still not acceptable. He'd feel a lot better once they'd returned to Nostravista.

Or not.

Evidently Natalia had been right about the sharpness of Janos' eyesight. It was he who saw them first as the three teenagers neared the village, he who seized Ben's arm and hissed: 'Look!'

Armed men. In the uniform of the Wallachian security forces. *Vlad's* men.

Ben tightened his hands into fists. They'd found him.

SEVEN

He ought to have been impressed by the speed with which Janos and Natalia acted, seeking cover behind a screen of undergrowth with the instinctiveness of Spy High students during Camouflage and Concealment training, the three of them in unison. But Ben was distracted by the security men loitering in Nostravista, entering houses as if they had a right to, as if searching for someone, a captain demanding information of Vissarion Vukic in full view of the village.

'They know I was here,' he concluded. 'Someone's informed on me.'

'Watch your tongue, outlander,' Janos cautioned with quiet ferocity. 'You don't know what you're *talking* about.'

'There are no informers in Nostravista,' expanded Natalia, more disappointed than angry with Ben's assumption. 'Surely you must realise *that*, Ben? We hate the devil Tepesch. Why would any of us help him?'

'Okay, okay.' Ben's wider experiences in espionage made him a little more cynical than either of his companions, but he thought any reference to the habit that financial reward and promises of power had of creating traitors in the unlikeliest places was not entirely tactful right now. He didn't want to start converting allies into adversaries himself. 'I'm wrong. I must be wrong, okay? They must have just got lucky. Let's keep our voices down and not help them out any more.'

'It's like the day they came for Daria and Dunia,' whispered Natalia gravely, and Janos squeezed her shoulder by way of comfort. Ben was tempted to join him.

But now there were high-pitched insults and raucous laughter from the nearby Vukic house. Two security men burst out with an irate Lyvia in hot pursuit, striking at them with a broom. 'Calm yourself, old mother!' one of them roared mockingly. 'Or you'll be sleeping beneath the grass by nightfall.'

'*You're* the ones to keep the worms fed!' pursued Lyvia hotly. 'Every last one of you!' She addressed her scorn to the security forces in general. 'You come here without a by-your-leave, force your way into honest people's homes, give our men an excuse to stop working. We're all good citizens of our beloved President *here*, you know. I've a good mind to let him know how his so-called security forces waste their time.'

'Peace, old mother. We're following the President's orders now,' the captain engaged with Vissarion placated her.

'Then he needs to give you better orders, and I'll tell him that too!' promised Lyvia. 'What's wrong with searching out those cursed outlanders, may they be taken in the night, hmm? Before good, honest Wallachian citizens wake in the morning with their throats cut.'

'I doubt anyone would dare to take a knife to you, old mother,' said the captain. He raised his eyebrows to his underlings and they shook their heads. 'And now again, I apologise for the intrusion. Yours is the second village my men have visited today and we have two more to go before we're finished. So you can rest assured, all of you, the enemies of Wallachia *will* be apprehended.'

'Yes?' muttered Natalia. 'Then search for them in the citadel.'

The teenagers stayed hidden until well after the last of the security forces had departed. Then, 'Let's check with Vissarion what's been happening,' said Ben.

But Janos held him back. His expression was beyond sullenness and suspicion now. It was contemptuous. 'A routine patrol and search,' he said. 'That's what it was. You heard him. No informant. No traitor.'

'Are you going to let go of my arm, please?' Ben enquired.

'Janos . . .' warned Natalia.

'But no, *that* can't be right,' Janos scorned. 'We can't have a village *full* of Wallachians without at least *one* of them being untrustworthy and corrupt, can we? Because that's what they're like, isn't it, these common peasants in backward countries. Unreliable. Faithless. Sell their mothers for a flagon of wine.'

'Janos,' frowned Natalia. 'Ben didn't mean *that* . . .'

'Oh yes he did,' Janos sneered. 'That's what you think of us, isn't it, outlander?'

'I think,' said Ben, coldly and matter-of-factly, 'that if you *don't* let go of my arm pretty much like now, you are going to need assistance in future every time you go to the boys' room.'

'Apologise first. Apologise for what you think of us.'

'Janos,' pleaded Natalia, 'have you gone mad? Ben is our *friend*.'

'Ah, Natalia,' chuckled Janos tolerantly. 'You see a handsome face and your mind turns to porridge. He's not our friend. He doesn't care about us or Wallachia. *Do* you, Stanton?'

'I'll count to five, Janos. One for each of your fingers I'm then going to break.'

'You may fool the others, old Lyvia with her spirits, but you don't fool a Mirescu.'

'And for the sheer hell of it I'm starting with three.'

'You'll side with us for as long as it suits your purpose, won't you, the purpose of all those big, important nations out there, America, Europa . . .'

'Four.'

'And when we've blindly, stupidly served your own agenda and you don't need us any more, you'll just turn your backs, won't you? Wallachia and our suffering will be as nothing again, a news flash at best. You'll destroy the starstone and leave Tepesch in place to destroy us.'

'Five.'

'No!' Natalia tore Janos' hand from Ben's sleeve, slipped her slim body between the two of them. 'Stop it, both of you. If the devil Tepesch could see you now he would be laughing. Janos, this is no way to talk to someone who's risked his life for us.' Janos thought otherwise. 'And Ben, tell him. Tell him you are our friend.'

'I am,' Ben declared, his gaze never wavering from Janos', but the Wallachian wasn't looking down either.

'I'm in this country, your country, to do a job that's in everyone's interests. We're on the same side, Janos. You have to trust me.'

'When you scarcely trust us? "Everyone's interests"!' Janos snorted. 'Prove your goodwill. Show yourself to be a Wallachian, by spirit if not by birth. Undergo the Rite of Manhood.'

'The what?'

'It's a custom, Ben,' Natalia explained, 'an initiation that marks the movement from childhood into adulthood. All Wallachian boys go through it on their sixteenth birthday.'

'Guess I'm two years too late,' observed Ben. 'So sorry, Janos, I *respect* your customs but I don't have time to *live* them.'

'Well, until you *do*, Stanton,' said Janos, 'I have no faith in you.' And he turned and stalked away. 'Natalia!'

'I'm coming, Janos!' she called. To Ben: 'I'd better go after him. He's a little . . . emotional. Wallachians are. Do you understand, Ben?'

Better than Natalia imagined. Because though it pained him to admit it, Ben knew that much of what Janos Mirescu had said was true.

That afternoon, Natalia took Ben to show him the dracul processors: 'I thought you might like to see these before you leave us.' After discussion with Vissarion, and now in renewed possession of a chameleon suit, Ben had determined that tomorrow he should make for Dracholtz and the final stages of his mission. Vlad's men had visited Nostravista and found nothing, but that did not mean that they wouldn't return. And the tensions between himself and Janos could only be resolved by the departure of one of them.

'I'm sorry about Janos earlier,' said Natalia. 'He had no right to talk to you like that.'

'It's okay,' Ben said. 'I've put up with worse. If you listened to my spycraft instructor during training, my name always seemed to have four letters.'

Natalia smiled. 'Only I wouldn't want you to think badly of him. Janos is a good person. He can be warm and tender when he wants to be. But he's deeply patriotic. He loves Wallachia more than anything.' And anyone? Ben wondered. 'He can't tolerate slights against our homeland and he's suspicious of the motives of outlanders.'

'Yeah, I think I got that,' said Ben.

'He hasn't got as close to you as I have.' Natalia seemed to stumble or *something* on the uneven path. She was pressing against Ben. 'And I don't know you yet as well as I'd like, Ben.'

'You were talking about Janos,' Ben reminded her gently. Why couldn't the dracul processors be nearer to the Vukic house?

'You see, what you have to understand about Janos is that if Wallachian history had taken a different route, *he* could have been our prince and president. The Mirescu family is very ancient and in times past was one of the six great noble families of Wallachia. After Kresniki's victory over the Magyars had preserved the nation, though, civil war broke out, and from years of bitter fighting one family only emerged to rule Wallachia.'

'The Tepeschs,' Ben deduced.

'Sadly so. And those defeated were lost to poverty and

humiliation. Janos is a peasant, a dracul harvester like the rest of us, but in his veins flows the blood of aristocracy.'

'I'll bear it in mind.'

They reached the dracul processors, modern machines in concrete buildings more usually to be found on a western industrial estate than by a peasant village in a forest. No wonder the Nostravistans kept them pretty much out of sight. They were more than a little incongruous.

'I think you know that the most important part of the dracul flower is its seeds or pods, don't you, Ben?' said Natalia. 'The scarlet seeds, the white petals. The white symbolises the purity of Wallachia, the scarlet the blood that its people are willing to shed in its defence.'

'Is that right?' Ben restrained his cynicism. He could have interpreted the dracul rather differently, with the white representing innocent lives, say, and the scarlet the craving for blood that was the terrible legacy of Drac and that destroyed those lives. But it was a reading that wouldn't go down well in Wallachia.

'The harvesters bring the flowers here for storage,' Natalia was explaining. A million dead blooms, like severed heads, heaped into giant circular bins. 'Then, after they've dried out, they're fed into the dracul gins that separate the pods from the petals. This used to be done by hand, but now the gin does it for us. I know Lyvia and even Vissarion prefer the old ways. "One day machines will make even men redundant." That's what Lyvia says.'

'Don't tell me,' Ben interrupted. 'The spirits told her.'

Natalia pursed her lips critically. 'Don't mock the spirits, Ben. Lyvia also says that belief can be stronger than truth.'

'Well, she's got a point there. And I'm sorry. That was a little bit too much of the outlander, wasn't it?'

'I forgive you,' said Natalia graciously. 'And *anyway*, the separated seeds we pack into jars' – she showed him some, circular plasteel tubes about half a metre long – 'suspended in a preservative fluid made from the crushed petals, and send them to Dracholtz once a week. Tomorrow's the next batch, actually.'

'Is it?' mused Ben. 'That's interesting.'

'Have I been interesting too?' Natalia asked coyly.

'My attention hasn't wandered once.' He was flirting. Flirting with a vivacious raven-haired beauty who clearly had the hots for him. Disgraceful! At least, it *was* if Cally still meant something to him, and she did. But not even Ben's self-control was limitless.

Natalia was taking his hand. She was laughing. 'Then come with me,' she was tempting. 'It's time for the first of your two exciting bonuses.'

And Ben went with her. To the dracul fields that sloped from the fringes of the Nocnitsa to the banks of the Krasnova, like a vast white canvas speckled with blood. Harvesters were at work in the distance – evidently this part of the process had not been mechanised – bending low to scoop the flowers up and thrusting them into sacks slung across their backs. No wonder Lyvia's back looked like half a McDonald's sign if she'd spent her life doing this kind of work. And what of Natalia, whose back, in keeping with her front and sides and pretty much every part of her, was presently as perfectly shaped as could be imagined? Would she be bowed and bent too by the time she was old? Ben began to understand her desire to travel.

The fumes from the fields were a cloying perfume, an opium for the senses, overpowering and entrancing. They waded through flowers to their knees, and Ben's trousers, Natalia's skirt were smeared with crimson.

'There's an old tradition in Wallachia,' Natalia said. 'When a girl is . . . attracted to a boy, she comes to the dracul fields and picks a single flower, then she presents it to the boy as a token of her . . . affections. In this case the white—'

'Yeah, I think I can work the symbolism out this time,' said Ben.

'Then close your eyes.'

'Pardon me?'

'Close them.' Natalia giggled. 'I've got something for you, Ben, something special. Your *bonus*.'

'I don't know, Natalia.' He was shaking his head, but amusedly.

'What? Close. Your. Eyes. Are you afraid?'

'I think I know what's coming.'

'Then you know it can't hurt you, don't you?'

'Okay,' Ben submitted. 'Have it your way.' He closed his eyes. 'What now? Hold out my hand, right?'

'Oh, Ben, you're *so* well trained. Now I'm going to put something *in* your hand but you mustn't look.' She closed his fingers over the object in question. 'You must count to ten, *slowly*, and then you can look.'

'All right,' said Ben, 'but I want you to know, Natalia, Ben Stanton wouldn't stand in a field of flowers with his eyes closed and counting to ten like an idiot for just *anyone*. Natalia?'

He heard her laughter fading into the distance. Could have opened his eyes then but honesty and integrity dictated he complete the count. He was generous with his definition of 'slowly'. 'Eightnineten.' Eyes open. Hand open.

A dracul flower in his palm.

Ben had known it would be, but he still felt his heart squeeze and an urge to break into purposeless laughter. 'Natalia.' Good name. It felt good shaping those syllables. Where was she? Disappearing towards the Krasnova, clearly inviting pursuit.

She'd given him a dracul flower. That was more potent than sending a Valentine. If he followed her, she'd be getting one message. If he didn't, if he returned alone to Nostravista, she'd be getting another. Which was the message he wanted her to receive?

Ben broke into a run, a run aimed at the river. What else could he do? He wasn't going to cheat on Cally, but Natalia deserved better than for him to simply walk away. He'd talk. She'd listen. She'd understand.

If he could find her.

She was in the river. 'Natalia!' He saw her head and shoulders above the shimmering surface of its waters. Her wet hair slicked back. Her *bare* shoulders. 'Natalia, I can't accept this.' He held up the dracul.

'Of course you can. You *want* to,' Natalia called from the Krasnova.

'But I told you,' Ben pleaded. 'I've *got* a girlfriend. Cally.' He was aware that he'd nearly stumbled over something lying on the ground. Some *things*. They looked disturbingly like Natalia's clothes.

'Cally's not in Wallachia, Ben,' Natalia pointed out. 'I am.'

And *how*, Ben gulped. There was no mistaking Natalia's

presence as she stood up in the river. Ben gaped. He'd been right about the clothes. 'Na . . . Natalia, what do you think you're doing?'

'I said you had two bonuses, Ben. This is your second.' She grinned in the sunlight, and the drops of water clung to her skin like jewels. 'Feel like joining me? Come on in, Ben. Oh, and it's an old Wallachian tradition. No costumes allowed.'

'Natalia, I don't think so.' He must be mad, but he thought of Cally. That made it easier. 'You're a stunning . . . you're a lovely girl and everything and I'm really, really flattered that you . . . but it's not going to work, Natalia. It's wrong.'

And then, simultaneously, 'Ben!' cried the girl, and 'The first truthful words you've *said*, outlander,' as Janos Mirescu battered into him from behind.

Stupid, Ben berated himself, thudding face-first to the stony soil. He should have been paying attention. Not even the alluring charms of Natalia should have proved so distracting that Janos could creep up on him. He spat out a mouthful of dirt and rolled on to his back. Oh well, he'd soon make amends.

'What's the matter, outlander? Good Wallachian earth not to your taste?' Fists clenched, the Wallachian was closing in.

Ben swept out with his leg, took Janos' from under him. 'I don't know, Janos. Why don't you try some for yourself?'

He leapt to his feet again. The Wallachian wasn't far behind him. They circled each other warily, Janos glaring.

'Janos! Ben! Don't!' Natalia splashed towards shore, the romance of the earlier moment rather forgotten.

'This isn't something we can just talk about, is it?' Ben said.

'Ogling my girl while she's bathing?' retorted Janos. 'I don't think so, Stanton.'

He signalled his first punch so early he might as well have put it in writing. And the second. Ben swayed with easy, economical grace to avoid them both. He didn't retaliate.

'I don't want to hurt you, Janos, I really don't. This is all a misunderstanding, so why don't you—'

Wasn't listening. With a yell of rage, where his fists had failed Janos now threw his whole body. Ben side-stepped. Janos crashed again to the ground.

'Stop it! Both of you!' Natalia, dripping wet, had tugged on her clothes. 'This is madness. Either of you could get hurt!'

'Natalia's right, Janos.' Though he might have quibbled over the 'either'. When someone who'd never enjoyed the benefits of Spy High unarmed combat training took on someone who had, only one person was ever going to need the medtechs. It would be unfair of Ben to fight on. He held out his hand to help Janos up. 'Here.'

Janos took his hand. And yanked sharply. This time his follow-up blow *did* strike home. And this time he wasn't going to give the outlander a chance to elude him. He grappled with Ben, struggling to throw him.

'I don't need your charity, Stanton,' he gritted. '*Wallachia* doesn't need it.'

'Is that right?' Ben slipped out of his opponent's grasp. He allowed Janos to press forward, deflecting the blows with his forearms. 'Maybe what you need is to listen to Natalia and just calm down. You're wasting both our times. I can keep this up all day.'

'Listen to him, Janos!' begged Natalia.

But listening to anyone seemed out of the question for Janos Mirescu right now. He was too far gone. Ben could see the madness in his eyes. If he wasn't stopped, the Wallachian might do something that in a saner moment he'd regret.

At the risk of damaging his pride further, then, Ben would have to stop him.

He struck so quickly and so decisively that neither Janos nor Natalia saw the blow coming, the heel of his hand driving powerfully against his opponent's chest, staggering him, leaving him gasping for air.

Janos dropped to his knees, bent forward, coughing, wheezing.

'It's okay. It's okay. You'll be all right. Deep breaths.' Ben crouched beside him, laid a hand on Janos' shoulder. 'I'm sorry, but you gave me no choice. You fight well.' A little magnanimity in victory never did any harm, Ben thought, particularly when you'd just defeated someone who wasn't really an enemy.

'Janos!' Natalia knelt beside him too. 'Did you have to hit him so *hard*, Ben?'

'Get away from me, both of you.' Janos shook Ben's hand from him. 'Leave me alone.'

'Indeed. It might be a good idea if you *did* keep apart from now on.' Vissarion Vukic, regarding the teenagers with bushy disapproval. 'Brawling in public like common thugs, is it? Janos, by deporting yourself like this you sully the name of Mirescu. And Ben, perhaps my mother's spirits were mistaken after all.'

'This was not the outlander's fault, Vissarion,' said Janos grudgingly. 'I started it.'

'Maybe not without cause, though. What say we split the blame fifty-fifty?' Ben adjusted.

'Hmm.' Vissarion still seemed far from impressed. 'I came looking for you, Ben, to tell you that your papers have been prepared. They're not as perfect as if we'd had access to Resistance resources at Karinthia, but it can't be helped. They should be more than sufficient to deceive the guards on the gates of Dracholtz. That is, if you still intend to pursue your mission as planned.' Vissarion glanced critically from Ben to Janos and Natalia.

'Of course. Thanks, Vissarion.' Ben dusted himself down, his expression turning grim. 'It's time I paid the devil Tepesch a visit.'

EIGHT

Morning, and the wheelless carts transporting dracul seeds from Nostravista to Dracholtz were well on their way. For most of the harvesters driving the route to the capital, it was a journey they'd completed many times before. For one of their number, however, it was all new.

As was the awkward silence Natalia Strepescu preserved for almost a full hour before she finally plucked up the courage to speak. 'Yesterday,' she ventured, 'you and Janos, the fight . . . that was *my* fault really, wasn't it?'

Ben, sitting in the passenger seat alongside her, smiled to himself. 'What makes you think that, Natalia?'

'You *know* what. The way I've been behaving towards you since I saved you from the Krasnova. The way I've been – how do you put it in the west? – coming on strong.'

'Strong? Like Muhammad Ali in his prime.'

'Who?'

'Twentieth-century pop-culture reference. To do with floating like a butterfly and stinging like a bee. It doesn't matter.'

Natalia blushed. 'It's just that in Wallachia, we don't like pretences, we're not good at hints and subtleties. We're an emotional people and we like to express our feelings outright and frankly, so they can't be mistaken. Sometimes that creates problems.'

Ben smiled reassuringly. 'Not with me it doesn't.'

'But if I hadn't thrown myself at you like I did then Janos wouldn't have grown jealous and he wouldn't have attacked you. And I wouldn't be feeling so ashamed now.'

'You've got nothing to feel ashamed about,' stressed Ben.

'Haven't I?' Natalia pointedly kept her eyes on the road ahead. 'I expect you think I only volunteered to be the one to drive you to Dracholtz so I could seduce you on the way. I expect you think I'm a cheap peasant girl who drools over anything in trousers.'

'Of course I don't think that, Natalia,' dismissed Ben, 'though as far as the drooling goes, if you feel it coming on I think I've got a handkerchief here somewhere.'

'Ben!' protested Natalia, but she glanced at him again in shy amusement.

'I'll tell you what I think, shall I? The old clear-the-air-and-cards-on-the-table routine before we get to Dracholtz.'

'If you like,' she said.

And in her voice Ben detected a little last hope. If he was going to let her down, which he was, he was going to have to do it gently. 'I think,' he said, 'that you're a gorgeous, exciting, wanna-be-with girl, Natalia. I think that any boy in his right mind and unattached would find you irresistible, me included . . .'

'I hear a but,' smiled Natalia ruefully. 'But Cally.'

'But Cally,' Ben acknowledged. 'I'm *not* unattached. You know that. I'm in a relationship and it's good and I'm happy and I'm not about to do anything to hurt it. I *am* sorry, Natalia.'

'You're not the only one,' the girl replied.

'And if it's any consolation, the prospect of taking a dip with you in the Krasnova yesterday, it *was* tempting.'

'Maybe it was just as well you didn't, though,' Natalia said. 'It was *cold*.'

Ben grinned, wondered if he shouldn't put the case for his rival while he and Natalia were being candid. 'What about Janos?' he suggested, a little unfortunately like a waiter assisting a diner with her menu selection. Natalia looked quizzical. 'I mean, you still have a dracul flower to deliver, don't you? And I'm sure I sense some kind of history between the two of you.'

'That's the trouble,' admitted Natalia. 'Oh, I know Janos likes me – he wouldn't have been jealous of *you* if he didn't – and I like him, and I *suppose* some people think we're going together, but we've known each other for so long, grown up together, that I can't tell whether my feelings towards him are those of a close and dear friend or . . . well, something more. If they *are*, then how do you explain that as soon as you arrived, Ben—'

'I'm an outlander,' Ben offered. 'A devastatingly good-looking one, I'll accept, but I'm someone new, Natalia, from somewhere different. That's what drew you to me, my novelty value.'

'What, like a new toy?' Natalia laughed.

'Something like that.' Ben laughed too. 'But just remember, the toy you love most is usually the toy you've had longest.'

Natalia suddenly grew wistful. 'And you'll be gone soon, won't you, Ben? You'll leave us and we'll never see you again.'

'I don't do predictions, Natalia,' Ben cautioned, "cause if there's one thing I've learned from the secret agent business, it's that you never know what's coming next.'

Vissarion had been right about the quality of the forged identification papers he'd prepared for Ben. The armoured guardsmen who checked the Nostravista party before allowing them to enter Dracholtz suspected nothing. They were not in any case, Ben surmised, intellectual giants. Something scrawled in crayon and in the name of Mickey Mouse would probably have fooled them just as easily. But the tall, blond Wallachian presenting his documents dutifully, almost humbly (and the guards liked humble – it made them feel important), was actually called 'Kresniki Stantiescu'.

'After our great warrior hero,' explained Ben. 'My family's always been patriotic.'

'If your parents wanted to show their patriotism they should have christened you Vlad,' opined the guard. 'Like mine did me.'

'I'll tell them. Maybe if I ever have a little brother . . .'

'Yeah, yeah. All right, Kresniki. Pass.'

The guardsman's partner was rather more taken by Natalia. 'Dracul harvesters from the Nocnitsa delivering to the Big City, huh? What if I offered to show you the sights later on? You'd need an escort. There's a lot of bad things can happen to pretty girls in Dracholtz if they're not careful.'

'Yes?' said Natalia with mock interest. 'I imagine the

worst of them is being shown the sights by a poor apology of a man like you.'

The guardsman threatened to take offence at that but his partner guffawed with laughter and he decided it might be better to cut his losses. Plenty of girls around who went for guys in armour and who *didn't* talk back. He waved Natalia and Ben's wheelless through.

They passed beneath the city walls and entered the capital. The narrow streets of Dracholtz were thronging with Wallachians going about their business, buying, selling, pressing from place to place. The buildings might seem as if they'd recently escaped from a museum, Ben thought, but the people resembled city-dwellers any-where. With one important exception.

The fear.

It was etched across their faces even when they were smiling, even when they were greeting colleagues or acquaintances or exchanging pleasantries with trades-men. Fear in the way they never stayed too long in the one place, never laughed or spoke too loudly, never dared to draw attention to themselves. The anonymous man is never arrested, Ben thought. And there was fear too in their furtive glances upwards, to the guardsmen on their flying platforms, in the catching of their breath as a patrol hovered close, as if *considering*, and in their thank-ful sighs of relief as it veered away again.

So this was what it was like to live in the city of Tepesch. This was what it was like to live under the rule of a tyrannical despot anywhere in the world. A perpet-ual condition of fear. And even worse, a permanent state of distrust, for how could you know for sure who was a friend and who a spy?

Never trust a Wallachian. Ben could remember thinking that. *They don't deserve us, Cal.* He could remember saying that. Now he looked at Natalia and he realised he doubted both sentiments. It wasn't right that people should live like this, and it wasn't their fault.

Lyvia's spirits. Maybe they had the right idea after all.

'I know,' said Natalia bleakly. 'It's horrible, isn't it? We have to come to Dracholtz to deliver the seeds, but we're better off in Nostravista. We can be ourselves there. The forest hides us even from the devil Tepesch. Here I feel his eyes upon me like crawling insects.' She glanced distastefully towards the citadel.

'Well,' said Ben, 'me he's *not* going to see.' Beneath his borrowed Wallachian clothes, he wore his chameleon suit. 'And it's time I started earning my money.'

'All right,' consented Natalia.

As had been prearranged, once in Dracholtz she and Ben had quietly peeled away from the rest of the Nostravistans. Instead of driving directly to the prosperous properties of the dracul merchants, Natalia had headed into the seedy, disreputable River District of the city. They were now in a cobbled street that was barely wide enough for the wheelless cart to enter, a shabby, slovenly, sorry-for-itself street lined with taverns where Wallachians in similar mood could come to find liquid comfort. Natalia drew up outside one such establishment. 'It normally takes us a couple of hours to complete business with our buyers. Will that give you enough time?'

Ben nodded. 'I just need to locate the starstone for the moment, learn what I can, *then* decide on a course of action.'

'So in two hours we'll meet back here, The Crown of Wallachia. It's a crown that's slipped over the years, I'm afraid, but it's as safe a place as any.'

'I'll be here.' Ben clambered out of the cart. 'And Natalia, thanks for the lift.'

'My pleasure,' she said, 'and at the risk of sounding too much like Cally, *take care.*'

There was no chance of anything less. But as Ben strode briskly and purposefully through the River District's increasingly decrepit, mouldering and ramshackle streets, he had to wonder. What kind of mentality made someone sign up for secret agenting? Why did they do it? Take his present situation, for example. Here was the citadel, looming blackly above him like an open coffin, and inside it somewhere was not only an alien artefact of possibly unimaginable destructive power, but also, seated on a throne maybe, a psychopathic madman with fangs and the strength of ten, not to mention, almost certainly, maybe kind of squatting at his feet, a white-faced female assassin with a similar dental profile, *both* of whom had already tried to kill him and would be only too happy to give it another go. Any person in their right mind would be fleeing the city, the country, resigning from Deveraux and becoming an attorney in their father's wealthy and prestigious law firm.

And what was he, Benjamin T. Stanton Jr, doing? He was gleefully slipping *into* a squalid, filthy but deserted alley and *out* of his exterior garments, wedging them behind a drainpipe for retrieval later (the dirt didn't matter – they belonged to Janos), and pulling on the gloves of his chameleon suit, its hood over his head.

Because, alone, unaided and entirely without back-up, he planned on infiltrating the citadel, entering the lion's den, so to speak, placing himself voluntarily within the grasp of perhaps his greatest enemy.

He had to wonder why. Did he have a secret suicide wish? Was it a macho thing, feeling the need to prove himself against all odds? Was it about playing the hero, impressing the chicks? Nah, he concluded, energising his chameleon suit. None of those.

It was just one *wild* ride.

The alley was deserted again. Kind of. Ben was physically still there, but the black fabric of the chameleon suit that now covered his entire body from head to toe also hid it from sight. The millions of nano-chips woven into the material were responsible. They assimilated and then replicated the immediate environment so as to erase the suit's wearer from it, the way a chameleon in the animal world takes on the colours of its surroundings for camouflage. Vital signs, heat signature, all masked. Instant invisibility. And yet the suit's wearer could see, more accurately than with the naked eye. The hood's infra-red viewing panels ensured that.

The suit came with one or two other useful features, too. Such as clingskin.

Ben slithered up the sheer wall of the citadel above the Krasnova. He didn't look down, but not because heights bothered him. The trick with clingskinning was to maximise contact between your hands and feet and the surface you were scaling, and that required sustained concentration. Ben had no wish to be plunging into the river a second time.

He heaved himself over the battlements, into the citadel, felt good, solid stone beneath his feet. There were guardsmen on the ramparts, stationed at strategic intervals, but none of them could see him, of course. And it occurred to Ben that even if they could, at the present moment they'd scarcely pay him any attention. Right now, the military population of Tepesch's citadel seemed rather preoccupied.

From the central tower, an eerie light was emanating. It emerged from the windows and embrasures of the turret like the green, questing tentacles of an alien being, and it was cold, chilling, redolent of deep space. Ben wondered if the unknown giants on the Moon had witnessed such a light before they died those unguessable centuries ago, because its source was obvious.

The starstone. Vlad's techs were activating it.

The guardsmen muttered warily among themselves, gripped their pulse rifles more tightly, as if anticipating their imminent use, and they were no doubt courageous enough given an enemy they could understand, but now, if they made any move at all, it was backwards, away from the tower.

Ben made straight for it.

The lower reaches of the tower formed part of the citadel complex, allowing him easy access. The curve of its stone meant that clingskinning was a little more treacherous, but Ben was an expert. He hauled himself higher, into the light that now enshrouded the tower's peak like a green mist. The sensory systems of his chameleon suit compensated for any changes in external temperature and quality of light: Ben could see as well as ever.

The embrasure nearby, designed to resemble the openings through which in times past arrows or other missiles might have been fired but in reality, like the rest of the central tower, a mere illusion of medievalism, was wide enough for intrepid secret agents to squeeze through.

Inside the tower, something was happening.

Ben absorbed the scene instantly, as he'd been trained to do. The mechanisms in the walls that allowed the construction to open and close. The computers and other scientific instrumentation that chattered and whirred tens of metres below him like a gaggle of excited gossips. The starstone itself, placed reverently on a raised dais like a religious relic on an altar, a trio of techs fussing at its control panels, the green light rising from the artefact like steam from an engine. And the people. Ben didn't recognise any of the techs, none of the dozen men and women busy with their monitors and screens, but there were three Wallachians present to whom he could put names. Craniescu, the regime's Head of Internal Security, he knew only from holographs, but of the whiskered Boris and Vlad Tepesch himself, he had rather more personal acquaintance. Funny how you always tended to remember those who'd tried to kill you. At least there appeared to be no sign of Modrussa. She was probably out assassinating someone, Ben thought grimly.

He needed to get closer to Vlad. The aural stimulators in his hood were good, but if he could give them a little bit of help, all the better. He slid his way down the internal wall, angling his path diagonally to avoid the strain a steeper descent would exact on his muscles. Keep *some* distance, though, Ben, he advised himself. You never know.

He was maybe twenty metres above the Wallachians' heads. He twisted his body so that he was facing down towards them, palms of hands and soles of feet pressed flatly and firmly against the stone.

Craniescu was talking, flattering his prince: 'When you have harnessed the power of the starstone, what further glories you will achieve!'

And Boris was muttering something under his breath that even the aural stimulators couldn't pick up, and whether his glowering expression was directed towards his sycophantic colleague or the alien starstone, Ben couldn't be sure.

And Vlad Tepesch, Vlad Tepesch was suddenly looking at *him*. Directly. Venomously. As if his chameleon suit had been stripped from him.

But how could that be? It couldn't be.

'My prince?' Craniescu seemed concerned. 'Are you well?'

Those magnetic black eyes were locked on to Ben's. The razor teeth, the taut white skin, the jagged beard, Vlad's features had not altered in the three years since Ben had last been in his presence.

'Do you . . . *see* something, my prince?'

And back then, they'd learned that Drac in its purest form heightened a man's senses to preternatural levels. Ben doubted that Tepesch could physically see him, but what if he could *hear* him or *smell* him – even though he was motionless and even though he'd been heavily into personal hygiene since his first date at the age of twelve.

Ben held his breath. Uncertainty was creasing Vlad's forehead like folds in the whitest paper. Play dead. Don't risk it for real.

'My prince,' a tech by the starstone was calling, 'we are ready for the demonstration . . . if it pleases you.'

All eyes on Vlad.

'My prince?' Even Boris now. 'Is something wrong?'

'No. Nothing.' The words cracked from Tepesch's mouth like lashes from a whip. His gaze snapped from Ben to the starstone. 'It's nothing.' And Ben would have breathed a sigh of relief if to do so hadn't been unnecessarily reckless. 'Proceed, technician. Let us witness the progress you have made.'

'At once, my prince.' The tech who'd spoken earlier, a man evidently so wrapped up in his work that he seemed to have forgotten to cut his hair or his fingernails for at least a year, made a great show of instructing his underlings to enter final information into the starstone's control panels. It was a new variation of computer language, he briefed his watching superiors. They had only the most rudimentary understanding of its complexities so far, but once they had fully mastered them, perhaps President Tepesch would permit the language to be named after himself.

'Languages and names will be the least of your concerns, technician,' Vlad Tepesch assured him, 'if this demonstration proves to be less than satisfactory.'

The tech bowed low and with a sickly smile.

At the same time, the starstone trembled. Vlad's techs *had* made progress, Ben realised, and that wasn't good news.

The starstone rumbled, like it was hollow and something mighty was booming deep inside. The techs stumbled backwards.

'Technician,' demanded Tepesch, 'is this what you expected to happen?'

'We didn't . . .' gulped the tech, 'we didn't know quite *what* would happen, my prince.'

As the rumbling became a dull roar. As the trembling became a shaking, a vibration that entered the very floor and walls of the tower, as if a power, an energy so long held in shackles was now striving to be free.

The sound, rushing to a crescendo. The green light, sucked back into the starstone. Ben almost rocked from his precarious vantage point.

'My prince, if there is danger . . .' Craniescu with an eye on the exit.

'Then I will face it like a true Tepesch.' Vlad drew himself up. 'Let this alien rock do what it can.'

And the tallest point of the starstone, the point that rose like a spire towards the roof, central and dominating, suddenly it was alight, suddenly its marble substance blazed like a green flame and flooded the tower in its dazzling luminosity. Everyone but Ben was forced to shade their eyes or turn away, even Tepesch, and the brightness filters in his suit's hood only barely managed to resist the glare. And still the green grew stronger. And still the whole world shuddered.

Techs cried out in panic. Several darted for the doors. 'Return to your posts!' commanded Tepesch, and to a man they feared the Prince of Wallachia more than the starstone. 'Technicians, *do* something!'

'I don't . . .' the long-haired man moaned forlornly. 'I don't know what *to* do . . .'

And then it didn't matter any more.

With a flash like lightning, the burning point of the starstone seemed to explode. *Seemed*, because the structure remained as solid and immutable as ever. Yet energy was indeed expended, rampant, destructive energy, an expanding ball of alien power that engulfed whatever it touched.

The techs closest to the starstone screamed and were swallowed. The long-haired scientist ran, but neither far nor fast enough. The green orb caught him and consumed him. It rolled outwards like the waters from a damburst. It was going to crash against the walls of the tower.

Vlad and his entourage were retreating now. Ben realised that he wasn't safe either. Like a swift-rising flood, the energy was lapping at his heels. He didn't think it was a good idea to let it touch him.

Ben scurried higher. The embrasure and his way out of the tower seemed further off than he remembered it. One slip now as the stone wall shook and he'd be *praying* for the Krasnova to be beneath him. Not this green, climbing energy field that didn't seem to want to let him go. Ben reached for the embrasure, slipped, for a second felt himself falling, but he thumped his hands and feet hard against the wall. He wasn't going to fall. But he wasn't scrambling for safety either and below him the light was . . .

Fading. As abruptly, as dramatically as it had been created, the starstone's energy was dissipating. The blinding green light became a glimmer, a glow, then not even that. Ben dared to look down. No sound from the starstone now, no vibration. It stood in the middle of the lab as remote and aloof as it had rested in the crater on the Moon, unchanged and unchanging.

The same could not be said of the room around it.

There was nothing left. It was as if the people, the computers, everything that until thirty seconds ago had occupied the tower, had been no more than sketchings in chalk, now erased by the energy burst from the star-stone. The floor and the walls had been smoothed to a featureless white, and nearly dissolved entirely. There were inches of difference in thickness between the surface where Ben clung and that just below him, eaten away by the alien energy. Of the instruments, of the techs, not a trace. Atomised. Ben hoped for the Wallachians' sakes that the process had been painless.

And all this, with just *one* of the starstone's many points activated, a single, solitary one, energised almost by accident. Ben didn't doubt that each of them con-tained the same obliterating potential. His blood ran cold. What if Tepesch managed to harness them *all*?

It was a thought that had obviously also occurred to the Prince of Wallachia, hence his triumphant exultation as he, Boris and Craniescu re-entered the tower lab. 'Hah! Magnificent! See, my faithful Boris, the power we have at our command! If only poor Trapiescu had sur-vived, we would have rewarded him well. Ensure that his widow receives a generous pension. And bring more techs, at once. Resume work on the starstone immedi-ately. The little demonstration we have witnessed today is only the beginning!'

Ben didn't doubt that, either. With the starstone in his possession, Vlad Tepesch was more dangerous than ever.

NINE

So what was he going to *do* about it?

In the dingiest, smokiest corner of The Crown of Wallachia, Ben pondered his options. He had to move to neutralise the starstone quickly – the advances that Vlad's techs had made with the artefact necessitated *that* – but operating alone and with the equipment he'd got made it difficult for him to see exactly how he could effect any kind of serious sabotage. His chameleon suit could get him close to the starstone, but it couldn't guarantee him uninterrupted time with it. He really needed back-up, a few of his old team-mates to make the play with him, but summoning reinforcements was out of the question. They'd take too long to get here, and if they were intercepted at the border they'd cause an international incident that could lead to war. No, if Ben was in need of allies – and who'd have thought the day would ever come when Benjamin T. Stanton Jr would actively seek assistance? – he'd have to look closer to home. The face of old Lyvia flitted unrequested into his mind. She was nodding and smiling an I-told-you-so smile, her toothless mouth wide with delight. Ben began to realise why. As a product of the twenty-first century, he didn't believe in spirits. As a product of Spy High, however, he *did* believe in the value of expediency.

The Wallachian Revolution. It had a certain ring to it.

The tavern door creaked open. Daylight peered inside and thought better of it, stayed out. Two of Vlad's guardsmen did not follow suit.

At the sound of their entrance Ben had looked up, expecting and hoping for Natalia. His first instinct when he saw the guardsmen was that they'd come for him, that Vlad had indeed spied him on the tower wall and had sent his men in pursuit. But of course, they hadn't and he hadn't. It was just that mission duty tended to make you paranoid. (On the other hand, as his former teammate Eddie used to say: 'Just because you're paranoid doesn't mean they're *not* out to get you.') Ben prepared himself for possible violence.

But when the guardsmen's eyes scanned the tavern, they saw only another dishevelled and decrepit drunkard slumped over his tankard just like all the other regulars of The Crown. Correction: like *nearly* all the others. Their gaze passed on to the two exceptions.

How the young peasant couple had found their way to The Crown of Wallachia was a mystery. Why they'd stayed there was more baffling still. Indeed, Ben was astonished that such a foul, wretched establishment had gained any custom at all – even the air seemed clogged with dirt, and prolonged exposure to the ale surely meant certain death (it was as well that Spy High regulations required its secret agents not to touch alcohol while in the field). But if the peasant couple weren't regretting their choice of hostelry already, they were about to.

Ben saw the signs. In the guardsmen's twin leers. In the nudges they exchanged, the knowing glances. In their arrogant swagger as they closed in on the peasant girl. Bullies in armour. Sleazebags with pulse rifles and position. The lowest of the low, exactly the kind of contemptible morons who'd sign up to serve under Vlad. For exactly *this* reason.

''Allo, darlin'. What's a nice girl like you doing in a dive like this?'

'What's your name, darlin'? Tell us your name.'

'M-Magdalena,' stuttered the girl. Fear in her voice, fear in her eyes.

'Thassa lovely name, that is. M-Magdalena. Suits you. M-M-Magdalena.'

The guardsmen roared with laughter. Small minds. Big mouths.

Ignore them, Ben instructed himself. Don't draw attention to yourself. Keep in your corner and wait for Natalia. *But if either of those scumbags ever talked like that to Natalia . . .*

The peasant man stood up for his girl, too. 'Excuse me, could you leave us alone, please?' But not very successfully. The guardsmen pushed him aside. He collided with a table, fell into a chair. He made no attempt to stand up again.

'Sure we'll leave *you* alone. What kind of men do you think we are? We're not int'rested in *you*, country boy. Your little girlie, on the other hand . . .'

'Talking of hands . . .'

'No. Please. Don't touch me.'

Ignore her. Poor, pretty Magdalena. Close your eyes to her anguished expression. Close your ears to her mews of protest and the vulgar, coarse laughter of the guardsmen. Mind your own business. Everyone else in this sink of a tavern seemed to be able to do it. Intervention here was not part of the mission. Intervention here could *jeopardise* the mission.

'It's all right, M-Magdalena. You ain't got nothing to worry about. We're the law.'

'No, please.'

'Why don't you come and sit with us for a bit, then maybe, if you're nice to us, we'll show you around. You want to be *nice* to us, don't you, country girl?'

'No, don't. I don't . . . Stepan, help me.'

But he wasn't going to. Ben regarded the peasant Stepan with mingled pity and contempt. The fear in him, it was palpable. He'd turned away from his girlfriend, fiancée, maybe wife. He'd turned away and he wasn't going to help her. Coward. Why should Ben put himself on the line for the likes of him? Why should he lead a revolution to liberate people who wouldn't even defend their own?

Benjamin White sighed and stood.

Because it was *right*. That was why.

And the two thugs were so intent on dragging Magdalena into a chair that they didn't notice his approach.

'Thassit, country girl, M-M-M-Magdalena. You sit with us.'

'You'll 'ave a good time with *us* and we'll 'ave a good time with *you*.'

'I don't think so,' Ben observed. 'I think the lady would rather stand.'

The first guardsman looked round quizzically. His puzzlement was increased when the contents of Ben's tankard slopped in his face. He spluttered: 'What?'

'You, though, I think you need a bit of a lie-down. Here, let me help you.' Ben followed up with his fist. A satisfying crunch to the guardsman's nose.

The man's companion was letting go of Magdalena and reaching for his pulse rifle. A kick from Ben sent the weapon spinning across the room. 'I don't think so, do you?' His second kick, connecting with the guardsman's chest, knocked him backwards on to a table, *through* the table in a crash of splintered wood and shattered tankards. 'They just don't make furniture like they used to, do they?'

'Who the hell . . .?' First opponent. Second pulse rifle.

This time Ben seized both it and the hands holding it, threw the owner of both on to his back, kept hold of the rifle only to cast it aside. 'Like I told your scumbag friend, let's keep the boys' toys out of it, shall we? Believe me, you're better off that way.' Though Ben didn't dare employ sleepshot or even his own shock blaster: if he did that, he might just as well send a note to Vlad telling him Ben Stanton was alive and well and – as the second guardsman renewed his attack – beating up his security services.

Elbow to the stomach. Guardsman doubling up. Thrown over his shoulder, over the bar. Wasn't likely to resume hostilities any time soon.

'Are you okay?' To a wide-eyed Magdalena.

'Be-be—'

'What?'

'Behind you!'

The remaining guardsman had used the few functional brain cells he'd been granted. He'd gone for a pulse rifle rather than his opponent. Now he was pointing it at Ben, grinning, beyond kicking range.

'That blood from your nose,' Ben said, 'it looks just like a moustache.'

'I'm gonna put a hole right through your middle, boy,' promised the guardsman.

'Yeah?' Ben was grinning too. 'I guess this is the day for behind yous.'

Natalia's business with the dracul merchants had obviously been concluded.

She leapt with a howl on to the guardsman's back, her black hair streaming. He managed to let off a shot but only the ceiling was wounded. Natalia tore at him with hands that in the murky light seemed taloned and un-naturally white. They startled Ben. So did the Wallachian girl's face, as pale as a Draculesti's, her eyes, like sudden nightfall, and the sharpness of the teeth Natalia was exposing in her violent fury. It was like she'd had a Modrussa Makeover in the last few hours. Ben could only stare as his saviour stood over the uncon-scious body of the guardsman.

'Just as well I was passing by, Ben, huh?' She laughed, and as she did so her features, the colour of her skin, returned to normal. *If*, Ben thought, they'd ever truly changed. Well, time for questions later.

'Great timing, Natalia,' he said. 'I was beginning to outstay my welcome.'

'Your transport awaits.'

Which was good. The guardsman Ben had thrown over the bar was no longer personally a threat, but as he hauled himself up he was summoning those who *could* be. 'Code Red. Code Red. Distur —'

Ben bringing the man's head into swift contact with the bar ended the communication. 'I'd sooner your Neanderthal pals *didn't* know where we are, thanks.'

'It doesn't matter, Ben. They *do*,' Natalia warned. 'Each guardsman wears a locator so Internal Security knows where they are at all times. Sounding the alarm was enough. Half the guardsmen in the city are going to be here any minute.'

'Is that right?' Ben squeezed Natalia's arm. 'You mentioned transport?'

They ran from the tavern, vaulted into the waiting wheelless. Ben had been pursued in a range of vehicles since he'd joined Spy High, sky bikes and more conventional wheellesses among them, but never thus far in a cart that on the surface looked as if it might be happier being drawn sedately by oxen or ageing horses. Still, as a patrol of Vlad's guardsmen appeared over the rooftops on their flying platforms, there was a first time for everything.

Ben drew his shock blaster, pulled up his sleeves to reveal his sleepshot wristbands. No point in disguise now. 'How fast can this thing go, Natalia?'

The acceleration all but spilled Ben from his seat. 'Fast enough, outlander?'

'I can shoot at this speed if you can drive.'

Natalia grinned. 'Oh, I can drive.'

They took the first turn at breakneck velocity, the cart veering ludicrously to the left. Down the next street Natalia gunned the magnetic engine so hard that the planked veneer of the wheelless rattled as if it was coming loose.

The first pulse blasts from the chasing guardsmen flashed close. Ben responded with fire of his own. He swayed to his feet to get a better aim.

'Ben, be careful!'

'Don't worry, I've got excellent balance.' Courtesy of Spy High physical training modules. 'You just watch the road.'

'Back-seat drivers,' grumbled Natalia.

Ben was bringing down the platforms. His blaster set to Materials, it was a safer bet to shoot for the flying discs themselves rather than the men who rode them. His marksmanship was unerring. To the right, a platform blasted and its rider bucked to the filthy streets of the River District. To the left, a disc's guidance systems shattered and the guardsman taken on an impromptu diversion through some hapless citizen's roof. Behind, ruptured steel ploughing into the road, hurling Vlad's men into unconsciousness. 'Ben!' Ahead, a kind of a roadblock kind of *un*blocked. Blaster in one hand, sleepshot pumping from the other wrist, men and machinery cleared out of their way in a barrage of shells both anaesthetic and explosive.

Through a curtain of flames the wheelless whooshed.

'You *told* me you could shoot!'

'You *told* me you could drive!'

'Hey, Ben,' laughed Natalia, 'so what do you do on a *second* date?'

Let's not get ahead of ourselves, Ben thought. There was at least one more obstacle for them to overcome.

The main city gate.

The area had been cordoned off to civilians but was nonetheless densely populated. By guardsmen. Not on fragile flying discs here. Behind more solid barriers of steel. At mobile gun emplacements. In full body armour. And fully aware that the consequence of failing to halt the rogues' escape would be to incur the wrath of Tepesch.

Small wonder they opened with a fusillade of fire-power before the wheelless cart was even in range. The ancient buildings of Dracholtz had clearly been deemed acceptable casualties.

'Ben, I'm thinking about a change of direction.' Natalia had manoeuvred the vehicle with dazzling dexterity so far, but even she could not perform miracles.

'No chance.' Behind them their pursuers were swarming like flies. 'It's now or never.'

'Then it looks like never. As in, we'll never fight our way through that kind of punishment.'

'Agreed,' said Ben tersely. 'But they taught me at Deveraux that if you can't work *through* a problem, work *around* it. As in, up, up and away.'

Natalia grinned. 'I think this relationship is about to hit new heights, Ben.'

She pulled back on the wheel, sharply, steeply. The cart soared. And now the enemy fire was all beneath them, and the guardsmen's shouting faces, their little pointing arms, their tiny guns like the weapons of toy soldiers. Their futile, failed attempt to stop them.

Natalia whooped as the wheelless passed above the walls of Dracholtz. The guardsmen's discs were good for short journeys only, designed for use in the city. By the time any serious pursuit could be mounted, she and Ben would be safe again within the embrace of the Nocnitsa.

'We did it!' she cried. 'We *did* it!'

Ben was already pondering Vlad's likely reaction to the news. 'I think we did,' he said.

Later, deep in the forest, they paused. In the golden light of the late afternoon the Nocnitsa seemed to be ablaze, not the most comforting of images, Ben thought. Natalia appeared contented, though. She stretched herself luxuriantly and lifted her face to the sun. Ben watched her.

'You want to tell me what back there was all about?'

Natalia turned to him innocently. 'Which "back there" do you mean? The two of us evading the entire garrison of Dracholtz?'

'The one of you doing a pretty convincing impression of a Draculesti in The Crown of Wallachia.'

'Oh, *that*.'

'Yeah, that. At one point I thought you were going for the throat. With your teeth.'

'Don't be silly, Ben.'

Ben grunted. 'I haven't been silly since I was five years old. Stantons are pretty much born serious. My eyesight's good, too, and I could have sworn you underwent some kind of physical transformation when you attacked that guy.'

'You mean like this?' Natalia said, and her flesh seemed to shiver. It paled and became parchment, bones cracking in her fingers to elongate them, making them like newly sharpened pencils. She laughed at Ben's discomposure, and it would be a brave boy who dared to lock lips with her with *those* teeth on the other side. 'This is nothing.'

'How?' The disturbing possibility occurred to Ben. 'Do you take Drac?'

'What's Drac? You've mentioned it before. Something to do with the devil Tepesch, may he be taken in the night?' Natalia smiled, Ben would have preferred not so broadly. 'No, my changes are the product of my work. Harvesting the dracul flower, coming into such close and regular contact with the raw seeds, they rub into your skin, get into your pores. In time they enter your blood-stream. There are' – she searched for the right word – 'side effects.'

'Some side effects,' Ben observed. 'More like head-on, full-frontal effects, if you ask me.'

'It's all right, though, Ben. It doesn't hurt,' Natalia assured him. 'Many Nostravistans can make the same change at will. One way' – her skin rippled like white water and she was human again – 'or the other. And don't look like that. You were grateful enough for my warrior self in The Crown, weren't you?'

'I guess so,' Ben acknowledged. 'I mean, yes.'

Natalia's smile was more attractive without the fangs. 'We made a good team, didn't we?' Ben didn't deny it. 'Without the *but Cally*, we'd have made a better one. We should be together, Ben, fighting the devil Tepesch side by side, together in the night of the Nocnitsa, you and I, outlander strength and Wallachian passion. Is there really no—'

No, there really wasn't. Ben was sorry. In the forest, shadows lengthened. 'But fighting the devil Tepesch side by side, if you still want to, *that* we can do.'

'What do you mean?' said Natalia.

'I mean I give in. I give up,' conceded Ben. 'Lyvia's spirits can have their way. I've seen enough today to change my mind. Nobody should have to live like the people in Dracholtz, but if Vlad's ever going to be beaten it has to be totally and absolutely. He has to be removed and his whole stinking regime with him.'

'You'll lead us? You'll lead the rebellion?'

Ben nodded determinedly. 'Whatever it takes, Vlad's going down.'

The Security Monitoring Centre in the citadel at Dracholtz was like the womb for Craniescu, the place where he felt most at peace, most at home. He reclined there now in his leather chair that was perhaps closer to a psychiatrist's couch. The chair rotated at the touch of a button a full 360 degrees to allow its occupant an unobstructed view of any of the dozens of screens that covered the conical walls of the chamber like tiles. Each one was the voyeuristic and unblinking eye of a camera concealed somewhere about the city and, in many cases, elsewhere throughout Wallachia. Big Brother might not have been watching Vlad Tepesch's down-trodden citizenry, but Head of Internal Security Craniescu certainly was, aided and abetted by the tubes that connected the helmet he wore to the Monitoring Centre's sound systems, like a bulge of umbilical cords.

'Craniescu.' The Prince of Wallachia announced his entry, flanked by both Boris and Modrussa. 'I trust the half-closed eyes and the simpleton's smile do not imply relaxation when there remains work to be done.'

'Indeed not, my prince,' said Craniescu. 'Locating Stanton has been my sole consideration.'

'Good. The renegade who brought chaos to our streets today *has* to have been Stanton. The description your abject excuses for guardsmen gave confirm it. I knew he was alive.'

'You know everything, my prince,' said Modrussa entirely without irony.

Boris harrumphed more sceptically. 'A pity the identity of his female companion is not equally transparent. A Wallachian girl, it seems.'

'Impossible!' retorted Modrussa. 'No loyal Wallachian would dare take the side of an outlander against their rightful prince.'

A bitter smile played at Tepesch's thin lips. 'Loyalty is an attribute in dangerously short supply these days, my dear Modrussa. It is a quality most effectively encouraged in the masses by fear, and fear can struggle to hold sway when outright challenges to our rule are witnessed in the streets, particularly when the perpetrators escape.'

'Let my Draculesti and me loose in the city, my prince,' urged Modrussa. 'We will have Dracholtz quaking by dawn.'

'My prince, such a move would be madness,' counselled Boris. 'The people need only to be reminded that the one man who can uphold their traditions and keep their country safe from outlanders is you. Find Stanton and the traitor, yes. Execute them, yes. Prove to the people that you are still their champion and protector.'

'A Tepesch needs to prove nothing,' scorned Modrussa. 'Power is his by *right*.'

'True, Modrussa,' agreed Tepesch, 'but as always, my faithful Boris sees with the eyes of wisdom too. Stanton is the key. Craniescu?'

Was chuckling quietly. 'I know the elders of Wallachia place their faith in spirits,' he said. 'They believe themselves to be guided by the ghosts of their ancestors. Senile idiots, all! It is science that solves all mysteries, science that learns the truth, from the origin of the Universe to the whereabouts of a single outlander teenager.'

'You've found him? Where?' Tepesch seized Craniescu's shoulder in his eagerness, so tightly the Head of Security almost cried out in pain.

Craniescu activated a control. The surveillance screens flickered and became a single giant map of Wallachia. Dozens of lines like scarlet threads flashed from Dracholtz at their source to a myriad of destinations throughout the country. 'The possible routes Stanton and his companion could have taken,' Craniescu explained. 'But after the computer's assimilation of all the relevant data' – one by one, the red lines vanished – 'the records of the peasants allowed into the city today, those towns and villages close to the Krasnova to which Stanton might have found his way' – 'Yes, yes,' snapped Vlad Tepesch impatiently – 'we can eliminate the merely possible' – four routes left, three, two – 'and deduce the incontrovertibly certain.' One. 'Nostravista,' smiled Craniescu wolfishly. 'You will find Stanton in the village of Nostravista, my prince.'

'Excellent, my loyal Craniescu,' Tepesch approved. 'Excellent. Modrussa, it appears there will be activity for the Draculesti after all.'

And they were both so enthralled by the revelation of the map that neither noticed the superior, triumphant glance that Craniescu cast towards an equally distracted Boris. They didn't see the expression of dismay and disbelief on the whiskered man's face. But Craniescu did.

He wondered what it meant.

TEN

IGC DATA-FEED: REGION WHITE
SUB-SECTION: WALLACHIA (FILE XL978)

The Wallachian crisis continues to escalate. The latest deadline by which the international community demanded that the Tepesch regime commit itself to weapons inspections has passed with no such undertaking given and none promised for the future. Many in government circles in the United States and Europa already view this missed deadline as the final one and are making contingency plans accordingly.

In America, all leave among the armed forces has been cancelled. A fleet of aircraft carriers is sailing towards the Mediterranean. In Europa, army units are being deployed close to the eastern border with Wallachia.

Despite crowd protests and marches in capitals around the world, the outcome of this massive military mobilisation seems inevitable. Unless either the western powers or President Vlad

Tepesch himself suddenly choose to back down,
which does not appear likely, there will be war.

He supposed it beat a night at the Pleasure Mall.

In traditional Wallachian peasant garb, leather waist-coat and leggings included, bare-headed to demonstrate humility, Ben stood at Vissarion Vukic's side in a forest clearing to the north of Nostravista. They were not alone. In fact, if any burglars chanced by this part of the Nocnitsa this particular evening, they'd find the village easy pickings. Every last Nostravistan was here, looking on from the rim of the great circle, their faces picked out in the flickering light of the giant bonfire at its heart. Eager faces. Expectant faces. In the eyes of the men, knowledge and memory of the night when it was they who had stood inside the circle.

Ben had elected to undergo the Rite of Manhood.

'It's the only way,' he'd told Natalia, Vissarion and Lyvia earlier. 'I need to be able to prove I'm one of you, that I can be trusted, that I'm not just an outlander who doesn't really care about Wallachia. How better to do that than to become a kind of honorary Wallachian.' He'd smiled faintly. 'Maybe then I'll even earn Janos' approval.'

Or maybe not. He noticed Janos now, as sullen and implacable as ever, still seeming more like an enemy than an ally. Next to him, Natalia, the opposite, gazing at him fervently, with frank adoration, wanting more from him than he could give. The rite would have to satisfy them both.

'So what do I have to do then?' he'd asked, and Natalia had told him.

'You have to drink of the dracul flower. The ceremony takes place at night and in the eternal circle sacred to the spirits of those Wallachian warriors who fought and died for our country.' There was no getting away from Kresniki, Ben had thought. 'The rite will reveal whether you are fit to join them, whether you are strong enough to be counted as a man or too weak to be considered anything but a boy.'

'How does it do that?' Ben had been pretty confident he'd make the grade.

'The drink. The potion,' Natalia had continued. 'It is distilled following a recipe known only to our wisest elders, the secret handed down from generation to generation. It forces the initiate to confront his deepest fears. In Wallachia, we know that fear is part of life, and we know that the true man is not the one who claims to feel no fear, but the one who masters and overcomes it. Such a one and such a one only is permitted to join the ranks of our warriors.'

'I hope I'm up to it,' he'd said modestly.

He was feeling a little more nervous about the whole thing now. The villagers in their silent ring and the dark hulk of the Nocnitsa beyond them. The bonfire crackling like breaking bones. Vissarion tall and proud beside him, like a worshipper in a cathedral.

And Lyvia, Lyvia in a gown so black it seemed to have soaked up the night. Her shrivelled old head appeared to be bobbing disembodied on a dark sea. In gnarled white hands she held the chalice. In the chalice, a liquid like blood.

'Where is the boy who wishes to be a man?' she cried out, though in the hush of the clearing her whisper might have been heard.

'He is here.' Ben had been taught the words of the rite.

Old Lyvia seemed to see him for the first time. 'What is his name?'

'His name is Benjamin Stanton.' He thought it best to leave out the T and the Jr for once.

'Who sponsors this child?'

'I do. Vissarion Vukic.' The bearded man stepped forward.

'Then bring him to the cup.'

The sponsor was supposed to be the initiate's father – a Wallachian bonding exercise, Ben thought, like Dad taking his son on a fishing trip or to the ball game, kind of – but there were alternatives. Particularly in times of war, a father might not have survived to sponsor his son, for example. In those instances a Wallachian boy could call on the services of an uncle or a cousin or even a friend of the family, any male who himself had success-fully endured the Rite of Manhood. It had been either Janos or Vissarion for Ben.

No surprise there, then.

Ben allowed Vissarion to escort him to Lyvia. The old woman seemed satisfied, vindicated as she raised the chalice above her head and locked her eyes to Ben's. She had what she wanted.

'Son of Wallachia, drink from this cup and gaze into your heart. Drink from this cup and gaze into your soul. Taste of the dracul and learn whether yet you are worthy to be called a man.' She offered the chalice to Ben. 'Your fears await you. Drink.'

Lyvia's last word echoed from the human walls of the circle. 'Drink,' the Nostravistans exhorted, in tones that might be used to lull a baby to sleep. 'Drink. Drink.'

And louder as Ben took the cup, almost conversational.

He lifted the chalice to his lips. The crimson dracul potion swilled around inside. He had no option but to gulp it down now. It was the only way. Besides, he wasn't going to be guzzling poison. It was *tradition*. Every male in Nostravista had done it or was going to do it, and if Janos Mirescu could emerge from the rite intact, so could Benjamin T. Stanton Jr.

'Drink! Drink!' More strident now. Demanding. A unified shout that could not be denied.

The rim of the chalice was resting against his lower lip. He was tipping it up.

'Drink! Drink!'

Ben obeyed.

And the concoction was thick, warm, a little bitter. He swallowed, mouthful after mouthful. The idea was that you downed the whole gobletful in one. It was a statement of intent. His mouth was crammed with the taste of dead flowers, his nostrils clogged with the reek of rotting vegetation.

'Drink! Drink! Drink!'

He'd done. He'd finished. A trickle from the chalice as he turned it upside down, but not even Janos could hold that against him. And he was feeling fine. He wiped the back of his hand across his lips. Looked like his mouth was bleeding. He doubted that.

The Nostravistans had apparently brought instruments with them. He could hear drumming. Or was it his heartbeat? No. Why would his heart be pounding that fast and that loudly? He was feeling fine. The dracul drink hadn't affected him at all, not a jot (good word, that – kind of English and posh). He obviously didn't have any fears to face. Good for him.

There was drumming and there was drumming. Those Nostravistans. Anything for a party. He turned to Natalia to tell her how fine he was feeling, maybe ask her for a dance as well, to celebrate.

Couldn't see her.

And he'd dropped the chalice as well. There it was, spinning through the air and into the Krasnova. Oops. He'd better tell Lyvia.

Couldn't see her.

And what was the Krasnova doing here anyway? Had it somehow flooded in the last few minutes, broken its banks? He'd ask Vissarion. Vissarion would know.

Couldn't see him, either.

In fact, couldn't see anyone. Couldn't see anything. (There was blood in his eyes.) Except the fire. The scarlet, boiling bonfire. He could see that all right. He could see the people hiding behind the flames, waiting for him, coming for him, the people who were laughing.

And somehow, maybe he wasn't feeling so fine after all.

Because they were surrounding him now and they were bigger than him and he was so small and helpless and even if he screamed out nobody would come, nobody *could* come. He was alone. With *them*.

Their bodies electric, distorted. Mouths open pits of jangling, jeering ridicule. Faces blurred, kneaded like dough, in common their terrifying emptiness. They filled the world.

Hallucinations.

And Vlad was here. He'd found him and his beard was red not black and his beard was the blood of his victims caked around his mouth. Vlad was reaching for him. They all were. Talons, scaled and serpent tongue flickering from his reptile mouth. Commander Krynor of the Diluvian Empire, his alien skin blue like frost because he was cold and dead but laughing too and keen for Ben to join him. Averill Frankenstein, hooting like a loon as he stretched out with his waxen fingers. Even Nemesis, even the cyber-spider, looming giant and black above them.

His enemies. His enemies had come to claim him. (Not possible.) Vlad had brought them all together. (Not possible – they were all dead.)

Hallucinations.

He'd defeated them once, in the flesh. Now he could conquer them again, in the *mind*. This was all in his mind.

Even Uncle Alex, shaking him with both hands. 'You're a failure, boy.'

Voice booming like cannon in his head. 'You're going to fail. You're no leader. You're no spy. You thought you were good but you're not. You're nothing, boy. Nothing.'

'It's not true.' He covered his ears but it didn't help. The voice was inside him. The fear of failure was inside him.

'Nobody likes you. Nobody cares. You think you're respected but you're not. You think you've achieved something but you haven't.'

'I have.' He *had* to have.

'They took the leadership of the team away from you and gave it to your girl. Failure!'

'No.'

'They took your girl away from you and gave her to your rival. Failure!'

'No, it wasn't like that. Lori—'

'Left you, boy. She wised up and saw you for the useless nonentity you are. She turned against you. They'll all turn against you.' And now Uncle Alex was speaking in the plaintive voice of Tolly Parker. 'Because you failed us, Ben. In the end you'll always fail us. You said you'd save me but you didn't.'

'I tried, Tolly. You know I tried.'

'Not good enough. Failure! I died and you did nothing.'

'No!'

'I died and you did nothing.'

'I did what I could.' Ben struggled to marshal his thoughts. 'No one can ask for more. Tolly wouldn't ask for more. So you're not Tolly. You can't be. You're not even Uncle Alex.' He clamped his hands around the figure's throat. 'Who are you? Tell me!'

And he was throttling a weak blond boy with watery blue eyes, eyes full of doubt and secret terror. 'I'm *you*, Ben. Don't you recognise me? I'm you.'

'No,' Ben denied. 'You might be a part of me but you're not *me*. I'm *more* than you, better, stronger.' He felt it with each word. 'I can control you. You don't rule me. I rule *you*.' And now the doppelganger seemed to be catching alight. 'And I'm sending you back to where you come from, do you hear me?' Maybe difficult with his head in flames. 'I know who I am and I know what I am and *you can't hurt me*.'

And suddenly the only fire was the bonfire in the clearing north of Nostravista, and Ben realised he was kneeling before it and the chalice was on the ground and on either side of him stood Lyvia and Vissarion.

Drumbeats thronged the night air. Hallucination, all of it. Induced by the dracul. None of it real. Ben looked wearily up at the old woman. 'Is that a pass?'

Lyvia raised her arms and silence promptly descended. 'Let the spirits of Wallachia rejoice!' she shrilled. 'The boy has become a man!'

There were congratulations then. Ben felt like a celebrity, his hand pumped constantly by people he didn't know. Men slapped him on the back; girls kissed him on the cheek. He was glad it was that way round. There were innumerable promises of support for the oncoming battle against Vlad Tepesch. Some of the Nostravistans, blades and even blasters hidden in the folds of their clothes, seemed ready to march on Dracholtz directly.

Vissarion remained alongside Ben, almost like a proud father, and he beamed in his beard. Somehow, it seemed less grey than before. A trick of the light, perhaps. 'You have done well, Ben,' he praised. 'You are one of us now. You have won the *right* to lead us. Let Tepesch tremble. We will tear the crown from his head and, if the spirits smile, the head from his cursed shoulders.'

Ben wasn't sure the Deveraux organisation approved of decapitations in the field, but he didn't say anything.

Natalia was flinging her arms around him. *Her* lips weren't content with either of his cheeks, which made conversation a little difficult. 'Ben,' she smooched, 'you were magnificent. You dealt with the rite like a true-born . . . I'm so proud of you.'

'Thanks, Natalia,' Ben grinned. 'Do you think I could have my face back now?'

'Enjoy your moment, Benjamin Stanton,' advised old Lyvia from somewhere close behind him. 'The spirits chose you. The spirits brought you here. They have further work for you to do yet.'

'But not *tonight*,' Natalia said. She tugged at Ben's sleeve. 'Come on, boy who's become a man. Prove it. Let's dance.'

The monotony of drums was now varied by the music of gypsy fiddles and a wind instrument similar to a flute. The clearing by the bonfire was filling with people dancing. All of a sudden, the ale was pouring.

Natalia was adamant and Ben was tempted. To dance with her here and now would be to remain the centre of attention. Ben *liked* to be the centre of attention: his training for that had begun long before he joined Spy High. But he resisted. 'You go, Natalia. Get warmed up for me. I'll be with you in a minute.'

'A minute? Why not now?'

Because there was one person who had conspicuously *not* come forward to offer Ben congratulations. He could see Janos slinking towards the forest now. 'I just need a word with Vissarion,' he lied.

'Well don't keep me waiting *too* long,' sulked Natalia. 'I might find another partner.'

'I won't,' said Ben, but as soon as she turned her back he was gone.

He intercepted Janos on the track back to Nostravista. It was a full moon, so despite their distance from the bonfire, visibility was more than adequate.

'Janos! Hey, wait up!'

'What do you want, Stanton?' Without pausing. 'I'd have thought you already *had* all you could want. The adulation of the entire village. The support of the spirits. Natalia.'

'I just want to talk.'

'Then find someone who wants to listen.'

Ben shook his head exasperatedly. 'Man, when you Wallachians get the hump with a guy you don't let up, do you? No wonder your feuds can last a hundred years. Let me rephrase. I *need* to talk. You *need* to listen.' He grabbed Janos' shoulder. 'Hmm, interesting. I can't *feel* the chip.'

Janos turned scowling to Ben. 'I promised Vissarion I wouldn't fight with you again, Stanton. Don't force me to break my promise.'

'You won't need to. Look, I didn't want to fight with you the first time. That's not what I'm here for. We need to get something straight.'

'And what might that be?'

'You and me,' said Ben. 'Where we stand. I'm not a threat to you, Janos. I didn't come to Wallachia to lord it over Nostravista and steal your girlfriend, whatever you might think. I came to do a job. Once that's done, once Vlad's been deposed, I'll be gone. *Gone*, Janos, back to my own life and back to my own girl. And it'll be up to you, then, what happens in your country, up to all Wallachians, and I've heard that the name Mirescu used to mean something pretty special around here. Maybe it could again.'

'If you think that flattery—' began Janos.

'I'm not talking flattery,' Ben corrected. 'I'm talking *fact*. And another fact is, Natalia's dancing back there all on her own and that seems kind of a shame to me. What about you?'

Janos considered. 'It does seem a waste.'

'So what are you waiting for?'

'Stanton,' said Janos, 'it's possible – *possible* – that I might have misjudged you, possible that I've even been jealous of you. Don't think that we'll ever necessarily be friends –'

'Perish the thought.'

'– but it *does* seem foolish for us to continue as if we were enemies.'

'Can I take that as a truce, then?'

'A truce,' consented Janos.

'With a handshake and everything? I've had a lot of practice with these tonight.' Ben extended his open palm. 'But let me tell you . . .'

Only he never did. A rustle of leaves on a windless night. A crackling of branches too heavy for an animal, high in the trees. First assumption in the field: anything unusual might mean danger. Ben's head snapped up.

'What is it?' Janos copied. Janos saw.

A dark shape in the foliage. As big as a man but winged like a bat. And then, caught by the moonlight, a face as pale as the dead. Black eyes. Bright fangs.

'Draculesti!' Janos uttered.

And before either of them could do anything more, the Draculesti attacked.

ELEVEN

The creature swooped from the boughs and for a shocking second Ben imagined that the vampiric metamorphosis wrought by the Drac was now complete, that the membrane stretched from wrists to waist that allowed the Draculesti to glide on the air currents, to dive snarling towards them, was a mutated part of his body. He thought of the transformation that Natalia could effect. Would *Natalia* too turn into this one day?

No time. He couldn't afford distractions. Not if he wanted to duck out of the way of those raking Draculesti talons. And, of course, he did. And, of course, now he could see that even Drac had its twisted limits. His assailant's wings, they weren't natural, or even *un*natural. Viewed up close, Ben could see that they were part of a flying harness, no doubt employed for its psychological impact as much as anything. He understood why. Fear created doubt, and a fighter who doubted was a fighter who died.

'Janos!' Had thrown himself to the ground. The Draculesti flitted in the night like a swimmer in dark waters. If his first assault had failed to draw blood, he would improve on his second as he wheeled in the sky and plunged anew at the Wallachian. Janos was scrambling to his feet, reaching inside his shirt, Ben assumed for a weapon. He wasn't going to be quick enough. The Draculesti's jaws opened like a trap-door. Collision this time seemed inevitable.

Sleepshot shells tore through the harness, studded the monster's pale flesh.

Collision was *still* inevitable, only now the Draculesti thudded unconscious into the earth, not Janos.

The Wallachian turned gratefully to his companion, the sleepshot wristband glistening around the blond boy's forearm. 'It seems I'm in your debt, Ben.'

'You'd have done the same for me.' Ben scanned the trees, the deeper darkness towards Nostravista. The shadows seemed to be moving now. 'He won't have come alone. This time I think they *have* found me.'

Janos drew a shock blaster. 'In Wallachia we dress for violence as some might dress for dinner.'

'That's cool.' Ben nodded. 'A tux won't help us now. We need to warn the others.'

Sudden screams and howls and gunfire from the direction of the clearing.

'I think they know,' observed Janos.

'Natalia.'

Janos inclined his head. 'Let us fight together' – with the thinnest of smiles – 'outlander.'

They raced back the way they'd come, and with every pace they pounded the shouts of conflict loomed louder, closer. Natalia, Ben thought again. And Lyvia. And the old and the young of Nostravista. Vissarion and the men could look after themselves, would even be *relishing* the combat, but what if his own presence in the village had doomed those incapable of self-defence? How many deaths after tonight would he be responsible for? Ben sprinted more quickly still. He'd save whoever he could. He'd do whatever he could. He was an agent of Spy High.

From either side of the track Vlad's guardsmen lunged, fired, flashes of pulse blasts in the night like exploding stars. Ben stabbed out with his arms. Sleepshot spat its contempt at those in the pay of the devil Tepesch. Charging guardsmen tumbled. Janos' marksmanship was nearly as good. If the Wallachian's blaster wasn't set to stun, Ben wasn't sure he'd mind.

And then they were surging out into the clearing and the only music now was the cacophony of gunshots as the frenzied light of the bonfire lashed across a scene of total chaos. Guardsmen struggled with Nostravistans. Draculesti wheeled in the sky in their harnesses, drop-ping suddenly, ferociously on targets who were putting up the sternest fight. Ben imagined that Modrussa must be among them but it wasn't she he was looking for. He and Janos side by side plunged into the mael-strom of battle. The children huddling together screaming. Their grandparents standing spryly against the invaders until clubbed to the ground. Armed Nostravistans, dracul harvesters exposing their teeth and claws, frantically protecting their fellow villagers. A guardsman taking aim; Ben made sure his finger didn't pull the trigger. A little girl fleeing the advancing enemy, two more of Vlad's men who'd advance no further tonight. But these were diversions only, keeping him from the one person he wanted to see more than any other.

'Natalia!'

She was transformed, of course, and in the thick of things, grappling with a guardsman who'd been slow to raise his rifle and was now regretting it. Ben's sleepshot made doubly sure of that.

'What did you do that for?' Not exactly the response he was expecting. 'I could have finished him off myself.'

'Staying alive's not a competition,' Ben pointed out. 'But it's good to see you too.'

'Are you all right, Natalia?'

'Janos? Are you two working as a team now?' Even in the midst of carnage, a slow smile crept along the Wallachian girl's lips. 'I like that idea. And I'm fine.'

'So far,' qualified Ben tersely. 'But we're outnumbered and outarmed. Our only chance is if maybe we can strike at their leaders . . .' Not too far away, on the edge of the clearing as if directing operations, a familiar figure, whiskered, bull-like. Boris. 'You stay and look after Natalia,' Ben directed Janos.

'Natalia doesn't *need* looking after,' the girl complained. 'She can look after *herself*.'

But Janos didn't need any encouragement to stay close to her. 'Where are you going?' he asked.

'Oh, to knock up an old friend,' Ben gritted. 'I doubt he'll be pleased to see me, though. Boris!' He yelled the man's name as he hurtled across the battlefield towards him. 'Hey, Boris! Remember me?'

Evidently so. The Wallachian barked orders to a brace of guardsmen, who opened fire with pulse rifles in Ben's direction. Deveraux agents were used to being shot at on the run, however, and practised at avoiding the blasts. They were also pretty good at deploying their own weaponry under such conditions. Boris' bodyguard sprawled in the dirt, courtesy of sleepshot. Vlad's chief adviser had no alternative but to combat the outlander himself, but he wasn't going to be fast enough. Fleetingly, Ben recalled their previous encounter, in Los Angeles. Then Boris had shot him point blank with a tranquilliser shell. *What goes around comes around, Boris old mate*, he thought.

But last-minute escapes are not the preserve of the righteous.

Ben heard the screeching above him, sensed it aimed at him like a missile, maybe should have reacted sooner. But Modrussa was slamming into him all too quickly, too irresistibly. He tried to roll with the impact but the wind was knocked out of him and his arms flailed wildly. He felt talons like steel scrape at his face. There was blood. There was fetid breath on his cheek as iron jaws dipped close, as feral fangs flashed.

Ben thrashed in the Draculesti's grasp, jerked his head away just far enough for those rending teeth to tear at the air rather than his throat. 'You ever thought . . . about a mouthwash?'

But he couldn't throw her off him. The assassin's arms were like vices. She had the advantage of height. Ben couldn't find a proper footing. He could hardly find *any* footing. The wind-borne Draculesti was virtually lifting him off the ground. *Was* doing so. Ben yelped inadvertently as he was swept into the sky in the grip of Modrussa.

'Are you afraid yet, boy?'

'I don't know about . . . afraid,' Ben retorted. 'I just don't usually fly economy.'

'You can beg for your misbegotten life if you like,' Modrussa invited, 'but it will do you no good.'

'Actually, I hadn't planned on —'

'I have no option but to kill you. Your survival on the Moon made me lose face.'

'Yeah? With that face you ought to be glad.'

Modrussa's pale lips peeled back. A glob of saliva dripped into Ben's eye. 'I will be glad, Ben Stanton, only when you are dead.'

Her arms were wrapped around him like a lover's. His were pretty much pinned to his sides. His room for manoeuvre was dangerously limited, particularly, his head lolling back, as they were more than a hundred feet in the air. 'Only when I'm dead, huh?'

She was going for the throat again, leisurely, savouring the moment. The blades of her teeth spiked towards the exposed flesh.

'Then I'm afraid you're in for a long life of disappointment.'

Ben fired his sleepshot, both wristbands. He knew the shells couldn't strike Modrussa's body. Didn't intend them to. But they could and did rip through both wings of the Draculesti's flying harness. Sizzles and sparks from damaged circuitry.

And they were suddenly *less* than a hundred feet in the air, spiralling to ninety, eighty.

'What?' Modrussa's white face clenching into rage. 'What have you *done*?'

Her mouth occupied with speaking rather than biting. Much more satisfactory, Ben thought. And her grip, too, in her startlement its strength was lessened. Ben felt his increase. The old adrenalin rush did it every time.

He pulled his right arm free, smashed his fist into Modrussa's face. Drac-infected blood spouted from the assassin's nose. Then he was reaching over her shoulder, grasping her tunic, as black as her hair, yanking her round. 'My turn to go on top, I think.' Deveraux agent and Draculesti twisted over in the sky.

Sixty feet. Fifty.

'Happy landings, babe,' winked Ben.

Modrussa's Drac-induced strength would probably ensure she survived the fall. Landing on her harness would help. With the benefit of neither, for Ben keeping all his bones from breaking was a matter of timing. He judged his moment. Guardsmen and Nostravistans alike scattered as the two of them plummeted earthwards.

Modrussa screamed something. It sounded like a word. It sounded unflattering. Ben didn't have time to ask her to repeat it. Like a pilot from a fatally stricken aircraft, he baled out.

The ground laid into him like a boxer. Its blows paid no regard to the Queensberry Rules. Ben was pummelled and pounded mercilessly as he tried in vain to cushion his fall. If this *was* the ring, he'd have been only too happy to be counted out. But it wasn't. His bruised, battered body came to rest but he couldn't allow himself the temporary bliss of unconsciousness. Not with the battle still raging around him.

Not with Boris standing over him. Boris with a blaster.

'You should have stayed in America with your little friends, Benjamin,' he said, with a sadness that seemed almost genuine. 'You could have been a hero there. In Wallachia, you are only an outlander who will perish unwanted and unlamented.'

What were the chances of there being tranquilliser shells in his gun tonight? They'd better be good. Ben's pain-racked limbs were not moving.

'You!'

Neither was his neck, a lot. But he could just about make out Vissarion, his own blaster pointed at Boris.

'You,' Vlad's henchman echoed, more quietly though, wonderingly. He redirected his weapon towards Vissarion but neither man made any attempt to fire. They looked as if they might be prepared to stand there like that all night.

And then Boris was gone.

Vissarion was kneeling by his side, helping him up. 'You had a shot,' Ben said. 'Why didn't you use it?'

'How bad are your injuries?' It seemed the Wallachian wanted to change the subject. His face was as grey as his beard.

'I've had worse. Nothing broken, but I'm not going to look good in swim-shorts for a couple of days. Did you see what happened to Modrussa?'

Vissarion shook his head. 'You've got to go.'

'Excuse me?'

'We can't hold out much longer and you more than any of us must not be caught. There is a place in the forest where you can hide. My mother knows it. Janos and Natalia are keeping her safe nearby while I searched for you. Come.'

'Wait a minute.' Ben winced to his feet. 'I don't do retreats.'

'Spoken like a Wallachian, Ben,' said Vissarion, 'but this is not the Kresniki Pass. Numbers *will* tell. We will fight for as long as we can but in the end' – the bearded man's blaster took out a pair of Vlad's guards by way of emphasis – 'we *will* be overrun. The only victory we can possibly claim is for you to escape.'

Ben felt a pain that was more than physical, that lasted longer and hurt more deeply. So he didn't do retreats. He'd been taught not to indulge in futile gestures, either. Vissarion was right. 'Come with us,' Ben urged.

The Wallachian declined. 'My place is here with the people of my village.' It was the response Ben had expected. He said no more but followed Vissarion to where old Lyvia, Janos and Natalia were waiting in the shelter of the Nocnitsa. 'Now go, and when the time comes, bring the battle to the devil Tepesch himself. As of this night you are a son of Wallachia, Ben Stanton. Be our hope, also.'

'I will,' vowed Ben.

By the time Vlad Tepesch himself appeared, the uneven battle was over. The dead of both sides littered the ground. The Nostravistan survivors, and there were still plenty of them, Vissarion Vukic included, slumped in a circle surrounded by guardsmen and Draculesti. They regarded their black-robed president with unalloyed hatred. Perversely, though, Vlad seemed to find the intensity of their emotion intoxicating.

Craniescu trailed him like a shadow. 'I promised you a victory, did I not, my prince?'

'You did, Craniescu,' acknowledged Tepesch. 'Let us see whether you have delivered one. Boris! Modrussa!'

The adviser and the assassin came forward, the latter's white skin unhealthily blue in places, blood trickling from her nose and lip.

'Stanton was here,' Tepesch deduced. 'Where is he now?'

'My prince . . .' For once, not even Boris dared to look his leader directly in the eye. 'The outlander appears to have . . .' He didn't need to say it.

'Let me pursue him, my prince!' Modrussa implored. 'The shame in me can only be expelled by the boy Stanton's death.'

'Then why does he still live?' snapped Tepesch. His black eyes blazed as if the night was on fire. 'How many opportunities do you need to eliminate one single teenaged boy, Chief Assassin of the Draculesti? And Craniescu, you dare to talk of victories with only Wallachians killed upon the field? Can I trust no one? Must I do everything myself?'

Craniescu bowed his balding head. Inside he was seething. Not only because Stanton had escaped, but also because no criticism had been levelled yet at Boris. Once again, Tepesch's favourite seemed unassailable.

'Well, we cannot afford to let these peasants live.' Tepesch regarded the defeated Nostravistans as if they were germs. 'They must learn the price of betraying their prince. They must become an example to any other misguided souls who might be tempted to take the outlander in.'

Boris blanched at his president's words. He could anticipate their conclusions. He looked to his countrymen and found himself staring into the eyes of Vissarion. Their gaze held.

'Raze the village to the ground. Kill everyone belonging to it. A Wallachian traitor is no Wallachian at all.'

'Yes, my prince,' said Craniescu.

'No, my prince.' Boris was turning back towards Tepesch, his manner urgent. 'Wait.'

'No? Wait?' Words that seemed unusual to Vlad Tepesch. 'Surely you are not going to plead for mercy for these renegades, Boris? What can their lives mean to you?'

'Nothing, my prince, and less than nothing.' Boris dismissed the Nostravistans with a wave of his hand. 'But what their lives might mean to *you* . . .'

'Explain.'

'My prince, Stanton has been sheltered here. Perhaps, in the naïve, sentimental way that Americans have, he feels a loyalty now to these people, a responsibility for what happens to them. Don't slaughter them yet. Transport them to Dracholtz. Let the nation know that they are your prisoners. Use them as bait to lure Stanton forth from his hiding place.'

'There's no guarantee that the outlander feels *anything* towards these peasants,' countered Craniescu. 'I say we kill them now.'

'I agree,' said Modrussa. 'And let my Draculesti lead the way, my prince.'

Tepesch considered. Boris' gaze flickered again to Vissarion. The Nostravistan had perhaps heard the previous exchange. That might explain his contemptuous sneer. For some reason Boris could not endure it. Instead, he scanned the assembled captives as if searching for someone. If that was the case, his expression denoted disappointment.

And Tepesch decided. 'Boris is right.' Much to Craniescu and Modrussa's dismay. 'Haste will gain us nothing. Perhaps the Nostravistans alive will work to our advantage. Have them taken to the capital, Craniescu.'

'Yes, my prince,' fawned the Head of Security. 'Most wise.' Teeth gritted.

'But the village must still be burned. And more,' Tepesch mused. 'Stanton cannot have fled far. Summon an air-strike, Craniescu. Fire-bombs. Let the Nocnitsa become his funeral pyre.'

'My prince!' Boris didn't require any external prompting to protest at this. 'You cannot mean to lay waste the Nocnitsa.'

'Not all of it, Boris,' placated Tepesch. 'A ten-mile radius from here should be sufficient, I think. And after we have left, of course.'

Craniescu and Modrussa laughed at their president's wit.

'But to destroy even an acre of the forest is unthinkable. The Nocnitsa is sacred ground. The dracul grows here and here alone, the source of Wallachia's strength. And our legends say that if the flower dies, the land dies with it.'

'Calm yourself, faithful one,' Tepesch said bemusedly. 'I am aware of our legends. I am aware that *that* is what they are, legends. We have no need for superstition now. Let the old ways die with the old. If the dracul is scorched here, what does it matter? The flower is no longer strictly necessary to us in any case. Our scientists have synthesised its benevolent effects. The powers that the dracul seeds grant can now be replicated artificially.'

He turned scornfully to the Nostravistans. 'We need no harvesters. We need no harvest.'

'My prince,' Boris burst out, 'you don't know what you're saying!'

'No, Boris. I begin to think that it is *you* who are unaware of the impact of your words.' Tepesch's features were cold with warning. 'Wallachia belongs to *me*. Not to our dead forebears. Not to the past. Wallachian legends and customs and traditions are acceptable only when they suit my purpose. Otherwise they, like everything and everyone else, must become subject to my will and its enforcement. That is the reality of Tepesch, my faithful one. You have lived it for nearly forty years. I am a little surprised you need to be reminded.'

'My prince.' Boris cast his eyes down, heard Craniescu chuckling. He glanced sideways as if compelled. Vissarion Vukic was shaking his head. His former contempt was now more akin to pity. And Boris closed his eyes.

'Craniescu,' Vlad Tepesch was commanding, 'let fall the fire-bombs.'

'How much further?' Natalia pressed. 'Lyvia?'

'A little way yet. Just a little way.'

Natalia Strepescu regarded her two male companions exasperatedly. 'A little way yet' was what the old woman had been saying since they'd first plunged into the Nocnitsa a time that seemed like hours ago. At first they'd encountered the occasional guardsman, whom they'd dispatched with little fuss. But they hadn't delved far into the nighted forest before all pursuit ceased and they were alone. The bonfire's light was extinguished by the trees, the yells of battle muted, finally silenced. The only sound was the party's increasingly laboured breathing as they forged ahead. At least, Ben for one hoped it was 'ahead', that they were groping through the dark in something vaguely like the right direction. They'd learned the art of tracking at Spy High from one of the last pure-blooded Apaches in America. Ben would put money on himself to be able to find his way anywhere. But tracking skills weren't much use if he had no idea where the 'anywhere' was. Only Lyvia knew. They were taking turns to help the old woman along while the other two flanked and watched for lurkers in the dark. Ben was sincerely impressed by Lyvia's wiry strength and determination. How long either could last, however, was debatable. Natalia was obviously thinking in similar terms.

'We've got to rest,' she said. 'Lyvia can't go on.'

'I can. I *must*,' the old woman declared, but her breath was rattling inside her like she'd swallowed a bag of marbles. 'We *all* must. The spirits will help me.'

'Yeah,' said Ben, 'only the spirits don't have to worry about legs and lungs any more. We mere mortals do.'

'What if we carry her?' suggested Janos. 'Or why don't we just stop here? It's not a bad place to hide out.' The ground was rising slowly but steadily as it had been doing for a while. The terrain was growing rockier. Nearby the sparse moonlight silvered a massive fallen tree-trunk that had evidently found the soil too stony to thrive in. 'We could defend ourselves from behind there if necessary.'

'No.' Old Lyvia had resolve enough remaining to lay down the law. 'This isn't the place. It's a little way yet. Just a little way. We'll be safer there.'

'Maybe Janos has a point, though, Lyvia,' ventured Natalia. 'What if we rested here just until morning, then carried on? Nobody's followed us. I think we'll be safe.'

'The spirits say no.'

Ben was almost tempted to ask what the spirits knew about possible pursuit that they didn't. He was glad he resisted.

From above, the scream of a jet.

'The devil Tepesch trying to trace us?' Janos cried.

'Not quite,' said Ben.

All around them, like sudden blooms in yellow and orange, the mighty Nocnitsa burst into flames.

TWELVE

Fireballs billowed into the night sky. The tallest and proudest of pines, trees that had taken years to grow, decades, that had towered grandly in their forest fastness for lifetimes, in a single second, as the flames flooded over them in a blazing deluge, were reduced to matchsticks, cinders. The furnace heat evaporated them.

And it rolled towards the exhausted party of four, the air like a blowtorch in advance.

'Vlad's not one to take chances, is he?' gritted Ben. 'Come on. Up!' All of a sudden, a lone fallen tree-trunk did not seem to offer any kind of protection. 'Lyvia, let me take you.' He stooped to lift and carry the old woman, cried out in pain. His injuries from earlier weren't conducive to swift and purposeful movement.

'Let me.' Janos stepped in. 'I can take her.'

'Okay.' Ben didn't argue as Janos raised old Lyvia in his arms, her hands clasped feebly around his neck.

'Ben, we can't make it.' Natalia was staring in horror at the walls of fire hemming them in. 'We're going to die. We're going to burn.'

Flames leaped like acrobats from treetop to treetop, and the crackle of exploding boughs was the applause of audience.

'Only if we stay here.' Ben seized Natalia's hand and pulled. 'Come *on*!'

They chased after Janos and Lyvia. The Wallachian boy possessed admirable strength in his legs, and was pumping a path up the slope almost as if unencumbered by the weight of a woman. Lyvia was pointing desperately with her bony finger. 'Just a little way. We're nearly there.'

Nearlys were good, Ben knew, but not always good enough. The fire was on Vlad's side. It seemed to be racing to outdistance them, to encircle them. It was a strangling noose of flame. Thick smoke belched through the Nocnitsa. The sweat was streaming down their faces. Ben longed for an enemy he could shoot. To be consumed by fire like this, he felt somehow so helpless, so anonymous.

Natalia stumbled beside him. He helped her up and when he glanced ahead again Janos and Lyvia had disappeared. Even in the foundry swelter, he almost felt a chill.

The rising ground split open where his companions had been. A hole in the rock. A stone slab slid aside. Janos beckoning madly from beyond. He and Natalia, rushing wildly. Fire above them like a sky. The grasses at their feet withering, incinerating. The clothes on their backs smouldering. A terrifying sense of imminent combustion.

Then they were diving forward and into cool and into dark and the air was moist and Lyvia was heaped against a wall like an unwrapped mummy and Janos was sliding back the door, shutting the inferno out.

'A cave! It's a cave!' Natalia half laughed, half sobbed with relief.

'I told you, just a little way,' insisted old Lyvia.

And it was rather more than a cave. The quartet's refuge proved to be a warren of interconnected chambers hollowed out of the rock.

'They were begun in the days of the civil wars,' Lyvia explained, 'designed as a safe retreat for the people of Nostravista in case the soldiers of any unfriendly Wallachian warlord should come pillaging and plundering. Now times have changed, we have a common enemy, the devil Tepesch, but still the caves can shield us from harm. Our ancestors were foresighted, though more recent generations have made their contribution too.'

A power generator, fully installed, allowing Lyvia to activate low-level lighting throughout the cavern complex, illuminating stores of other useful equipment. A videscreen. Light-rods. A small armoury of shock blasters and pulse rifles. A quantity of plastic explosives.

'It's a real home from home you've got here, Lyvia,' said Ben.

'We can strike back.' Natalia seized two of the guns as if she was preparing to rush outside and tackle Vlad this very minute.

'Don't worry,' Ben said grimly. 'We *will*. But we also need to rest up, recover our strength.'

'Agreed,' nodded Janos. 'Besides, we're going nowhere until the fires have burned themselves out.'

'I suppose so,' Natalia said grudgingly, reluctantly returning the weapons to the armoury. 'I'm not sure it's that much fun having you two on the same side after all.'

There was a rudimentary medkit available which enabled the group to tend their wounds. There was bedding which enabled them to get some sleep. Then, the next day, at an hour when Ben judged that the forest inferno, if not entirely extinguished, should at least have abated sufficiently not to burn them to a crisp the instant they appeared, he, Janos and Natalia ventured outside.

They'd survived. The Nocnitsa had not been so fortunate. Small fires still flickered here and there in the way that carrion beasts linger at the kill long after the predator has eaten its fill and moved on. The acrid stench of the blaze hung nearly as heavily in the air as the thick pall of smoke, like that of countless cremated corpses. The blackened bones of the Nocnitsa were all around them. Its verdant flesh had been stripped clean.

'This is one habitat that's going to take a while to recover,' muttered Ben. He stamped out an anaemic flame at his feet. It didn't improve his mood. 'But I guess at least we can move about again. I reckon it might be wise to stay put for today, though. Vlad could be sending guardsmen to hunt for bodies. What do you think . . .?'

He turned to his companions and was struck dumb. Natalia was crying. She was doing it silently and she was struggling not to be doing it at all, but her slim body was visibly racked with sobs and her eyes were filled with tears.

'Natalia?' Ben wanted to hold her. He wanted to comfort her. 'What is it?'

Janos got there first, enfolding the girl in his arms.

'It's the forest.' He even answered Ben's question for her. 'The Nocnitsa is sacred to Wallachians. Its devastation like this . . . it's hard for us to endure. You can't understand, Ben. You're not one of us.'

And Janos was right. The destruction of Nature by Man was not something of which he approved, but his thoughts were all of Vlad and the starstone, not the forest where the dracul flower grew. He *didn't* understand. He *wasn't* one of them. The Rite of Manhood, that had been nothing more than window-dressing. Bottom line: he was still an outlander.

'I'm sorry, Ben,' said Natalia.

'For what?' he said. 'There's no need.' He saw her press against Janos, twine her arms around his neck. They were Wallachian and he was not. Novelty value over. In a time of crisis, she'd instinctively known where to turn. 'There's no need at all.'

He wished Cally was here.

Later, they watched Vlad's broadcast on the videscreen. It was an old model, the picture was not good, but they got the message all right. 'The conspiracy against your president and prince has been smashed,' Tepesch announced with sadistic self-satisfaction. 'The renegades responsible are even now contemplating the folly of their deeds in the dungeons of Dracholtz. Further arrests are continuing throughout our beloved country. I tell you this so that you know, your concerned prince will not rest until every last traitor has been brought to justice and every guilty party punished. I tell you too, those who may be watching this with sedition and rebellion in their hearts, give yourselves up, throw yourselves upon our tender mercies.'

'I'd sooner throw myself off a cliff,' said Ben.

'May the devil Tepesch be taken in the night,' added old Lyvia.

'Come forward. Acknowledge your crimes. Beg for forgiveness. If not for your sake, for the sake of those whose lives may depend on you . . .'

'He's talking to us,' said Natalia. 'It's as if he can *see* us.'

'. . . your fellow traitors whom we will otherwise execute in the market square of our noble capital. One by one. Beginning the day after tomorrow. You can . . .'

'You can go to hell, that's what you can do.' Janos switched the videscreen off. 'I'll listen to no more of your poison.' He got up and paced the chamber restlessly.

'What are we going to do?' Natalia seemed torn between Janos and Ben. 'We can't let our friends be slaughtered. We have to help them.'

'How?' Janos demanded. 'Can we conjure an army out of thin air, bring Kresniki back to life? No one will dare ally themselves with us now, and what hope can we three have of toppling the devil Tepesch?'

'Four,' corrected old Lyvia.

'If it pleases you then, old mother, four.' The increase in their manpower made Janos no more optimistic. 'And what do we have to fight with? A mere handful of weapons. No longer even Ben's invisibility suit.'

'Chameleon suit, actually. We don't want to offend the trademark people,' said Ben. 'But no, that would have been useful. It could at least have gotten me into the citadel.' His suit, like his mission-belt and all the other equipment from his pack, everything but his wristbands, had been left in the village while the Rite of Manhood took place; all was certainly now lost. 'But one thing I learned at Spy High, and I reckon it's something your Kresniki would have known as well.'

'I hope you're not going to tell us that any odds can be overcome,' said Janos sceptically.

'No. Just that it's a poor spy who trusts only to his gadgets. I guess, by extension, it's a poor warrior who hides behind his armour. It's what we have inside that counts, our own courage, our spirit, our discipline and resolve, not weapons and materials and equipment. And we've still got those, and it's *those* qualities that'll see us through and that Vlad can't match, nothing else. We can still win this, Janos. It can be done.' Ben's blue eyes blazed with conviction. 'There's got to be a way to get to him.'

'Ah,' chuckled old Lyvia, 'I think I can help you there.'

'Boris,' smiled Craniescu politely, 'if I might have a word?'

Smiles and politeness. Two reasons to trust Craniescu even less than usual. But still Boris followed the Head of Security into an otherwise unoccupied room in the citadel. Keep your friends close, he remembered hearing once, and your enemies closer. Your enemies who wore the *guise* of friends, he might have added, keep them closest of all.

'A clever idea of yours to spare the Nostravistan peasants for the moment, my friend,' Craniescu said. 'I'm sure that if Stanton is still alive their situation will draw him out. Then they'll have to be executed anyway, of course.'

'Of course,' Boris ratified coldly.

'Unless, perhaps, you might in your fertile imagination be able to find some further use for them that will delay their deaths, hmm?' Craniescu raised his eyebrows speculatively.

'I don't know what you mean, Craniescu,' said Boris. 'The fate of all enemies of the state is death.'

'Indeed it is.' Craniescu seemed rather pleased at the fact. 'No, but what I wanted was to congratulate you on your wit. Nobody but you could have changed our prince's mind over the Nostravistans, not even myself or Modrussa.'

'Our prince can recognise sense when he hears it.'

'Oh, you're too modest, Boris,' tutted the Head of Security. 'You know as well as I do that your influence with Vlad Tepesch exceeds all others'. But then, how long have you stood stalwart by his side? Forty years?' A shrug from Boris suggested general accuracy in Craniescu's estimation. 'Forty years as the strong right arm of our homeland's undisputed leader. Quite a feat. Quite a legend.'

'I appreciate your kind words, Craniescu, but if you'll excuse me . . .'

'Your names enshrined together in the annals of Wallachia. Vlad and Boris. Tepesch and . . . now there's a thing.' Craniescu seemed suddenly puzzled. 'I'm not sure your family name is known.'

'I *have* no family name,' Boris said impassively. 'I have no family. I was orphaned as a boy. That much *is* known, by you and everyone else, *my friend*.'

'But of course.' The smile refused to go away. 'And highly traumatic your bereavement must have been. No wonder you're so reticent about your past. You must have wanted to block it all out completely, even where you were born . . .'

'I was born in Wallachia,' said Boris. 'That is enough.'

'Some rumours say in the Nocnitsa,' offered Craniescu helpfully. 'Some rumours say in a poor peasant village. Of course, it flatters the common people to believe that one of their own could become arguably the second most powerful man in the country, and I suppose it doesn't much matter –'

'Correct, Craniescu.'

'– not even if you were born in such a nondescript, inconsequential backwater as, say, Nostravista itself.'

'What do you want, Craniescu?'

'Nothing. Nothing. We're simply conversing, are we not? One loyal servant of Tepesch to another?' The smile was so fixed by now that his lips could hardly move to form words. 'There's no reason why anyone should be interested in your origins, my friend, I'm certain you're right. Not even our prince. I'm sure he knows all he needs to know, yes? He must do. He's trusted you for forty years, hasn't he? Now if *you'll* excuse *me*, Boris, I have work to do in the Security Monitoring Centre. I thought I might browse through some old records, births, deaths, that sort of thing. You never know what you'll find. Goodbye, Boris,' Craniescu concluded meaningfully.

'Goodbye, Craniescu,' Boris repeated.

'Catacombs? Under the city? Reaching directly to the citadel?'

Lyvia shook her head pityingly. 'Are you sure your tussle with Modrussa didn't damage your hearing, Ben? It's worse than mine. Yes, yes and *yes*.'

'I always like to hear good news twice,' said Ben.

'The present city of Dracholtz was erected on the site of earlier towns and settlements,' Lyvia went on, 'as far back as the primitive camps of the first tribes to live on the banks of the Krasnova. At various times in our history our architects have built beneath the ground as well as above it. Certain of my ancestors assisted in the construction of the catacombs – some even died there, a sacrifice to which the spirits grant meaning only now. Their knowledge has been passed down through generations of the Vukic family. The catacombs exist, though few others are aware of them and perhaps none have entered there in a lifetime. But I know their design and they *will* take you unseen to Tepesch.'

'We'll need a map,' said Janos.

'My fingers aren't so feeble that they can't draw a map, young Mirescu,' cautioned Lyvia.

'Good,' said Ben. 'Then I'll memorise it. We don't want to be burdened by anything that can't be used in a fight, because sooner or later we'll be in one.'

'And massively outnumbered,' said Natalia. 'I don't like to remind you boys, *but.*'

'Maybe not,' mused Ben. 'If we can infiltrate the citadel, if we can locate the dungeons and open the doors . . .'

'I like the sound of everything but the ifs, Ben,' commented Natalia.

'That's the most difficult part of my job,' the Deveraux agent accepted, 'converting ifs into realities. But if – *when*, Natalia, better? – when we do reach the dungeons, we also reach major reinforcements. Vlad's got 'em packed full of rebels and Resistance, hopefully including Vissarion.' He glanced towards Lyvia.

'My son still lives,' she assured him. 'If he did not I would feel it.'

'Vlad's going to regret rounding up the dissidents. He's given us an army, *inside* the citadel.'

'An excellent plan, Ben,' Janos approved. 'Kresniki himself could not have conceived one more audacious.'

'I'll take that as a vote of confidence.'

'But might it not be better if Natalia remained here with Lyvia?'

Immediate protest. The girl's eyes flashed emerald fire. 'Janos,' she warned, 'that's one if neither Ben nor you will be converting into reality. You need me. I'm coming.'

'So,' said Ben, 'that's weapons for three, I think, Lyvia.'

Vlad Tepesch, Prince of Wallachia, himself discovered the body.

It wasn't surprising to find Craniescu in his chair in the Security Monitoring Centre with his eyes closed. He tended to find eavesdropping such blissful entertainment. The hole in his chest where the dagger had plunged in, however, that was more unusual. No blade present now. No killer either.

Vlad regarded his late Head of Internal Security with contempt rather than sympathy. He'd never liked Craniescu. Who could warm to a man whose job was to spy on other people? And he'd enjoyed watching them so much. A pity he hadn't been a little more vigilant in watching his own back.

Vlad stood thinking for a while, his black eyes and stern features betraying nothing. Then he summoned

Boris and Modrussa. They arrived within minutes. Both appeared shocked by Craniescu's murder, but neither seemed likely to shed tears.

'Who can have done this, my prince? Stanton?' Modrussa's best shot at a theory.

Tepesch shook his head. 'No. The westerners like to think that they are above cold-blooded assassination. That is why they are weak. No, Craniescu's death is not the work of Stanton.'

'Had we better not sound the general alarm?' Modrussa pressed. 'Whoever the killer is, my Draculesti will hunt him down.'

'Boris?' said Tepesch.

'The alarm will serve no purpose, my prince,' the whiskered man considered. 'For someone to attack Craniescu here, in the heart of the citadel, and without being detected, suggests that the culprit *belongs* here, is one of us.'

'Indeed,' Tepesch concurred. 'You echo my own conclusion precisely, faithful one. Redouble security around the starstone. Monitor all possible access points into and out of the citadel. It seems we have a traitor in our midst.'

'So that's the plan,' Ben told Cally. 'Lyvia says she knows people in the neighbouring village who'll lend us one of their wheelless carts, so we can get to Dracholtz with no problems. Then we're on our own.'

He was on his own now, in one of the many underground chambers to which Lyvia had led them. The Cally who was with him, the half a Deveraux lab she'd brought with her, both were products of the holographic communicator attachment that had been sent with his replacement pack and was now incorporated into his wristband.

'It sounds risky,' Cally said.

'What's a mission without a little risk?' Ben tried to sound upbeat. He wasn't sure he made it. The trouble with the holocom was that, by enabling you to see as well as hear your interlocutor, it became that much more awkward to shield what you might truly be feeling from them and vice versa. Cally could detect the doubt in Ben's eyes. Ben could perceive the anxiety in hers. 'Risk is what we train for,' he added.

'Of course. Of course it is. Anyway,' Cally turned away and led him towards a computer console whose screen was alive with indecipherable symbols and notation, 'my turn to update you. The starstone. We think we've just about resolved the final lexical nuances of the alien computer language. We think if we had the starstone here at Deveraux we could control it. But we don't. Not *physically*, anyway.'

'No,' said Ben, 'but *holographically*, that could be another matter, right?'

Cally nodded. 'You just need to get us close to the starstone, Ben. Activate the holocom. Then myself and the other langtechs, we can tell you what to do to put the thing out of commission permanently.'

'Sounds good. It'll be almost like having you on the mission with me for real, Cal.'

'I wish I was,' Cally said.

I'm glad you're not, Ben thought. 'Yeah,' he said. 'Okay, well' – reluctantly – 'I've got to go. If we don't make our move now, Vlad'll start executing the Nostravistans and enough innocent people have died already. I don't want any more.'

'No. Well.' Cally reached out but her hand went through him. 'There are things I want to say but—'

'There'll be time,' said Ben. 'Save them for later. I'll see you at the starstone.'

'I'm not leaving this lab until then. And Ben?'

He was already deactivating the holocom. 'I know. See you, Cal.'

His girlfriend vanished. In her place, Lyvia. 'It seems I'm not the only one to commune with spirits,' the old woman remarked drolly.

'Are the others ready?'

'Yes.'

Ben frowned. The way Lyvia was looking at him, like she was trying to memorise his features, preserve them for posterity. 'Is something wrong?'

'Yes.'

'What?' Draculesti at the door? Guardsmen with guns just waiting for them to emerge from their hiding place?

'The spirits have spoken to me again,' revealed Lyvia.

Ben relaxed a little. No immediate danger, then. He'd come to admire the old woman for her tenacity and resourcefulness, but her obsession with the so-called spirits he still found difficult to take seriously. 'And?'

'Your mission will be a success. The devil Tepesch will fall.'

'I'm pleased to hear it. But how is that something wrong?'

'There will be sacrifice,' Lyvia said. Her eyes narrowed as if she was reading words that were written far off in the distance. 'You are brave and idealistic, Benjamin. You remind me of my own sons when they were your age, all of you willing to risk your lives to fight for a cause you believe in. No end is more glorious than to perish for a noble cause.'

'Lyvia?' She was rambling. Maybe it was a delayed reaction to . . .

'You are strong enough to know. You have a right to know.'

'Know what? Lyvia, you're not making sense.' And it seemed colder in the caverns now.

'The spirits have shown me. You will leave here, Benjamin, but you will not return.'

'Not . . .?' So that was it.

Old Lyvia was shaking her grey head sadly. 'In Dracholtz, Benjamin, you will find only death.'

THIRTEEN

Religion was not an aspect of life that was encouraged in Vlad Tepesch's Wallachia. His people, his reasoning went, should have no greater loyalty than to their prince, and should conceive of no being more powerful. Denied priests and deprived of congregations, the properties belonging to the Wallachian Orthodox Church over time fell into disrepair, neglect and ruin. It was generally considered unwise, un*safe*, even to go near them, even at night.

So nobody was around to notice three youthful figures slipping inside the crumbling shell of the Church of Our Lady in the poor outer district of Dracholtz, an area home to people so insignificant the city wall itself spurned to embrace them. But it was here, according to old Lyvia, that the catacombs could be entered, and from here the devil Tepesch's stronghold was not so very far away.

Ben, Janos and Natalia stole into the crypt. They carried light-rods to guide their way, but at the moment still only dared to set them on low power. Shadows hung about them thick and black.

'Whose tomb are we looking for?' Janos hissed.

'Lyvia said a single name – Matthias,' Ben hissed back. Even in Wallachia, the crypt of a disused church was unlikely to be bugged, but somehow the eeriness of the setting encouraged whispers.

Janos set about searching for the appropriate tomb. Natalia kept her gaze firmly and worriedly on Ben. 'Tombs are over there, Natalia,' he directed her.

'Something's troubling you,' she observed. 'You've been different ever since we left the caves, more tense and withdrawn.'

'I always tend to turn tense and withdrawn when I'm about to put my life on the line,' Ben claimed.

'No, there's something the matter. You can tell me, Ben. You can trust me. Did Lyvia say something to you?'

Only that mine's a one-way ticket to Dracholtz, Ben thought. But he didn't want to burden Natalia with the spirits' latest bulletin, nor Janos, come to that. They had enough to concern themselves with simply staying alive. 'No,' he lied professionally. 'Nothing, other than what she told us all, that we're going to succeed. With the spirits in our corner, what's to trouble me? A little tension – just keeps you on your toes, that's all, ready for anything.'

'Well, if you're sure.' Natalia sounded doubtful.

'I'm better than sure,' Ben said.

But he was relieved nonetheless when Janos called over, 'I've found it!' and Natalia excitedly turned to join him. She was too perceptive and he didn't like keeping things from her, but it wasn't as if he *really* believed Lyvia's gloomy prediction anyway, was it? How could he? He didn't believe in spirits or ghosts or any kind of phantom presences, so how could he possibly have faith in anything they might say? To be honest, Ben didn't believe in God or an afterlife either. The Stanton family creed was purely materialistic. You were born. You made as much money as you could. You spent as much money as you could. You died. You had a museum or an art gallery or a hall at Princeton named after you. End of story.

'Ben,' Natalia beckoned. 'Matthias.'

The name inscribed on an oblong of stone as high as the teenagers' waists.

'Help me slide the lid off,' urged Janos.

Ben heaved to. But he wasn't like the rest of his family, was he? Maybe he had been once, obsessed by wealth, driven by the desire for status and position, needing to be the best for its own selfish sake, but he'd changed since he'd joined Spy High, hadn't he? He'd learned. He was Benjamin White now, not Benjamin T. Stanton Jr. And white was the colour worn by heroes. And heroes did what they did for the good of others, not for themselves. And sometimes they died doing it. The cemeteries were full of heroes.

The stone slab sealing the resting place of Matthias scraped protestingly as it was shoved to one side. 'What's in there?' Natalia thrust her light-rod over the gaping tomb like a dentist shining a torch into a patient's mouth. 'What's *in* there?'

So, Ben thought, what if, somehow, Lyvia's spirits *did* know their stuff? What if his time *was* running out?

'Lyvia was right!' Natalia was exclaiming. 'Look!'

Why would she have told him the bad news unless she herself believed it? To tell someone they were about to face certain death wasn't the likeliest way to boost their morale. What could she gain by doing so?

'Steps,' wondered Janos, 'cut out of the rock. No Matthias was ever interred here. It's a staircase leading to the catacombs, just as Lyvia said.'

She'd done it for his sake, Ben thought, to give him time to make his peace with life, to prepare himself.

Janos climbed into the tomb, in the dim light like a dead man returning to his grave. He disappeared inside.

She'd done it to allow him the choice. He could go to the citadel or he could turn his back. He could be Benjamin White or Benjamin T. Stanton Jr. He could follow or he could stay.

Natalia was in the tomb. She was looking at him. Her eyes were bright with adventure. 'Are you coming, Ben?'

Certain death? He'd confronted it before, many times, and he'd always survived. His enemies underestimated him, Vlad included. So did the spirits. He'd *prove* it.

Ben smiled purposefully. 'Oh yes,' he said. 'I'm coming.'

And soon, in the Church of Our Lady, the crypt again was empty.

The slanting, uneven steps that led downwards were hardly the work of Michelangelo, but Ben supposed they served their purpose. He joined his fellow explorers in a narrow, low-roofed tunnel that snaked ahead into impenetrable darkness. He sensed Natalia and even Janos looking to him for guidance.

'I think we can afford to turn our light-rods to full power now,' he said. The additional illumination drove the darkness back considerably. 'According to Lyvia, there's a hundred yards of tunnel and then we're straight into the catacombs. I know most people only get to visit catacombs once, when they're dead, but just in case there's anything living waiting for us up there, and just in case it's hostile, we'd better check our weaponry.'

It didn't take long. They didn't have much. Ben of course still wore his sleepshot wristbands, and had opted to supplement those with a brace of shock blasters. One he held, the other was thrust under his belt. Wrapped around his waist as well were several bricks of plastic explosive, their task to remove any unforeseen barriers that might otherwise block the group's path. Janos and Natalia both carried shock blasters and had pulse rifles slung across their backs. They were as well prepared as they could be, given the limited resources they'd had to draw on. Ben hoped it would be sufficient.

One way or the other, though, 'Let's go,' he said.

The tunnel seemed to have been hewn by a drunk trying to keep in a straight line. The roof began to dip, became so low that they almost had to stoop. The walls closed in on them like pincers. 'This can't be right,' Janos muttered. 'Ben?'

And then, abruptly, like someone leaving the dinner table without excusing themselves, the tunnel ended. The three teenagers emerged into an altogether vaster underground cavern. Ben's life seemed to be *full* of underground caverns just lately. This one was the most striking yet. 'Welcome to the catacombs,' he said.

Their light-rods sent the darkness skittering like startled animals in the night, or like dirt suddenly shovelled from a grave. They saw the coffins. They saw the tombs.

Down among the dead men, Ben thought bleakly. Natalia coughed. Janos spat. The air was not good.

The catacombs, where the dead of centuries past had been stored and long-since forgotten. Ben ventured forward, cast his gaze around. Some attempt had once been made to create a mood of spirituality and commemoration. Here and there the walls of the vault had been planed smooth, names carved upon them, unreadable now, plaques and shields and coats of arms hung upon them by men and women now dust themselves, the relics rusted and spoiled and ruined by the passage of time.

'I can see why people don't come *here* any more,' Ben said.

'I don't like it,' Natalia shivered. 'The place of the living is *with* the living. Let's move on.'

'Sure.' Ben accessed old Lyvia's map in his mind. The chamber in which they stood was only one of many that comprised the catacombs as a whole. They'd sprawled outwards from the citadel like suburbs. All he, Janos and Natalia needed to do was to retrace their expansion. Before long they'd be under Vlad's very feet.

The decor didn't improve, however. They passed through galleries where skeletons in rotted finery reclined on shelves built into walls, like goods that no one would ever buy. They picked their way across chambers where stone tombs seemed to have grown randomly from the floor, like a strange crop of corpses. They passed through caverns that were a sickly green with damp, like vomit, and where the ill-advisedly wooden coffins had sagged like wet cardboard and the skulls inside, peeping out from a layer of fungus, looked most

aggrieved to have come to this. They saw the first sta-
lactites and stalagmites here, like an old man's bad teeth.
They heard the first, lonely drips of water, as if the rock
itself was weeping.

'The water,' Janos observed. 'That means we must be
directly beneath the Krasnova here.'

'And that means we're close to the citadel.' Natalia
brightened. It wasn't solely the artificial light from the
light-rods that made her appear pale and wan. Natalia
was designed for sunlight and open spaces, not coffins
and catacombs.

'Correct,' said Ben. 'According to Lyvia, there's only
one more chamber after this and then another stairway
that should lead to the lowest levels of the citadel itself.
Guess we *may* need to blast our way in, but we're ready
for that.' Ben patted his explosives.

But he wasn't prepared for Janos' sudden strangled
cry. The Wallachian boy was standing transfixed before
an upright stone sarcophagus bearing the carved image
of a Wallachian warrior. Ben thought it looked like
Kresniki.

'Janos, what is it?' Natalia rushed to him concernedly.

He wasn't looking at the carving. He was gazing at the
inscription beneath it. It was ancient, faded, but
somehow still legible.

'Janos?' Ben was worried too. Unexpected problems
they could do without.

'Mirescu,' Janos read reverentially. 'Nikolai Mirescu.
My ancestor. The most famed of all my ancestors. In the
civil wars he was betrayed. He was murdered by a
Tepesch – his death marked the beginning of my family's
decline – but his body was never returned to us. We

never knew what happened to it. *Now* we know. I take this discovery as a sign that my family's time has come again.'

'That's terrific, Janos,' hastened Ben, 'but old Nikolai's not going anywhere in a hurry. *We* need to. He'll still be here after we've dealt with Vlad.'

'The citadel at last,' Natalia anticipated. 'May the spirits be praised.'

'The spirits cannot help you, girl,' rasped a cold, malignant voice. 'Look only to join them in death.'

'Modrussa!' Ben snapped round. Modrussa indeed, her hideously white face more like a grotesque mask than ever. She was not alone. Half a dozen Draculesti accompanied her. All bore light-rods which they now threw to the floor. All carried pulse rifles. They'd come from the direction Ben's party wanted to go.

'Did you truly imagine, Stanton, that the Prince of Wallachia was not aware of this possible means of access to his citadel? Faithful Boris told him of it years ago.'

'I guess it's no good asking you politely to move aside,' said Ben.

'I think a young man's last words ought to be more memorable than that, don't you?' responded Modrussa. *'Kill them!'*

The Draculesti opened fire. 'Down!' Ben cried, purely instinctively. Anyone who didn't *already* know that this was the kind of time to seek immediate shelter wasn't worth saving. Janos and Natalia were diving to the floor with him. The Draculesti's pulse blasts scorched over their heads, struck the walls instead.

Sleepshot wasn't going to be Ben's best option here. He unleashed his shock blaster instead, aimed for

Modrussa. She moved with the speed of thought. One of her followers wasn't so lucky. One up to the rebels.

'Are you two okay?' Ben yelled to his companions.

'So far so good,' Natalia returned. Janos was too intent on shooting to comment.

But the Draculesti's tactics were different this time. They were making no attempt to move forward and engage the enemy hand-to-hand, as seemed their usual way. Taking no chances, Ben thought grimly.

Hence the shock grenades.

'Scatter!' he shouted, the grenades in the air. One was not about to be avoided. Leaping up, Ben fired his blaster directly at it. The grenade detonated in flight, the shockwave knocking him off his feet. He cracked his head against rock, felt his senses lurch. Explosions reverberated through the chamber. The old tombs shook. Some split open and disgorged rattling bones. Ben fought to keep his consciousness.

Was that blood on his face? He thought he'd struck the *back* of his head. Not blood. Water. Leaking from the Krasnova. The grenades. Their impact had fissured the fragile roof of the catacombs. Through widening crevices the river ran.

Ben saw Natalia, stunned among the rubble of a sarcophagus. He saw Janos, his head gashed but groping for his pulse rifle, still able to fight. That was good.

Here came the Draculesti.

'Janos!' He was closer to her. 'Natalia!'

The Wallachian boy understood. Laying down a covering fire with his rifle, he scrambled towards her. But it looked as if a male Draculesti might get there first. He was already howling at the scent of blood. Natalia was stirring, recovering. She only needed seconds. Ben's shock blaster gave her those seconds, pitching the Draculesti forward into unconsciousness.

'Don't save your friends, Stanton,' snarled Modrussa, 'when you can't save yourself!'

She was there, in front of him, an apparition from a nightmare. How could she have moved so *fast*? It wasn't . . . Taloned fingers slashed at his hand as he brought the blaster to bear. Disarmed. Then claws at his face, a raking assault on his body. Ben felt the assassin slicing through his clothes, scourging his skin. He had to defend himself, retaliate. He raised his arms, blocked some of her blows, but there was no doubting the truth. As Ben's legs barely held him up, as they almost buckled under the frenzied attack, it was Modrussa who was in the ascendancy, forcing him back. He knew it. She knew it. Her fanged jaws slavered like a beast's about to feed.

'At last! At last!' Lashing Ben relentlessly. 'I will tear out your heart as a present for my prince.'

'Don't you think,' Ben strained to rally, 'he'd prefer chocolates?'

He threw a feeble punch. It glanced harmlessly from Modrussa's black-clad shoulder. His arm she clamped and twisted, shooting agony through him. Ben's pain pleased her like a smile from a lover. 'Your final attempt at wit, outlander,' she promised. 'Now you die.'

Ben felt himself thrown. He felt himself flying through space, slamming against the ground a second time. He was on his back. He was helpless. Above him, cracks were gathering in the roof, water beginning to spill and spray and gush through as the rock weakened. If

Modrussa didn't finish him off, the Krasnova would. Both had tried before. He saw Natalia and Janos, battling bravely back to back.

'Whatever gods you worship in the decadent west, pray to them now.' And Modrussa was advancing on him, filling his vision with black and white. He was scrabbling backwards on elbows and heels. She was a hellish predator ready to pounce. He was bracing his muscles for one last effort. She was launching herself at him, in for the kill.

Ben rolled hectically, desperately to the side. He was still rolling when he heard Modrussa scream. It was raw, intimate, somehow obscene. It was a sound that would haunt him for ever. In reality, though, it didn't last for long. Not even the chief assassin of the Draculesti was capable of continued utterance with her body impaled by a stalagmite.

Ben winced. He hadn't realised how close he'd been to the spike of rock. Clearly, neither had Modrussa. The stalagmite had skewered her through the breast with as deadly an effect as any stake in a flickering twentieth-century vampire movie. Her limbs jumped and twitched, but she wasn't going to be reaching for Ben any time soon.

It looked like there was an opening at the head of the Draculesti.

Those of her comrades who'd seen Modrussa die didn't seem keen to volunteer for it. Leaderless, their morale was lost. They fled, some back the way they'd come, others further into the catacombs.

'Tolly,' breathed Ben, 'maybe you can rest a little bit easier now.'

'Ben, are you all right?' Natalia was beside him, her tone anxious. She'd been fighting in her mutated form, but now returned to normal. 'Did she hurt you?'

'Not as much as she hurt herself,' Ben said. 'Now let's get out of here. I don't know how long this roof is going to hold.' As he stood, he was aware that they were already sloshing in water to the ankles. 'Janos, come on!'

The Wallachian, however, showed no interest in moving on. He'd returned to the tomb of Nikolai Mirescu. A stray pulse blast had shattered the lid of the sarcophagus. Janos had probably never imagined that one day he'd be staring at his ancestor face-to-skull. 'I can't come,' he said. 'Not yet.'

He's losing it, Ben realised with dread. Chunks of rock were now falling from the roof, with water, icy-cold and limitless, not far behind. 'Not yet's not good enough, Janos. The catacombs are flooding.'

'Janos, what are you doing?' Natalia cried.

He seemed to be leaning down, into the sarcophagus. Ben had this crazy idea that the Wallachian was going to kneel and kiss his ancestor's feet, or at least the tarsal and metatarsal bones that were all that remained of them. Luckily, he was wrong. Janos reached inside the tomb, and when he withdrew his hand, something gleamed in his grasp.

'A Wallachian warrior must be buried with his sword,' he said, 'and it is so. The sword of the Mirescus!' He flourished the blade triumphantly. 'A gift from Nikolai to Janos, from the Mirescus dead to those living, from the past to the present.'

'Yeah, well the present's all we'll have if we don't move ourselves,' Ben warned. 'Bring the sword if you want,

Janos, but grab a blaster as well, *and* a light-rod' –
retrieving one himself from the floor beneath the water –
'and be *quick*. The future's *that* way.'

They waded forward as rapidly as the roof above them
crumbled. The Krasnova cascaded in, swirled to their
knees, their waists. Bodies that had not glimpsed a river
in hundreds of years decided to go swimming.

Ben had to shout above the roaring flood. 'There it is!
Lyvia's stairway.'

Broader than that from the tomb of Matthias, easier to
scale. Ben began to think he was doing a pretty good job
of cheating the spirits. Up the dozen or so steps, through
the door that Lyvia promised would be there, and he'd
be doing an even better one.

They dragged themselves out of the water. 'No, Ben,
look!' Natalia's despair was almost physical. And, of
course, he should have realised things wouldn't be that
easy.

There *was* a door. If it was opened, it probably *did* lead
into the bowels of the citadel. But it wasn't the kind of
door that Lyvia had envisaged. The old woman had been
thinking in terms of stone. This barrier was wrought
from a more modern material, a metal that Ben suspected
would be impervious to shock blasts.

'There's no way in,' Janos observed. No mechanism,
no control. Obviously, the door could only be operated
from within the citadel.

'Your explosives, Ben,' Natalia prompted.

He felt at his waist. The plastic explosives were not
there. 'Modrussa,' he realised. 'When we were fighting,
the belt must have snapped.' He glanced back at the
fast-rising waters, sucking again at their ankles.

'They're gone.' Maybe the Draculesti had doomed them after all.

'What are we going to do?' Natalia gazed nervously at the flood.

'No use crying over spilt plastic explosives,' Ben gritted. 'The door might be a no-go, but let's see if we can blast our way through the wall.'

Janos and Natalia nodded. They saw the sense in Ben's idea. The old weathered stone certainly seemed to pose less of an obstacle than the steel-alloy door.

All three teenagers opened fire with everything they had. The wall was pulverised, chips of fractured masonry shooting off in all directions. A trio of voices prepared to whoop with success. Prematurely.

The stone they'd stripped away, no problem. But behind the wall was steel, unmarked, undented, undamaged steel.

'I don't believe it,' groaned Natalia. She turned searchingly to Ben: 'So what now?'

He wished she hadn't asked. As the flood waters swallowed them to the stomach, he didn't have a clue.

FOURTEEN

'**W**e can't just stand here and drown!' Natalia pursued. 'We're not *going* to just stand here and drown.' Ben was insistent.

'Then where are we going to go?'

Ben glanced back the way they'd come with trepidation. The catacombs were now almost entirely submerged. 'How good are you at swimming underwater?'

Janos, meanwhile, was remaining remarkably calm, more interested in his sword than their predicament. 'The spirits are with us,' he said. 'We will not be abandoned.'

'Janos,' rebuked Natalia, 'now isn't the time to go all religious on us. The spirits help those who help themselves.' She turned back to Ben. 'Do you think we'll be able to hold our breath for long enough?'

'We'd better,' said Ben. 'Start preparing now. Deep breaths. Use your lungs.'

They breathed in. Breathed out. Breathed in . . .

The door to the citadel slid open.

The waters surged through the gap like the Red Sea

crashing down on Pharaoh's head. They carried the three
teenagers with them, spilled them shocked and soaking
on to a metal floor. Ben was aware that the flood was
now trickling away, becoming a depth that might invite a
child to paddle, soon not even that, the legacy of an over-
eager cleaner. The door had closed again. Drowning was
no longer on the agenda.

Death, however, came in many forms. Boris standing
over them with a shock blaster qualified as one.

Ben reckoned his reflexes could match those of a guy
of sixty, even given his recent exertions.

'It's all right. It's all right.' Boris, inexplicably, was
lowering his weapon. 'I'm not your enemy, Stanton. Not
any more.'

'What?' Ben was on his feet. What kind of game was
the Wallachian playing? His own blaster did *not* waver
from its natural target. Neither did Natalia's. Janos
looked ready and willing to wield the sword of the
Mirescus for the first time in half a millennium. 'Forgive
me if I don't shake hands and order drinks all round
immediately, but I tend to be a little distrustful of guys
who for no apparent reason suddenly swap shock
blasters for olive branches.'

'It's a trick. He's just trying to delay us until reinforcements arrive,' Janos theorised. The corridor in
which they found themselves *was* distinctly unoccupied
in both directions.

Natalia looked at the screen above the door. It showed
the catacombs beyond, the Krasnova in complete possession. 'But why would he even let us in? He could have
left us to drown.'

'We *wouldn't* have drowned,' countered Janos. 'We'd

have found a way to escape. Now he can make sure.'

'Good point, Boris,' said Ben, 'and I'm not clear as to why Vlad's right-hand man should suddenly switch sides. You've got a minute to convince us, and if we hear the patter of tiny guardsmen's feet in the meantime . . .' He indicated his shock blaster warningly.

'Very well, Stanton.' Boris smiled ruefully. 'Your scepticism does not surprise me. Neither, if I may say so, does your victory over Modrussa and the Draculesti. I watched it from here.'

'You *may* say so,' Ben allowed, 'but you're down to fifty-five seconds already.'

'Then perhaps my name will grant me more time.'

'Boris?' queried Natalia.

'Vukic,' said the whiskered man. 'Boris *Vukic*. Brother to Vissarion. Son to Lyvia. I take it you two' – Janos and Natalia – 'are Nostravistan. Those names should not be unfamiliar to you.'

'Lyvia's second son?' Natalia frowned. 'But that's not possible.'

'She always claimed you were dead,' added Janos. 'Vissarion, too.'

'To my family I *am* dead. To them I died the day I entered the service of Tepesch as a boy of your own age, more than forty years ago.' Something stirred in Boris Vukic. 'But now, perhaps, I can be alive again. My mother?'

'She's well,' said Natalia. 'It was Lyvia who sent us through the catacombs.'

'Of course. I should have guessed. Vukic family knowledge.'

'What about Vissarion?' Janos pressed.

'Well, too. Dungeoned with the others. We have half of Wallachia under lock and key. I assume you seek to release them.'

'You assume right,' said Ben, 'but even if you're who you *say* you are' – he recalled the stand-off between Boris and Vissarion during the battle at Nostravista, their mutual reluctance to shoot – 'and okay, let's make another assumption that I believe you, you still haven't explained why the change of allegiance this late in your career. And let's say, thirty seconds.'

Boris inclined his head. 'My actions have always been ordained by my love for our country,' he said. 'Always. A man is mortal, a man is but a moment in time, but his country is time*less*, his country endures for ever. I was born in a new century. I saw that it was a century more than any other in which science and technology would sweep away the old order and the old ways, a century in which the military and financial strength of a few nations would allow them to swamp and stifle and finally to dominate and control the many. I looked at Wallachia, fiercely proud but on a world scale tiny, insignificant, and I feared for her future. To survive at all in the twenty-first century we needed a leader who was strong, even ruthless, who would have no qualms about doing whatever was necessary to preserve Wallachia's uniqueness, her independence, her traditions.'

'So you made a pact with the devil,' said Ben. 'The devil Tepesch.'

'I did. And I made no protest at the killings, the murders, the assassinations that kept Vlad Tepesch in power. I welcomed them. I played my part. I actively assisted in the repression of our people for what I believed to be the greater good, for the homeland itself.'

'So what's changed?'

'The devil Tepesch fired the Nocnitsa,' guessed Natalia.

Boris admitted it. 'The burning of our sacred land. The corruption of our greatest gift, the dracul flower itself. An alien weapon brought into the heart of our nation. Vlad Tepesch no longer rules for Wallachia. He rules only for himself. Perhaps he always did. Perhaps I was stupid, blind to dedicate my loyalty to him for all these years, but I did what I believed to be right and no man can ever do more. *That* is why I have turned against my former prince, Ben Stanton. That is why your enemy is now your ally.'

'Okay, well that was slightly over thirty seconds,' noted Ben. His eyes met Boris', though, and he'd been trained to detect falsehood and lies in others' expressions, to recognise deception even in the features of the finest actor. In the lines of Boris' face, and for the first time he realised how many there were, he read only sincerity. Ben nodded. 'But I'm convinced. Janos? Natalia?' Agreement, if cautious. 'Then let's get moving before Craniescu does his rounds.'

'You needn't worry about Craniescu,' said Boris. 'I have already closed his eyes.'

Ben winced. Another Wallachian euphemism. Revolution made for strange bedfellows, it seemed. But the greater good was what mattered.

Boris was demonstrating little remorse. 'And I have taken steps against Tepesch too, as he will soon discover.'

❈

Vlad Tepesch, Prince of Wallachia, had learned long ago that the life of a leader was a lonely one, and the more absolute a dictator you became, the more isolated you grew. Who could you trust? No one. A ruler such as he knew only two types of people, flatterers and rivals. No smile – if anyone dared lift their gaze from the floor to smile at him – could be depended on: smiles were either hollow and empty with sycophancy or masks for envy and ambition. No, Vlad knew, the only way to survive as ruler was to surround yourself not with people but with power.

He reflected on this as he sat in the vault of his throne room, alone. In the pursuit of power, power itself had to become everything to you. Your parent. Your lover. Your child. The only relationship you could safely have was with power. All else betrayed weakness and would eventually destroy you. All else had to be subordinated, rejected, dismissed. And if you could do it, if you could devote yourself to power and nothing else, power for its own sake to be wielded as you wished without restraint or restriction, the rewards were immense.

Vlad Tepesch sat in the vault of his throne room, alone.

He permitted his brow to furrow. How long had he ruled Wallachia? Forty years? Fifty? His consumption of the dracul kept him younger than his true age. Regardless, it seemed to him that his reign had never been under such threat as now. Outlander armies massing on his borders. Dissension and rebellion rife within them. Stanton still alive, like a wound that would not heal. And Craniescu murdered. A traitor in the citadel.

There were only two people the traitor could *not* be, Vlad reasoned.

'Modrussa?' He tried contacting her yet again over his communicator. Yet again there was silence. 'Modrussa?' A permanent kind of silence.

'Boris?' Different tack. Same result. 'Boris, answer me.'

Two people who couldn't be the traitor. Two people who couldn't be raised.

Vlad Tepesch sat in the vault of his throne room, alone.

And for how many years had he done this? Forty? Fifty? Long years. Years in which he'd ensured Wallachia's survival and prosperity. And now the ingrates were turning against him. He'd show them. He'd show his enemies at home and abroad the cost of defying a Tepesch.

He'd show them *power*.

The word dungeons evoked in Ben's mind deep, dark cells of stone, riddled with rats and with impossibly old prisoners wearing impossibly long beards chained to darkly dripping walls. It was more than possible that once such accommodation had existed beneath the citadel, but no longer. Confinement now took the form of fixtureless metal rooms locked electronically, lit relentlessly by pitiless light-ceilings and monitored constantly by bored guardsmen from the adjacent control room.

Guardsmen who might have expected a visit from Boris, but not necessarily in the company of three peasant teenagers, one of whom looked suspiciously like the Benjamin Stanton the whole country was looking for.

'New prisoners,' announced Boris. 'I'm sure we can squeeze them in, can't we?'

'But aren't they still,' ventured a guardsman, 'armed?'

'Most observant.' Boris added his own shock blasts to those of his new-found allies. 'Remind me to recommend you for a promotion when you wake up.' He stepped over the bodies, activated the cell-door release mechanisms. 'Time to rally your troops, Stanton.'

As Vlad Tepesch's broadcasts had made clear, not only Nostravistans were held captive in the citadel. Resistance fighters and other dissidents from all over Wallachia, particularly places like Karinthia, had been brought together and crammed into the dungeons in advance of the proposed mass executions. It was a policy that was beginning to look like a mistake.

The liberated prisoners emerged gratefully but uncertainly into the control room, Vissarion Vukic at their head. '*Ben!* Janos! Natalia! I knew you wouldn't let us —' The sight of his brother silenced him.

'Greetings, Vissarion,' Boris said. 'It's been a while, has it not?'

'What is this?' Vissarion protested. 'What kind of ruse? Do you not realise who this traitor is?'

'Boris is on *our* side now,' said Natalia.

'We could not have reached here without him. He saved our lives,' said Janos. 'It seems you have got your brother back, Vissarion.'

The two men faced each other warily.

'Is it true?' Vissarion asked. 'Does the prodigal return?'

'He does,' said Boris simply. 'If his family will accept him.'

'Sorry to intrude on Vukic business,' Ben interjected, 'but we've got a regime to topple, don't we? And I think we'd better get on with it.'

'We're ready to fight,' Vissarion declared, 'but we need weapons.'

'I can find you weapons,' said Boris.

There was only ever a token guard on the armoury. It was hardly surprising. Conventional wisdom denied the possibility of any enemy of the state penetrating this far into the citadel. Conventional wisdom, as has so often been the case, was a fool.

The rebels fell upon the guardsmen. Vissarion had his weapons.

'Now for Tepesch,' he vowed darkly.

'Vissarion, wait.' Ben could tell that the Wallachians, many of whom had never seen *him* before, would follow Vissarion Vukic to the death, and maybe they'd have to, but there was one factor in all the turmoil that he couldn't allow to be forgotten. 'There's still the starstone. I told you what it can do. We have to secure the starstone first.'

'Very well,' consented Vissarion. 'We'll take the central tower, then the throne room. Death to the devil Tepesch!'

The insurgents took up the shout. Their infiltration techniques obviously left a little bit to be desired. Ben closed his eyes as if in pain. 'So, no need for an alarm, then.'

Vissarion turned to Boris. 'Brother,' he invited, 'shall we fight together?'

'Nothing would make me more proud,' said Boris.

And to begin with, the ragtag army did well. The element of surprise and their passion for their cause combined to devastating military effect. Vlad's guardsmen were swept almost effortlessly before them. The upper echelons of the Tepesch regime, Boris, Modrussa, Craniescu, none was there to rally and direct the citadel's defence. Indeed, the former's intimacy with the building's geography helped them make progress towards their final destination even more rapidly than they might have done. Ben was beginning to think he'd have good news to tell Cally on the holocom.

Then things changed.

Resistance to the rebels' charge stiffened. The guardsmen became more organised. The battle for each corridor intensified. Casualties increased.

Worse was to come.

A blistering barrage of fire from ahead of them made any advance in that direction impossible. And now the enemy was behind them, too, in numbers.

'This way!' Boris led them down a corridor which seemed to have been virtually forgotten by Vlad's men, a handful in permanent retreat encountered only. 'This is good! We have a courtyard to cross and then the tower.'

A courtyard? Ben's heart froze inside him. 'No!' he cried. 'Boris! Vissarion! They *want* us to come this way. It's a—'

It was indeed. The rebels burst out into the courtyard without heeding the intense blond boy who wasn't even *Wallachian*. They raced directly into a hail of pulse blasts from guardsmen lining the ramparts above it. The tower, less than sixty metres away, might as well have been on the Moon.

'Back! Get back!' Ben yelled until he felt his lungs would burst.

Natalia obeyed him, and Janos. The majority retreated.

'No, we can go on!' Boris Vukic did not. 'We have to go on!'

'We have to live!' Vissarion's eyes were sharp. He saw the pulse blast aimed at Boris almost before the guardsman squeezed his trigger. He lunged recklessly forward. 'Brother!'

The shot thumped into Vissarion Vukic. It shook his massive frame like a mighty tree felled.

'No.' His brother's body slumped into his arms. Boris stared in disbelief. 'No no no.'

'Cover me,' Ben urged Janos and Natalia. Firing his own shock blaster, he darted out into the courtyard.

'Ben, don't!' Natalia cried after him. 'It's suicide!'

Ben sincerely hoped not. Somehow, he reached the Vukics. 'Get him back under cover, Boris.' The whiskered man seemed incapable of movement. 'Boris, listen up! We have to get Vissarion back under cover.' The pulse blasts were going to get lucky sooner rather than later. 'We might still save him.' Though sadly, he doubted it.

He'd kindled enough hope for Boris to take action, at least. Together they dragged the limp form of Vissarion to shelter if not safety. Guardsmen were closing in behind them. They couldn't go forward, couldn't go back. Ben surveyed the faces around him. Apart from Janos and Natalia, they suddenly seemed to have lost their belief.

'Vissarion. Vissarion.' Boris was crouching at his side. 'Why did you do that? We've been opposed for so long. Why did you save me?'

Vissarion's lips parted, struggled to shape words. 'You're my brother,' he said. 'My brother.' Not that he seemed able to see him. Not that he could see anyone now.

'Oh, no. *Vissarion*,' mourned Natalia.

Ben felt the collective groan of the insurgents. He shared it. He'd liked Vissarion too. He only wished there was time to pause. There wasn't.

The corridor, the courtyard, the citadel itself trembled.

'What's that?' said Janos.

Ben knew. He felt himself plunging helplessly towards disaster. 'The starstone,' he said. 'Vlad's activating the starstone.'

FIFTEEN

It was almost beyond belief. Boris, faithful Boris, Boris who'd been at his side and carried out his orders without question for nearly half a century, Boris was with the insurgents. There could be no mistake. The anonymous guardsman who'd stumblingly informed him of the fact would not have dared to lie. But now one or two matters became clearer. Craniescu's murder. Modrussa's disappearance.

Boris and Stanton were fighting as one. Vlad's jagged teeth clenched in his rage.

Yet all was not lost. Far from it. The Prince of Wallachia stood in the tower laboratory and looked on as his techs scurried around the starstone like mice around cheese. The control panels flashed as if in warning. Light like green ghosts was exuded from the artefact, drifted upwards. The vibrations began.

They'd told him that they understood the starstone's energy now, that they could direct it in a beam of disintegrating power to destroy his enemies. That was good. If the rebels *did* happen to reach the tower, if they *did* overrun the elite security force that he'd gathered around him, their defeat was still assured.

Let them come, Vlad Tepesch silently declared. Let the traitor Boris and the whelp Stanton come. One way or another, today it ended.

'It's no good, Ben. We're pinned down. They can pick us off at will.' Janos summed up the situation rather succinctly.

'We've got to move. We've got to make the tower.'

'Nobody'll go out there again.' The courtyard was still littered with bodies from their last attempt.

Ben thought desperately. What made men voluntarily risk death? A cause. Motivation. A leader who inspired. It couldn't be him: he wasn't Wallachian. Vissarion was dead. Boris was still bent over the body. There was maybe another candidate.

'Janos,' Ben urged, squeezing his shoulder, 'it has to be you. You're a Mirescu. Your name means something in Wallachia. They'll follow you like they did Vissarion. You can do it, *only* you. You can lead us to the tower.'

'You think so?' There was pride in Janos' eyes. He weighed the sword of his ancestors in his hands.

'Ben's *right*,' Natalia put in. 'Janos, it's your *time*.'

'Perhaps it is. Will you be with me, Natalia?'

'Always,' she said, and pride was in her eyes too.

'Then let us try.' He stood tall in the blaze of gunfire and thrust the sword high like a beacon, called out to the beleaguered Wallachians. 'I am Janos Mirescu. I wield the sword of my ancestors, the sword of victory. Who will follow me and bring an end to the devil Tepesch?' Murmurs of willingness. Jaws setting. Eyes narrowing.

'In the name of a new Wallachia, who will follow? The moment is now. Our time is *now*.' The rebels seemed to believe it. Hopelessness was stirred to hope again. Despair became belief.

Ben watched Janos in humble admiration. The peasant boy seemed visionary, a warrior prophet. And to think, this was the guy he'd been brawling with over a girl just a few days ago. Maybe it *was* his time after all.

'Who will follow?' The sword flashed like fire above Janos' head. He didn't have to ask again. His answer was clear.

Everyone.

'My prince,' reported the guardsman, 'the rebels are breaking through.'

'Then stop them,' snapped Vlad Tepesch. He was aware that the soldier's gaze was travelling over his black-robed shoulder. 'What are you looking at, Captain?'

'N-nothing, my prince.'

'Then return to your post and fight to the death for your prince.'

'Y-yes. Yes, my prince.'

Tepesch doubted the man would. He'd seen not commitment in his eyes but surrender, not courage but fear. He glanced back over his shoulder to view what had so preoccupied the underling.

The starstone, throbbing, existing now in an emerald haze. The techs were yelling at each other in a display of intemperate and most uncustomary animation. Their agitation was so extreme they were almost assaulting one another, pulling at each other's coats, shaking their comrades by the lapels. One of them was crying out in some kind of denial.

The starstone's central point flared into eldritch light.

As it had done before, Vlad Tepesch reasoned. It only meant that an energy discharge was near. He hoped Stanton and his insurrection would be here in time to witness it.

A second point was suddenly blazing too, to the right of the first. A third, to its left. The tower shook as if rocked by an earthquake.

A tech floundered towards him. 'What is happening?' snarled Vlad Tepesch.

'My prince, we can't . . . we couldn't . . .'

Tepesch seized the hapless man by the throat. 'I repeat, what is happening?'

'It's out of control,' the tech panicked. 'We can't stop it. It's started a chain reaction. The starstone will kill us all!'

The good thing about battles, once you were in them you had no time to worry. The past and the future, those twin causes of human anxiety and regret and fear, were reduced to irrelevance. In battle you no longer existed as a thinking, coherent human being. You became a creature who acted purely on instinct, whose only concern was the present. At least, you did if you wanted to survive.

And they were at the doors to the tower, blasting the barrier into scrap. Men had fallen in the courtyard but as a body they had not faltered, and Janos was still swinging the sword of the Mirescus around his head, rallying the rebels. The tide was turning. Ben felt it. At the last, the guardsmen on the ramparts had seemed to fire only as an afterthought, their minds elsewhere. Resistance on the lower floors of the tower was quickly overcome. He realised why.

It was the green tincture to the air, like the sun refracted through a forest. It was the shuddering of the ground beneath their feet. The guardsmen knew as well as Ben the kind of damage the starstone could inflict. They knew that if they waited around, they could go the way of the unfortunate techs before them. They were disturbed by the past, dismayed by the possible future.

They were going to lose.

'Hold our position!' Ben barked to Janos. 'You've got to give me time to deactivate the starstone or else none of this is going to matter.'

Janos understood. 'It'll be done.'

'Natalia?' He remembered their escape from Dracholtz, the team they'd made.

'I have to stay with Janos, Ben.'

Of course she did.

'I am with you, Stanton.' Boris.

Ben nodded. Not as pretty as Natalia, but easily as focused. Those Wallachians Janos could spare as he tightened the insurgents' grip on the tower joined him too.

The final stairwell to the lab. A guardsman falling, screaming past him. The scorch of shock blasts on steel. The clamour and cries of combat. Pushing forward. Always pushing forward. Vlad's defenders driven to retreat.

Ben's force stormed into the lab and he remained not even wounded, not even scratched. He felt a told-you-so to Lyvia's spirits might be in order.

Two shocks.

The starstone: five points lit, almost its entire upper half. And Vlad: like a dark statue immune to the panic and carnage around him. Vlad, recognising certain of the invaders and smiling as if in welcome. The Prince of Wallachia's hospitality, however, was likely to prove hostile.

Only Tepesch's most ardent loyalists were battling on by now. The rebels engaged them.

'Vlad's mine,' vowed Ben icily.

'No, Stanton.' Boris Vukic placed a restraining hand on his shoulder. 'He's *ours*.'

'Well, well,' chuckled Tepesch, like an undertaker with a full order book. 'The boy and the betrayer. Shall we fight like men?'

'If only we had the time, you piece of slime.' Ben raised his blaster. Stun Vlad quickly, then deal with the starstone.

Good plan. If it had worked. 'Make time,' said Vlad.

And sprang. His cloak was like ink thrown across a room. His body was solid enough. His fist crunched into Ben's face, cruel nails drew blood beneath his eye. He was as strong as ever, superhumanly strong. Ben saw Boris go down in the first attack. He tried to bring his blaster to bear again, or his sleepshot. Vlad seized both his wrists, forcing him to drop the gun, squeezing, crushing.

'Did you think you were a match for Tepesch, Stanton, did you? You've *never* been my match, boy. You've only ever been lucky. And now your luck has ended.'

'Dream on, scumbag,' gritted Ben.

Boris was on his feet once more, pounding Vlad's back and neck with his fists. Tepesch lashed behind him with his left hand. Ben twisted, kicked, thumped his boot against the Wallachian's chest, making him stagger. He wrenched his wrist free. It was bruised but not broken.

And he'd made Vlad stagger. It wasn't only the Prince of Wallachia who was surprised.

'Your rule is finished, my prince,' Boris snorted. He tried to renew his own attack, but this time Vlad was prepared. He bludgeoned the older man ferociously, without mercy, beating him to the floor. For the second time Boris tried to rise. Didn't make it. Instead, with an agonised groan he collapsed, writhing, clutching painfully at his chest.

'Perhaps,' Tepesch spoke bitterly. 'Perhaps not. What does it matter?' Defending himself against a frantic flurry of blows from Ben. 'Look at the stone, Stanton.' More than half illuminated, each energy-charged point passing its power to the next. 'Do you know what this means? The full might of the starstone is about to be unleashed.'

'I can stop it! I know how. Let me stop it,' Ben pleaded.

'I don't think so.' Vlad struck back.

'But the people who might die. *Your* people.' Somehow, Ben still stood. Was his foe *weakening*?

'What do I care for *people*? If Tepesch is to fall this day, then he will take Wallachia with him. And *you*, Stanton.'

Vlad lunged for Ben's throat. Ben sidestepped. Vlad flailed at empty space. He was vulnerable to a well-placed karate chop. Incredibly, Vlad Tepesch, Prince of Wallachia, was on his knees.

'Bit of a new position for you, Vlad, huh?' taunted Ben. 'Get used to it.'

But the *starstone*. The fighting in the rest of the lab was over; the guardsmen had surrendered. Wallachians from both sides stared awestruck at the alien rock. It was turning the lab to jade. Only three points remained to be lit. The tower shook like a rocket ready for lift-off.

Forget Vlad. He was beaten. Get to the starstone.

A steel hand around his ankle. 'You're going nowhere . . . boy. Saving . . . no one . . .' Not steel. Flesh and blood. Ben pulled himself free of Tepesch's detaining fingers and he saw them trembling like an old man's, like an addict's. Vlad's whole body was suddenly racked by seizure. 'What . . . is . . .?'

'You never cared for our country, did you?' sighed Boris. His breathing was ragged, excruciating, his face ashen. 'I should have done this years ago, for the sake of Wallachia.'

'What . . . have you . . . done?' Vlad's death-mask face was horrified.

'The dracul preparation you drank today, my prince,' Boris confessed. 'I poisoned it.'

'No . . . no . . .' The Prince of Wallachia convulsed. 'Boris . . . but I . . . trusted you . . . I . . .'

His back arched impossibly, as if the vertebrae would snap. His mouth gaped wide, fangs bared a final time. Then the man who'd tyrannised Wallachia for half a century slumped back and there issued a rattle from his throat and he moved no more.

Ben wasn't sorry but he wasn't glad either. He didn't gloat. To celebrate the death of any man was to become less human yourself.

He crouched beside Boris. His old enemy looked far from bull-like now. The rattle was in his throat, too.

'My heart . . .'

'Vlad did this.'

'No.' A rueful smile. 'My heart has been dead for many years. I killed it myself and now I must pay.' He gripped Ben's sleeve. 'Go to the stone, Ben. Save Wallachia.'

'I will.' He eased Boris Vukic back. 'You rest awhile.'

'Ben!' Janos, accompanied by Natalia and most of the others. 'The devil Tepesch's men have either fled or . . . My God.' He'd seen Vlad's body.

'May the spirits be praised,' said Natalia, in a way that Cally never would.

'I'd keep the praising on hold for the moment,' Ben cautioned. 'Janos, you've got to get everybody out, like now. Evacuate the entire citadel. I need to disarm the starstone and I need to do it alone.'

'But do we really have to leave the *citadel*?'

'Janos, if I *can't* deactivate this thing you'd probably need to leave the *city*. Now will you go?' An ominous boom from the interior of the starstone. Three unenergised points had just become one. 'You're still here?'

Most of the men didn't need Ben's exhortations. They fled. The techs, too. It was as well that the Deveraux agent had not been expecting assistance from that quarter.

'I'll stay,' Natalia said boldly. 'You can't be on your own, Ben. I'll stay with you.'

'No. Thanks, Natalia, but no.' Even on the brink of death, there was time for warmth. Maybe it was more important at moments like this than any other. 'If something goes wrong . . . You've got to go with Janos. Your place is with him.'

Natalia hugged him, kissed him as if it was her final kiss. 'I'll see you soon, outlander. Promise me.'

'Go. Go. *Natalia*. Take Boris.'

'Boris is dead.' Janos was kneeling, checking the body. 'Natalia, come. Ben, good luck.'

Ben didn't look back to see them leave. He was activating the holocom even as he darted to the starstone, bounded on to the dais and confronted the control panels. Cally had been true to her word. She was by his side again. Several langtechs were by hers. He'd opened what was like a doorway, a portal from Wallachia to Deveraux. If he could only pass through it and actually be with Cally, everything would be all right. But he couldn't. The starstone was in his way.

And this close he felt it pulsing, beating like a heart, like it was alive. Without the brightness filters of his chameleon suit, its savage green was blinding. The world around him was green, green like the poison gas of the Great War.

'Ben! What's . . .?'

'No time for updates, Cal. If you don't tell me how to switch this sucker off soon, Ben White is history.'

'Arrest the progression,' a langtech declared.

'*That's* real helpful.'

'The central control panel,' Cally directed. 'I'll tell you what to key in.'

She did. Ben let her guide his hands as if he was a puppet and Cally the puppet-master. His concentration was absolute. The kind of symbol, the sequence, he entered the information into the starstone as promptly and precisely as Cally uttered it. Her words became his own thoughts. They were almost simultaneous.

And then she stopped.

'Is that it?' Ben didn't dare to hope.

'We've arrested the progression,' Cally said. 'The last point won't light.'

'That's it.' Secret agent supreme or what?

Though the starstone still throbbed and Ben could hardly keep his balance on the dais.

'Tell Agent Stanton the energy will *still* discharge.'

'What?' That langtech was a joy to listen to.

'Ben, we still have to shut the whole thing down or else—'

'I know about or else, Cal. How do I shut it down?'

'We think there's a disengagement sequence.'

'You *think*?'

'There *is* a disengagement sequence. Feed it into the central control panel. You'll have to do it once for each point energised on the starstone.'

'Understood. The sequence?'

Cally told him. She only needed to do so once. Ben made no mistake. A second point on the artefact was doused, was harmless alien marble again. Ben repeated the process.

'Get those glad rags out, Cal,' he grinned. 'It looks like Agent Stanton's going to be coming home just *covered* in gl— What's that?'

A panel to his right was doing something it hadn't done before. It was suddenly displaying a series of successive symbols. They weren't Arabic in origin, but with a sinking heart Ben guessed they were numerals nonetheless.

'Automatic countdown.' At least the langtech sounded dismayed this time.

'Tell me he's wrong, Cal.' Ben's fingers didn't pause. It was like they were programmed.

'He's not.' Cally's voice was grim. 'The energy in the starstone can't be contained indefinitely. Once the power's been generated, it has either to be defused or discharged. Automatic countdown's a warning . . .'

'How long have I got?' With half the starstone neutralised.

'The numerals were easy.'

'Let's hope my deadline is.'

'*Ben*.' He could tell from Cally's tone that it wasn't. 'You've got just over a minute.'

Numbers and timing and symbols all juggled in his mind. Seven points still green. It was taking him ten seconds to key in the disengagement sequence. He needed to do it in eight.

Inside the starstone, imprisoned energy thrashed to be released.

'Ben . . .'

'I know, Cally, I know.'

Six to go. Five.

At least Janos and Natalia should have cleared the citadel by now. If he could reduce the starstone's power to just one point, he knew that would only affect the lab. That would incur just a single casualty. Admittedly, it was a casualty with whom he was more than familiar.

His *fingers*. Clumsy. Fumbling. He was too slow.

Four. Three. He was nearly there, nearly there.

'Ben, there's no time. You've got to run. Get out. Save yourself.'

Save himself with his work not done? That wasn't very Benjamin White. 'I can do it, Cal.'

'Ben, it's no good. Get out *now*!'

In Dracholtz, Benjamin, you will find only death.

Lyvia's blasted spirits. He wasn't about to give *them* the last word.

Two points remaining. Just two. He needed maybe nineteen, twenty seconds. The countdown in his mind told him he didn't have them.

'Ben! Ben! For *me*!' Cally was a phantom pulling purposelessly at his arm.

'All right. Just let me . . .' Down to one. The spire of the starstone. 'Cal . . .' He gazed at her in longing.

'Ben, *please*.'

He stabbed at his wristband. Holocom off. Cally gone. For ever?

Depended on how fast he could run.

Ben hurtled across the lab. He didn't look back. No point looking back. He sprinted for safety. In his mind, though, the countdown reached zero.

Time up.

There was the lightning flash behind him, the detonation. And exit an uncrossable distance away.

He'd saved lives, though. He'd done that. He could be proud of that. *Cally* could, eventually. It was just a pity about his own.

But Ben Stanton was no coward. He turned, defiant. The green blast of energy hurricaned towards him. No chance to scream. No chance to close his eyes. He wouldn't have done either, anyway. He felt himself *changing*.

The starstone consumed Ben Stanton.

Cally Cross glared at the artefact with cold hostility. She'd seen it before, obviously, though only holographically, and she hadn't been forced to see it again now, not after what had happened to Ben. Nobody had ordered her to be part of the clean-up operation in Wallachia. She'd volunteered. She'd wanted to come.

Now that she was here, she wondered why.

No trace of Ben, of course. No body. No remains. Not even the flimsiest strand of Stanton DNA could be combed from the tower lab. The starstone had removed him entirely from existence, along with the bodies of Tepesch, Boris Vukic and the others which the surviving Wallachians had sworn were in the lab.

So. Nobody had actually *witnessed* Ben's death. Again, there was no physical evidence of it. Cally had been taught at Spy High that, at least as far as the Bad Guys were concerned, if you didn't see a body you didn't assume a death. She hoped the same held true of heroes. But it was a hope from the heart, not from the head.

Whatever way she looked at it, Ben was gone.

The starstone was departing too, across the Atlantic to a new home in a Deveraux-sponsored scientific research installation. They kind of knew what it *did* now, but not really what it was *for*. The nature of the energy it released required much further investigation. The walls of the tower had opened up. Helicopters with stasis beams hovered in the sky above ready to lift the starstone.

Cally turned her back. Goodbye and good riddance.

'You're Cally, aren't you?' A Wallachian girl was addressing her. A strikingly attractive Wallachian girl, all green eyes and dark gypsy curls.

'You must be Natalia.' The boy at the girl's side Cally already knew from the news feed. Janos Mirescu, tipped by many to be the next ruler of his country, the new Prince of Wallachia.

'We didn't want to intrude,' said Natalia, 'but we thought you'd like to know . . . about Ben.'

'He fought bravely for Wallachia,' said Janos. 'I was proud to be his ally, I hope his friend. He did everything he could for us and more. If not for Ben, the devil Tepesch . . .'

'We'll never forget him,' Natalia promised. '*I'll* never forget him.'

'No.' Cally smiled wanly. 'Me neither. And thanks. I appreciate it.'

'We're about to eat,' Natalia said. 'Would you like to join us? Come with us, Cally. We can talk some more. We can drink a toast to Ben.'

Cally glanced up as the starstone, locked within diagonal stasis beams, began its journey west.

'I think I'd like that,' she said.

In the Wallachian village of Nostravista, newly rebuilt now but occupying its traditional site deep in the great forest of the Nocnitsa, an old woman sits by the fire and talks to the dead. She's always done this, according to those who know her, but these days she does so more than ever.

It's her sons, you see. Her sons have joined the spirits. Sons *plural*. And she misses them both.

So she sits in the flickering firelight, long into the night, and sometimes she smiles, and sometimes she laughs, and always her lips mouth words that no one living can hear.

And sometimes she frowns. Sometimes she seems

puzzled. There is a third spirit old Lyvia seeks, but no matter how hard she tries, that third spirit she cannot find.

She calls to him: 'Where are you, Ben? Where are you?'

But her only reply is silence.